Praise for

WHERE YOU ONCE BELONGED

"Compelling and timely, *Where You Once Belonged* is a gripping story of an executive's journey back to her past and toward an awareness of her current, flawed self. As she did in her first novel, Lorna Graham uses the supernatural to excellent effect, with historical characters holding modernity to account. "

—**Daphne Uviller, author of** *This Was Not the Plan*

"*Where You Once Belonged* is a brilliant tale of abandonment, betrayal, and friendship that winds back and forth in time, illuminating the ways in which a woman's past have tragically affected her present. Mysticism lends its hand, and life-shaping misunderstandings surface—leading to truths that bring clarity and grace. Lorna Graham's writing is mesmerizing, empathetic, and so absorbing that readers will find this novel impossible to put down."

—**Karen Uhlmann, author of** *Intersections*

"With sharp dialogue and some unconventional plot twists, Graham writes about the challenges faced by a woman chasing corporate success. Things are more complex than they seem, and getting ahead also requires delving into the past. A profound exploration of ambition, sacrifice, compromise, and (last but not least) finding love."

—**Jude Berman, author of** *Shot*

"*Where You Once Belonged* Pulls you in like a beach read, makes you think like a book club pick, and delivers a whopper of a twist like the best TV magazine show. I couldn't put it down, and the ending—that's somehow both shattering and uplifting—still haunts me."

—**Andrea Canning, correspondent,** *Dateline NBC*

WHERE
YOU
ONCE
BELONGED

WHERE YOU ONCE BELONGED

A Novel

LORNA GRAHAM

SHE WRITES PRESS

Published 2025
Printed in the United States of America
Print ISBN: 978-1-64742-902-7
E-ISBN: 978-1-64742-903-4
Library of Congress Control Number: 2025900996

For information, address:
She Writes Press
1569 Solano Ave #546
Berkeley, CA 94707

Interior design by Stacey Aaronson

She Writes Press is a division of SparkPoint Studio, LLC.

Company and/or product names that are trade names, logos, trademarks, and/or registered trademarks of third parties are the property of their respective owners and are used in this book for purposes of identification and information only under the Fair Use Doctrine.

This is a work of fiction. Names, characters, places, and incidents either are the product of the author's imagination or are used fictitiously. Any resemblance to actual persons, living or dead, is entirely coincidental.

For my mother, Judy Pool, who taught me what family is.

For Charley McKenna, who teaches me that anew, every day.

And for my four brothers, as well as my numerous, marvelous pockets of relations across the US, the UK, and Norway, who've shown me that definitions, like family itself, are worth expanding.

PROLOGUE

T he envelope slips out of her hand and falls to the kitchen table where it sits, looking as though it is breathing. It's made of thick cream paper and the writing on the front bears flourishes like that of an ancient text. She squints at the return address, surprised that she still knows it by heart after all these years.

Ev slides her index finger underneath the flap and moves it along, creating a soft *kssst* as the rich paper gives way. Inside is a single card bearing the silhouette of a Victorian house in the upper right-hand corner. It doesn't take long to read what's on it.

June 4, 8 p.m.
Foster House Recommitment

On the other side it says "RSVP" with an email address she doesn't recognize.

Recommitment. *Re*commitment. It takes a few moments to get the reference.

She takes a sip of wine, contemplating the original "Commitment" ceremony, the night when May had beckoned her, Dilly, Tina, and Cam to the hidden parlor in the basement. Sometime after the little speech about how lucky they were to take their places among the women who'd come before them—*Elizabeth Cady Stanton and Lucretia Mott stood right here!*—and before having a few drops of blood taken, they were advised of a particular membership obligation: Every Foster woman was to return to the House for a single evening, two decades after graduation. She remembers how romantic it all sounded as a teenager, when you'll do anything to be part of something bigger than yourself.

Ev shakes her head. Why would she be expected to go to this thing? She didn't graduate with the rest of them.

The sky outside, the part that's visible between the surrounding high-rises, darkens from navy to black, but Ev doesn't turn on a light. She goes to a cabinet and reaches past the cups and saucers, deep into the back where her hand alights on a handmade ceramic mug. There's a crumpled pack of cigarettes inside.

She eases herself back into her chair, kicks off her shoes, and lights up. She inhales, coughing before the old feeling of comfort sets in.

She picks up the card again and is about to toss it in the trash when lights begin to come on in the building across the courtyard. A large window reveals a woman arriving home, a man springing up from his laptop to greet her. Other neighbors enter their apartments, embracing children and dogs, filling pots with water and chattering about their days.

She can still hear the rhythmic banging of the screen door at Foster House, the girls shouting up and down the stairs. She can smell the maple pheasant and succotash of Sunday dinners and see the indigo light of the backyard when they slept outside on hot nights. She remembers the strange sensation, as an only child, of gaining eleven sisters overnight. She remembers being told that there was nothing stronger than the bond they shared.

It was only at the end that she realized what a crock that was.

She takes another puff on her cigarette, remembering Dr. Long, the Iroquois woman who owned the house and smoked a pipe while brewing elixirs over a fire in the garden.

She'd been sipping some of the doctor's ad hoc medicine, fighting a cold, that night she was home alone. She'd dozed off in front of the fire and awakened to see something that simply could not be.

Even now, the image, as it reassembles itself in her mind, confounds.

She takes a last drag, then exhales slowly, feeling herself empty. The smoke pours out of her mouth and curls like a beckoning finger in the dark. Then it disappears.

ONE

Ev hides in the stall and crams another antacid into her mouth. Her private washroom, the one that adjoins her corner office, is on the fritz, so she's using the regular ladies' room. She's resting gingerly on the front edge of the toilet hoping she's not going to need to turn around and throw up in it. She scoots forward and leans her forehead on the stall door, closing her eyes.

The shriek of a metal door opening pierces the peace. Ev leans back and lifts her feet off the floor, not wanting to alert whoever it is to her presence and risk having to chat.

She peeks through the narrow gap to the left of the stall door but all that's visible is a sliver of brown hair falling over a black sweater. This describes half her staff. The tap goes on. Maybe the woman's just come to wash her hands and go, which is good because Ev has a conference call in six minutes. But then she hears the unzipping of a makeup bag and some low humming, and she wonders how long this primping session will take and how long she can keep her feet up to avoid detection; her thigh muscles are beginning to ache. This is stupid. She should have left her feet on the ground. Now she's stuck.

Her stomach clenches again, a result, no doubt, of today's troubling lunch with Gareth. When you're singled out by the president of the News Division, you can never be sure what's going on. There's a chance it's something good. More likely you're in some kind of trouble.

Which was to be expected after the interview she gave to Channel Surf, an industry website, a couple of weeks ago. She doesn't usually do interviews but lately she's noticed that the people who move up the ladder seem to be the ones who get out there and "brand" themselves. All she'd said was that in a time when the country seems rocked by everything from political chaos to the aftermath of a deadly virus to unprecedented weather events, all while failing to agree on basic facts, she hoped that her news-magazine show, *Breaking*, would use its primetime real estate to do fewer sensational stories and more informative and investigative pieces. They used to do a lot of hard-charging reporting, but over the last few years Gareth has insisted that focus groups reveal the audience prefers revisiting infamous crimes, scandals of the past, and celebrity profiles. An escape, perhaps, from the divisive environment they're in. Maybe she stated her displeasure about this a little too baldly, because the headline on the piece blared, "Network EP Keen to Finally Do 'Good' Work."

It's the "finally" that screwed her. She heard through the grapevine that the network's new parent company thought she was implying that ARC News didn't practice real journalism, potentially denting its cachet, a key part of its contribution to the company's public image.

But by the end of the salad course at the blond wood midtown restaurant favored by the media elite, Gareth hadn't mentioned it, so she'd figured something else was afoot. And boy, was it.

. . . . .

The steaks arrived and they carved silently for a few moments before he looked at her directly. "Two pieces of news for you."

"Ah."

"The West Coast is trying a new show—a late-season addition to the schedule—Thursdays at 9." Ev sat up straighter. That's the hour before *Breaking*. Whatever runs in that slot can dramatically affect her ratings; the better the show does, the more eyeballs there are to sample her wares at 10. She may be a newswoman to her core but as executive producer, her primary responsibility is to deliver ratings, which can mean millions of dollars to the network's coffers.

"*Interrogation Room* is going away?" she asked. An old-fashioned but polished police drama, *Interrogation Room* had been a solid draw for years. The people who watched it enjoy the work of detectives, of which *Breaking* serves up plenty. They were a natural fit.

"It needs some time off to retool, add some younger characters. It'll be back in the fall, though maybe not in the same time slot."

"What am I getting instead?" Ev asked, not bothering to hide the fact this was personal for her.

"*Chill*," Gareth said. She raised an eyebrow at her boss, a man too old and too formal for this kind of language. He gave her a pointed look. "Or perhaps I should say, *Chillll!*"

Ev put down her fork, checking Gareth's face for a smile, a hint he was kidding. "The game show?"

Chill! had languished in development forever, seemingly fated to never make it to air. The conceit was that contestants, secured in a chair, are put in stress-inducing situations like having bees released nearby while being asked a string of trivia questions that escalate in difficulty. Their vitals are monitored throughout. Contestants must answer the questions correctly *and* keep their heart rate below a certain level. The potential for lawsuits has kept it from airing, but the show has stayed in contention because a beloved sitcom star is attached to host. Now they've decided to bite the bullet and run it. But why did they have to dump it on her?

"Try to see it as an opportunity," Gareth said. "*Chill!* will bring a new audience."

Gareth surveyed the room's power clusters from under a high forehead and a thinning iron crown of hair, expertly cut to make the most of it. When he turns sideways, he looks like a coin.

"What if it brings no audience?" Ev asked.

"People will sample it out of curiosity if nothing else," Gareth said. "Try to reach those people. *Breaking* needs to break out of its slump."

Ev looked at him sharply. "Slump? That's a little strong." She knew she wasn't matching last year's numbers, but she wasn't *that* far off.

"People upstairs are starting to get concerned, Everleigh. You need to know that."

This surely refers to the new parent company. It bought a majority stake in the ARC network a year ago, and while the top brass promised to be "hands off" when it came to the News Division, remarks like this make it clear that they're paying close attention.

"Now, this, I'm afraid, is less pleasant," Gareth said, as if that were possible. "We need staff cuts. Real cuts. Something in the neighborhood of six or seven percent." He motioned for the waiter, and his watch, gold and a good half an inch thick, caught the light, throwing little spears in all directions.

"Six percent," Ev repeated, her mind spinning. It felt like a bullet to think of laying off even one of her staff.

"Let's just say seven. Don't want corporate to think we're unenthusiastic about meeting their needs." The waiter came by to pour

7

the rest of the silky red they'd been drinking. Gareth did a little spin with his index finger to indicate they'd have another bottle. Each was $175. "The overhauling for 4K cost a fortune, and they're dangling all kinds of juicy carrots in front of Ken to get him to sign his new contract," Gareth continued, speaking of Ken Chang, the network's superstar 6:30 anchor. "Every show and every department has to slice and dice."

Ev put down her fork. *Oh, I'll bet.* She sincerely doubts that anyone else will be asked to sacrifice as much as she will be. Most of them are men who know each other from places like *The Crimson* and disappear into a private room for cigars at senior management retreats without inviting her. Theirs is a glossy bubble that protects them from many of the vagaries of the business.

There is one other woman EP in the News Division, Candy Wallace. She's head of the morning show but largely because her father held the job two decades ago and turned the show into a powerhouse. Candy plays the legacy card for all it's worth, enjoying her status as a one-person protected class.

Ev, having no such special status, has to play ball. Just like most women do. You don't get the luxury of pushback. You may advocate for your principles or turf, but if you're too aggressive, count on it, you'll be out.

Ev took a drink of water and ran calculations in her head. Laying off seven percent of her staff would mean roughly one correspondent, two producers, three associate producers, and a writer or no correspondents but then one more each from the other categories. The producers and APs are the workhorses, but a healthy squad of correspondents makes the show look robust.

No matter whom she fires, it's going to make it harder to pull out of her alleged "slump." The staff is already streamlined after years of shedding jobs to keep up with the changing business model of the industry. Those still left are working full tilt as it is.

And, of course, firing people, even if you have staff to spare, is brutal. They say that to the person let go, it's like a death. Ev has always tried to shield her employees from bean-counter onslaughts by finding other ways to economize—but from Gareth's tone it seems like that's going to be impossible this time.

"I'll get on it," was all she said, pulling her clutch onto her lap and surreptitiously rooting around for the roll of antacids inside.

"Good girl." He looked at her almost fondly and Ev felt him appreciating her "go along" attitude. She guesses it doesn't hurt that she also provides a checked "equal opportunity" box and, with her trim frame and sheet of white-blond hair, an attractive companion on awards evenings.

"Just the check," Gareth said to the waiter who appeared with the dessert menu. They left soon after, half the second bottle of wine remaining.

Ev becomes aware that the woman on the other side of the stall door is speaking. She's momentarily confused before realizing that the woman isn't talking to her, but to herself.

"I will not sacrifice my self-worth for acceptance. I will not sacrifice my self-worth for acceptance. I will not . . ." the girl says.

Christ.

A loud clacking ricochets around the bathroom. It takes Ev a moment to realize that her heels have slipped on the porcelain of the toilet rim and hit the floor.

"Someone in here?" asks the girl at the sink, clearly startled. Ev flushes the unused toilet, straightens her skirt, and comes out with as much dignity as she can muster. At the sink is Tab Morales, an assistant producer.

"Oh—hello," Tab says with evident surprise that her boss has apparently been hiding in a bathroom stall. "You all right?"

"Hello, Tabitha. Perfectly." As someone only recently made staff, Tab will almost certainly be one of those let go.

Ev waves her hands under the automatic faucet of the sink next to Tab's and it springs to life. Briefly, she takes in their shared reflection, recognizing once again how tempting it is to think you look quite youthful—even in your forties—until you stand next to a twenty-five-year-old.

"So glad I ran into you," Tab says. She wears glasses that are too large for her small face and her black sweater has animal-shaped cutouts sewn on the front. "I wanted to tell you I signed up for your writing clinic."

"I thought you had a conflict."

"I was supposed to help my mom," Tab says, rifling through her makeup bag. "She's taking in some freelance bookkeeping work. You know, for extra cash? But my sister's going to do it."

"Ah."

"They both thought it was cool that you were teaching a class for, like, free."

"You realize the clinic will have homework?" Ev asks, feeling a prick of guilt about the layoffs and knowing that Tab will only attend a handful sessions at most. "You're already pretty busy, you sure you want to take this on?"

Tab nods vigorously. "I'm working with Sandra Keaton on a story now. Her scripts are amazing—not a word wasted—and she says she learned it all from you."

Ev's mouth feels dry from the antacids. She scoops some water into her hand and sloshes it inelegantly into her mouth. The kid is quirky but she's picking up some basics about broadcasting. Ev wants to hint to Tab that in the roiling job market of TV news, maybe she should poke around, see what else is out there. Much easier to get a job when you have one. But she can't risk Tab figuring out what's up and telling others.

As Ev starts to leave, Tab's eyebrow pencil lands on the ground, bounces lightly, and rolls away. Her head lolls to the right as if she's trying to get water out of her ear. Before Ev can say anything, the girl's knees buckle and she's falling toward the floor.

"Jesus!" Ev catches Tab just in time. The two of them are splayed on the cool tile, Ev cradling the girl's head in her lap. Tab's eyelids are fluttering and her body is clammy. "Tabitha? You there?" says Ev, tapping Tab's cheeks lightly. She grabs her cell phone from the counter and punches in the number for the network medical center, telling them to hurry. She uses her paper towel to dab Tab's forehead. Tab opens her eyes and blinks a few times but doesn't speak.

In a few minutes, two young men arrive. They give Tab a glucose tablet and help her up. Ev ignores their outstretched hands and pushes herself to her feet.

Tab appears fully back now though very pale. "Your shirt," she whispers hoarsely.

Ev looks down. Her blouse is damp, presumably from Tab's sweat.

"Sorry," Tab says, looking shaken and embarrassed.

"It's fine," Ev says. "Are you all right? Should I call anyone?"

"No," says Tab. "I'll be okay in a few minutes. I found out I'm diabetic a few weeks ago and they don't have my medication sorted out yet. I'm going to see a specialist next week." She offers a weak smile. "You know, now that I finally have medical."

Ev makes understanding noises, dabbing at her wet shirt so she won't have to look Tab in the eye.

. . . . .

Her office is spacious, with large windows, a bank of TVs, and a small round conference table. It's saved from total corporate blandness by the wainscoting she had put in with the decorating money that came with her promotion to EP. She actually went a little over budget and had to pay some out of her own pocket but it was worth it. The place feels like home. It has a cupboard with real plates for her frequent late-night takeout meals and a large closet with extra clothes in case of an impromptu business dinner or trip. She's never been so glad for the closet, even if the silk blouse with bell sleeves that her assistant, Meryl, brought to the ladies' room is a bit much for three in the afternoon.

After the conference call, she has Meryl print out a staff list that contains her hundred or so employees' contract status, yearly review scores, and salaries. She scans the names, running a mental calculus of money versus performance. There's no one on her staff who deserves to be fired. At this point, she hired many of them herself. They are hardworking, professional, and unusually supportive of one another.

A few possess annoying habits. Like the production manager who uses interoffice email to send chain letters. A few producers' expense sheets are always a mess and usually late. And of course Tabitha, she of the oddball getups and bathroom self-help sessions. Though all in all, she's a good kid.

Ev puts a check next to each of their names to mark them as possibles but her heart's not in it. She puts down the pen and pushes back from her desk, thinking. It would be a lot more fun to expend her efforts on finding a truly meaty story, an investigative piece with the potential to become a national water cooler moment. Gareth may have his doubts, but for the right story she bets he'd be willing to pour some real resources into promoting *Breaking*. Which might help them turn things around.

Maybe she wouldn't have to lay off anyone.

She looks up at the monitors on the opposite wall, which are tuned to the other networks and cable news channels. The bottom right one, however, angled away from her office door, flickers with the Mac 'n' Cheese Channel. It airs nothing but cooking segments, each with a different chef preparing macaroni and cheese. There are "quick 'n' easy" ones with processed cheese and bacon bits as well as elaborate ones with truffles or lobster. There are stovetop versions and baked. Some have a bread crumb topping, some don't. The chefs are men, women, nonbinary, old, young, fat, thin, Cajun, Yankee.

It's not like Ev even cooks. But there's something soothing about these shows: the butter bubbling gently in a pot, the flour sprinkled over the top, the rhythmic whisking of a silky sauce.

The only problem is she sometimes fails to mute the sound when Meryl comes in. Meryl, who wears her slate-gray hair in a pert ponytail, is a seasoned executive assistant who's a good ten or fifteen years older than she is. Whenever Meryl catches Ev watching this stuff, her expression makes clear that she can't believe Ev toils in the same business as Edward R. Murrow once did.

Two cable channels break into regular programming and Ev leans forward, elbows on her desk. A partial mine collapse in Kentucky. The banners beneath the video blare "Men Trapped" and "Time Running Out." Ev looks at her watch. It would be tough to rejigger tonight's broadcast, but the show isn't called *Breaking* for nothing. Most of their pieces actually take weeks to produce but her team can crash a report with the best of them. It's expensive, though, with resources spent in the field and on overtime, and right now she has to pinch pennies.

Ev drinks in the footage, trying to decide whether to pull the trigger. The helicopter shots of a mountain crawling with emergency vehicles are wonderful, as is the pan of families waiting and hugging and the close-up of a little girl's tear-stained face. As a third channel picks up the story, Ev calls one of her senior producers and tells him to get on the phone with their affiliate in the area. She refocuses on the screens in front of her, the bright colors like a big bowl of candy.

She loves news. Loves the tension between mystery and revelation, the dance they do with one another. And she loves that, eventually, the truth will come out.

The only question is, when.

Ev arches her back and stretches her arms overhead. Her eyes are closed and she can hear Sean's pencil scratching against the paper. "Thigh," she says. "Inner right."

"Mmm," he murmurs from the chair across from his bed. Ev hears him take a sip of wine.

Whenever Sean sketches her she swears she can feel his pencil on the part of her body he's drawing. It's a gentle, tender sensation with a bit of steeliness behind it. She rolls sideways, the sheets wrapping around her legs. It's fun to see if he can keep up with her changes.

"Now?" he asks.

"Jawline," she says, scratching hers. "It tickles."

"Not even close," Sean says, creating a lot of noise with his pencil, as if he's shading a section of the drawing. "So the mine collapse. No go?"

"Nope," Ev replies, biting at a hangnail. "Everybody got out. I called back the crew before they even got there."

"You sound disappointed," he says with a wink.

"Ha ha." She tosses a pillow at him. "But there was a lot of interest on social media. If it was still going on at ten, we could have led the show with it. And that would have boosted the audience for everything else we had."

Sean nods and keeps drawing. "What about the Gareth lunch?" he asks. "What was that about?"

"Nothing," Ev says.

"Gareth Smyter doesn't take two hours out of his precious day for nothing."

Ev sighs. "I'm getting a new lead-in that's going hurt me." She brushes some hair off her face. "And—" She stops herself.

"And?"

But Ev doesn't want to go into the layoff thing. Sean will want to know how she's coping and want to talk her through each and every option for whom to cut, dissuading her even though he hasn't met them. He's never been a boss, let alone a female boss, and doesn't know that this is part of the territory and it's best not to sentimentalize it.

"And I just . . ." she starts, rooting around for something to offer instead. "I just have to figure out how to adjust my programming around the new lead. That's all."

"Hmm." Sean wets his fingertips and rubs them over the tip of the pencil, shaking his head. "You sounded almost wistful there for a sec."

He's not buying it and when he doesn't buy something, he's guaranteed to hound her about it.

She sits up, flexing her muscles in exaggerated fashion like a body builder. She kisses a bicep.

"Cute," Sean says. "But it's not an answer."

She hunches and places her chin on her fist, forehead knit, à la *The Thinker.*

"Ooh, an art reference," Sean responds dryly. She lies on her stomach, reaches back and grasps her ankles. "That looks painful," he says.

Ev collapses and lies flat. She pats the mattress. Sean rolls his eyes but at least there's a smile.

"I'm cold over here," she says. Finally, Sean drops the sketchpad and comes over to sit beside her.

"Let the record show there is more to the Gareth-lunch story," he says, before pinning her with a kiss. She pulls off his T-shirt and soon she's lost in that place he takes her, where it's just breath and soft colors behind her eyelids, where she escapes everything including, wonderfully—briefly—her own mind.

Afterward, they lie close, facing one another. Ev hears Homer, Sean's Labradoodle, pad in. Seconds later his cold nose presses into her behind. She pats the bed, letting him know it's okay for him to come up. There's a soft thump, then the gentle pressure of a furry back against her own.

In their silence, the only sound is the ticking of the grandfather clock that once graced Sean's childhood home. His parents sent it from Illinois. They're always sending him things, from homemade chocolate bark to packs of T-shirts, like he's a kid at summer camp and not a successful forty-six-year-old graphic designer in Manhattan. It's all very sweet but the truth is, this habit irritates her. It's like they need to be "present" in his life at all times.

Not a problem she has with her own father. Anton rarely even emails. He's actually forgotten her birthday three out of the last five years.

Ev can't get used to the clock's baritone beats; they call to mind parlors and verandas and pies cooling on windowsills, all quite incongruous in Sean's sleek, modern apartment.

Sean rolls toward his side of the bed and sits up. Cool air settles between them, chilling Ev's skin. She pulls the sheet up and her eyes follow Sean as he finds his sketchpad on the floor. He rips out the top page and props the new picture of Ev on a long metal shelf on the wall. He's in a phase of experimenting with light and shadow and Ev looks like a yin-yang version of herself. He's rendered her rounder than she really is, but artists like curves.

Sean's placed her next to several sketches of his family, who are all, thankfully, clothed. His parents are yin-yang too: Erik, his father, fair, with his high forehead and thin lips, while the strong-boned Caribbean face of his mother, Carmen, is capped with a profusion of graying dreadlocks.

Ev's picture sits between a portrait of Sean's younger brother, Peter, and younger sister, Annette, who appears to be wrinkling her nose at Ev's pedicure.

"Maybe I belong somewhere else?" Ev says.

"Actually," Sean comes back to the bed and sits, "I'd like to see you with my family in the flesh. Okay, maybe not *that* much flesh," he says.

"What do you mean?" Ev asks.

"My parents' fiftieth is coming up."

"Mmm," Ev says. She pushes herself up into a sitting position and slips into one of Sean's T-shirts.

"Just a long weekend in Evanston." Sean's parents are professors at Northwestern: his mom, chair of the anthropology department, and his dad, associate chair of history. "But I'm sure you and I can sneak down to Chicago on our own one night."

Ev presses her lips together. A whole weekend with the Andersens? A single evening had utterly exhausted her.

"Who'll watch Homer?" she asks.

"The dog walker. Not Homer's favorite thing but I'll pack extra treats. He can manage it for one weekend."

Ev nods but doesn't say anything.

"It won't be any fun without you," Sean prompts, touching his index finger to the tip of her nose. It's sweet of him to say, but she knows it's not true. "And my parents would think it was a little, I don't know, strange if you didn't come. After two years together. Plus I think you and Annette are one girls' night out away from being besties."

Ev frowns. He's completely wrong about Annette. Plus, Ev has work to do—more than ever, if she's going to get her show back on top while slicing her budget. She'll need weekends to make it happen.

But she wants to make Sean happy. Not many men are interested in a workaholic like her. At least the weekend is by definition a one-off; how many fiftieth anniversaries can his parents have?

"Sounds amazing," she says, kissing his shoulder.

He sighs as though he really wasn't sure what she was going to say. "After our run in the morning I'm going to make you the best waffle ever. Sri Lankan cinnamon." He turns off the light and within moments is breathing deeply. But Ev stares into the blackness. Most women would be thrilled that their boyfriend wanted to bring them home.

Her cell rings, of course, just as the color goes on. The hunched young woman doing her manicure instantly withdraws her hands. Even though Ev doesn't recognize the number, she accepts the call, leaning over and speaking into the phone.

"Hello?" she says warily.

"Leigh?"

Ev blinks. She hasn't been called this in twenty years. "Hello?" she says again.

"Leigh, it's me."

Ev realizes she knows this voice; it echoes deep in her brain, from a place that is mapped but that she never visits. "May?"

"That's right, May Jessup. From Foster House. Is this a bad time?" she asks. "It sounds like you might be at dinner."

"No, I'm just . . . it's fine." Ev isn't sure why she doesn't just say she's getting her nails done except it suddenly feels small, banal.

Though the topcoat has not yet been applied, she stands, pointing to the drying area by the window. The manicurist nods and swoops up Ev's bag and sweater and carries them over. Ev parks one hand under the air and uses the other to hold the phone near her ear.

"How are you?" asks May.

"I don't know how to answer that."

May laughs lightly. "I know what you mean. Not easy to sum up two decades, is it?"

"Where are you calling from?"

"Washington."

Ev settles back in her chair and her breathing starts to normalize. "Is that where you live?"

"Yes."

"What do you do there?"

"I'm a lawyer, consulting with the Southern Poverty Law Center."

"Exactly what you said you'd do," says Ev. She remembers May arguing on the house phone with her parents about how she was going to do something worthwhile with her eventual law degree even if it meant leaving money on the table.

"What about you?"

Ev tells her about *Breaking*, feeling a small surge of pride.

"So you stayed in journalism," May says. "Exactly what you wanted, too."

"Yep," Ev says, thinking that after what happened to her in college, it's a wonder she has a journalism career at all. But May probably doesn't know about that, since she was a year older and everything happened after she graduated. Ev waits for May to continue but she is silent, as if unsure of her mission.

"What else? You married?" May finally asks.

"No," Ev replies, waving her red nails under the fan. She doesn't usually opt for such a deep color, too much maintenance. But Sean thinks it's sexy. "You?"

"I was, for almost fifteen years. Three kids. But we're getting divorced."

"Sorry to hear that."

"It's fine. Turns out I like women better." There's a short pause. "But maybe you knew that."

The intimacy of this remark catches Ev off guard. But May is right, eventually most people at Foster House suspected there was something between May and Belina.

"Do you have a girlfriend?" asks Ev, realizing she's being nosy but unable to stop herself.

"Yes."

"Who's the lucky lady?"

"Belina."

"Really?"

"Long distance at the moment, but we'll see."

"Let me guess," says Ev. "You saw each other at your reunion last year and sparks flew?"

"*Recommitment*, not reunion. And something like that."

"I suppose after a few too many cocktails these things happen," Ev says. She expects May to laugh but she doesn't.

"Speaking of Recommitment, I assume you realize why I'm calling," May says.

Ev had actually not thought that far ahead but this makes sense. "Of course."

"Did you get the invitation?"

"Yes."

"We didn't get your RSVP."

Ev doesn't even know where to begin, but she decides not to lead with anger. After all, it's not May she's mad at. "I guess I didn't understand why I was invited."

"What do you mean?"

"I didn't graduate with everyone else. You were gone by then, but you know that, right? I was thrown out of school."

There's a pause before May answers. "But Recommitment isn't tied to graduation. They hold it in June because it coincides with the college's reunions, when alumni are generally back anyway. Easier for everybody." May exhales. "The name *Recommitment* tells you what you need to know, right? It's connected to the Commitment ceremony you went through when you became part of Foster House. It's . . . the bookend to it."

"Why does it need a bookend?"

"Maybe it doesn't. Please don't get hung up on this. Let's just say it's about coming back and . . ." May trails off.

"Seeing old girlfriends?" Ev offers teasingly, trying again to lighten the mood. But this is only greeted by silence. "May I at least ask what happens at this thing? The card didn't include any details."

"I'm afraid I can't, either." May exhales.

"Why would you expect people to drop everything to show up for something you can tell them nothing about?" Ev asks.

"I realize some might think it's a lot to ask," May says in a tone that suggests she really doesn't. "But as you may remember, details of Recommitment are kept secret by design."

"Why? Now that you've been through it, I presume you know."

"Excuse me a moment." May puts her hand over the phone to converse with someone, her voice sounding strained through the muffle.

Ev starts to feel annoyed by this conversation, the presumptuousness of it. Not everyone's a joiner, and those who are never seem to respect those who aren't. One isn't inherently better than the other. And yet, she thinks as she lightly presses a nail to see if it's set, she has to concede that May has every reason to remember Ev as a joiner herself. Before everything went wrong, she had drunk the Foster House Kool-Aid. Buckets of it.

May comes back. "Sorry about that. You'll understand once you're there. I promise."

"I could just Google it," says Ev. "I'm sure somebody's let the cat out of the bag over the years."

"You could," May says with an offhand tone as if it doesn't concern her. "You keep asking about what happens but you haven't asked me who's coming. Aren't you curious?"

"No."

"Not even a little? These were your best friends. You couldn't get enough of each other."

"*Were* best friends. You weren't there . . . you don't know."

"I know some things."

"Like?"

"Like before whatever happened *happened*, Dilly was very good to you. Good for you."

"What are you talking about?"

"Are you really going to pretend you don't know?" May sounds exasperated.

Ev does know. She just doesn't want to admit it. "Fine. Is she coming?" she asks, like a sulky child repeating something at an adult's command.

"Yes. They all are."

"All of them?"

"Tina, Cam, and Dilly. All coming."

Ev still remembers the last time she set eyes on Dilly. It wasn't long after she left the dean of students' office, her heart pounding. She'd gone back to Foster House, packed up her things, and called a taxi. On the way to the train station, she'd passed Dilly hurrying to class, head tilted into a stiff wind. She looked like a stranger.

"Did they ask about me? Whether I'm coming?" The questions escape before she can stop them.

May seems to consider. "I don't think it's for me to share that with you."

In other words, no. They'd rather not have to deal with her. Maybe she should go to this thing, just to spite them.

"What about Foster House itself?" May presses. "Wouldn't you like to see it again? We had some very happy times there, all of us."

"I don't get attached to places," Ev says.

May sighs. "How about this? *I'd* like to see you. I always felt we had a special bond."

Ev sighs. She'd felt this, too. In those years when she still missed her mother so much, she'd been comforted by May's nurturing ways.

"I've thought about you often. You probably don't believe that but it's true. I'll even pick you up in Albany if you want to fly up. Just to remind you, it's Saturday, June fourth."

It's the weekend of Sean's parents' anniversary. She tells May that she'll be in Chicago for it.

But May is undaunted. "Seems like something could be worked out. Maybe you could come up to Lawton Saturday night and fly out first thing Sunday morning," she says.

"The big party's Saturday evening."

23

"You remember that you promised, right?" says May, sounding flustered. "On Commitment night. You took an oath to come back for Recommitment with your sisters."

"It was sophomore year. We were nineteen—kids."

"Were you really a kid, though?"

Ev can't tell whether May is asking whether any nineteen-year-old is really a child or whether she in particular was.

"I can't stress enough how vital it is that you come. It's a once-in-a-lifetime opportunity."

"For *what*?" Ev says impatiently. She pulls her nails out of the dryer only to see that the thumbnail on her right hand has a big gash in it, an obstinate white slice through the deep red.

There's a long silence. "All right," sighs May. She sounds like a person who's been desperately treading water and now realizes that the sea will win.

"But the next time you're in New York, let me know," Ev says, meaning it. May was always good to her. The only one she can say that about.

"Sure," May says.

But Ev can tell by her tone that they'll never see each other again.

TWO

As a child, everyone had called her Everleigh but when she arrived at college, she decided she'd go by Leigh. Less girly, cooler, she'd thought, though during the first few weeks of the term not many would have cared one way or the other.

For a roommate, she'd been paired with Fran, a preppie, outdoorsy girl from Rhode Island. Leigh had assumed that your freshman roommate was, if nothing else, an automatic friend for things like orientation events, meals, and laundry. But Fran had arrived with her high school best friend, Caroline. Caroline's mother thought it best that her daughter make new friends at Lawton and had forbidden her and Fran from rooming together. It didn't matter, though, because Caroline spent all of her time at their place, even sleeping on their floor some nights. When she and Fran were together, they egged each other on into almost stratospheric levels of brattiness, speaking exclusively in a combination of twin-like shorthand and private jokes, making Leigh feel like a party crasher in her own room.

One day during the third week of classes Leigh came home, as she always did, during a mid-morning break. As she pushed open the door, she heard what sounded like a brief scuffle. Inside, she found Fran and Caroline sitting cross-legged on Fran's bed, Caroline's fingers at her temples, kneading at the pale flesh.

"Oh god . . . *oh god*," she murmured.

"What's wrong?" Leigh asked, letting her book bag fall to the floor.

"Migraine. Just hit," whispered Fran.

"The light . . ." Caroline shut her eyes tightly.

Fran yanked the drapes shut and plugged in the electric kettle on her desk. From a shelf, she pulled down a box of teabags and placed one inside a mug.

Leigh sank down on her bed. "Does she get them often?" she whispered.

"She didn't used to. But since tenth grade, it's been more and more, especially when she's stressed. Last year she had one that lasted a whole weekend." Fran sighed, then began again, quietly. "I've spent a lot of time at her house, so I've learned how to deal with them."

The kettle screamed and Fran hurried to unplug it. She poured the water into the mug. She perched on the edge of her bed and touched the mug lightly on her friend's upper arm. Caroline took it from her and drank, grimacing, Fran rubbing her back.

"I hate to say this," Fran said, looking at Leigh. "But I think Caroline needs to move in here."

Leigh's heart sank, but what could she say? Caroline was clearly in a bad way.

"A third bed might block the closet but we could work around it," she said, feeling like the soul of generosity.

"Not with us. With *me*," Fran said.

"What?"

"Look, you're great," Fran said in a soft voice. "And I know I've sucked as a roommate. But I think Caroline's going to need special care while we're here. Either that or she'll be in the infirmary every week."

Leigh wasn't following. "But where would I go?"

"Housing," Fran said. "They'll set you up. I heard there's lots of moving around in the first few weeks and that people who switch usually get a single. Maybe they'll put you in that new dorm, the one with the mini fridges and views of the woods."

Leigh tried to take it all in. She looked at Caroline's swaying body and nodded slowly. "You're a good friend," she said, standing.

"You are, too." Fran crossed the floor and pulled Leigh into a hug. "Thank you," she whispered into her ear.

Leigh reached for her bag and headed out the door. A few feet down the hall, she paused, trying to remember where the housing office was. A moment later a sound came from the room she'd just left.

A peal of laughter.

"What—the fuck—was that shit? It—tasted—disgusting!" Caroline broke off into a fit of giggles and *gacking* noises. "Why didn't you just tell her to move out like I said?"

"Because she's hopeless. I don't think she's made any friends yet. And those sad-kitten eyes. If I'd asked her to leave without the migraine excuse, she probably would have killed herself."

"Get me some water, will you?" Caroline said. Seconds later, the door swung open and Fran came out, holding an empty glass. Leigh met her gaze and held it, determined not to make "sad-kitten eyes," whatever those were.

She lasted about two seconds before she turned and headed down the stairs.

. . . . .

27

At the housing office, a girl with short henna-red hair and a bangle around her upper arm was embroiled in conversation with a harried-looking woman at a battered desk.

"What do you mean, gone?" the woman was saying, peering at the girl over her glasses.

"She partied all weekend then packed up her stuff and left," the girl said. Her voice had a southern smokiness to it that made a person want to eat whatever she was saying. "Like, every last diet pill and tampon. Poof. Gone."

"Did she go home?"

"How should I know? *You* paired me with her. Her name is Marianne Becker. Maybe her parents contacted the bursar or something. I just want to—"

"And your name?"

The girl cleared her throat and took a long, exaggerated breath. "We went over this, remember? It's Adele Dechanet," she said. "That's, A-D-E-L-E—"

"Right-right-right," the woman said, mostly to herself. "How can kids be leaving school and not telling anyone? Jiminy." She threw her hands up in the air and disappeared through a door behind the desk.

Adele turned to Leigh. "These people, huh?" She sighed. "What's your deal? Your roommate bailed, too? They're dropping like flies."

"Um, no," Leigh said. "It's—"

"Wait, don't tell me. She was obsessed with you." Adele widened her eyes dramatically. "*Single White Female.* You had to kill her to get away."

"She told me to leave."

Adele shook her head and pulled a pack of cigarettes from her jeans. "That's cold," she said finally. She offered Leigh a cigarette and Leigh took it though she'd never smoked before.

The first drag felt like fire being applied directly to her throat. Between coughs, she explained about Fran, Caroline, and Caroline's "headaches," though she was too embarrassed to reveal that it was all a trick.

"Hmm," said Adele, exhaling a delicate plume of smoke up towards the ceiling. "Sounds like some serious bullshit to me. If you don't mind me saying."

Leigh shook her head. She didn't. It was.

"You know what?" Adele said. "Fuck her. Fuck both of them. They're going to get bad karma and you're going to get a single. And by the way, you can call me Dilly."

"Who said you could smoke in here?" the housing woman squawked as she reentered the room, waving a sheaf of papers in front of her face, though the smoke was nowhere near her. "Put. Those. Out." She pointed at a trash can in the corner. "Honestly, the entitlement . . ." She mumbled a series of outraged pronouncements as Leigh gratefully stubbed out her cigarette and Adele took another leisurely drag.

The woman beckoned Adele back over to the desk and slid the papers at her. "You need to fill these out."

"Marianne left and *I* have to fill shit out?"

"Someone has to. And she, as you yourself say, is not here." The woman rolled her shoulders and shifted her attention to Leigh. "Now. What do *you* need?"

"I have to move out of my room." Once again, Leigh explained about Fran, Caroline, and their caregiving arrangement.

"Not that anyone's asking me, but I would send this Caroline straight to the infirmary," Adele cut in, nodding to the housing woman. "Sounds like she's very ill. Like she needs lots of testing. With needles and maybe a rectal thermometer."

Leigh stifled a giggle.

The housing lady closed her eyes as if trying to summon inner peace. After a few moments, she roused herself and handed a sheet of paper to Leigh. "Here's the form you need to fill out to get a new roommate."

"I was told I'd be getting a single."

"This girl *has* to get a single," Adele said, like she could decide these things. "After what she's been through, this complete nightmare? It's probably disrupted her sleep, not to mention her studying. She needs peace and quiet for the rest of the semester."

The housing lady rolled her eyes. "Are you done yet?"

"Not remotely," Adele said with the brio of a stage actress. "Because I, too, will require a single. Being abandoned by the roommate I'd come to love, having to start my college career amid this emotional trauma . . ." She looked at Leigh. "Wouldn't you say?"

"Absolutely," Leigh said, nodding. "You're going need time to heal and—"

"Girls, *girls*. I have news for you. No freshman gets a single."

And that's how it started.

THREE

Ev boards the uptown subway at Christopher Street at 7:30 a.m., but it's even more crowded than usual and she has to stand, her hand wrapped around a pole, her body wedged tightly between those of fellow passengers. She's holding the *New York Times*'s main section, folded into quarters. She skims an article about a large company leaning on a premier social media company to help it spy on employees organizing a union in a private chat.

The officials and users quoted in the piece sound utterly stunned. Ev wonders how in this day and age anyone can be surprised by anything. Are they not paying attention? Betrayal, both macro- and micro-level, is part and parcel of the human condition, especially now. Every day her fellow journalists uncover terrible deeds: corporation against citizen, church against flock, husband against wife.

What Ev does, generally speaking, is assume the worst. It rarely fails as a life strategy.

Space is tight, so it's hard to refold the paper to the international page. As she struggles, a strange feeling comes over her. It manifests as a certainty that someone she knows is nearby.

She glances around, looking for a colleague or neighbor but all the faces nearby belong to strangers. Most everyone is absorbed by a small screen except for a man with a hand down his pants standing under one of those security posters saying, "If You See Something, Say Something."

Ev almost says something.

At Thirty-Fourth Street, a stream of new passengers presses in. Someone bumps her and she turns reflexively. As her eyes sweep across the car, she catches sight of a young woman about halfway down. She wears a black dress and has long buttermilk-blond hair. Nearly white with just a hint of yellow, it's Ev's exact unusual shade. She cranes her neck, trying to see the woman's face, but jostling commuters conspire to block her view.

She gives up and becomes lost once again in the paper. But within minutes, the odd feeling of familiarity returns. She twists, looking under the arm of the tall man next to her, trying to find the blond. Finally she spots her. What she sees next makes her stare even harder: The woman lifts her left hand and brings the pad of her ring finger to her left eye, appearing to lightly brush it back and forth along the tips of her lashes. It's done with the distracted deliberateness of habit.

A habit Ev herself had when she was young.

She stands on tiptoes trying to see the woman's face, but can't.

At the next stop, Forty-Second Street, a surge of riders gets off and Ev thinks she spies pale locks glinting among the sea of black suits on the platform, but the train pulls out before she can see much more.

It's not until they're deep in the tunnel again that she notices the strange feeling has disappeared.

. . . . . .

Ev steps into the elevator and hums impatiently as it carries her down to the fourth floor. She's about to meet with Aviva Abramowitz, a veteran producer who's been in the Midwest for a couple of weeks working on a story she's been keeping under wraps. She said she wanted it to be a surprise. Ev wouldn't approve the expenses for this with any other producer, but the two of them go way back.

Aviva's facing the back of her office, hanging a framed painting on the wall.

Ev raps her knuckles softly on the doorjamb. "Another ode to Picasso, I see," she says. Aviva and her husband, James, have a pre-teen daughter who churns out a remarkable amount of art.

Aviva swings around. "Come in!" she says. "Yep. Michaela has officially moved into her cubist phase."

Ev steps carefully around the stacks of files, tapes, and books that rise like a model city on Aviva's floor.

"You should send her to one of the art schools. Isn't there a great one on the Upper West?"

"York Prep? Unless you're handing out raises, I don't think that's in the cards," Aviva says with a chuckle as she slides an elastic band off her wrist and uses it to pull her curly black hair into a high ponytail.

Ev shakes her head. "Where were you, again? Iowa?"

"Ohio."

"And why?"

"I think I got what we need." Aviva leans forward and begins clicking and unclicking a ballpoint pen. "For the drug story."

Ev raises an eyebrow. They've spent years, on and off, pursuing this one without ever getting quite enough to go to air. She admires Aviva's tenacity but this story feels like a losing prospect. "Maybe we don't throw good money after bad on that one," Ev says. "Maybe we go forward, not backward."

33

"Maybe we have to go backward *to* go forward." Aviva reaches for a binder on her desk and starts flipping through it.

The "drug story" is about how the process for testing prescription drugs is deeply flawed, freighted with potentially deadly consequences. Testing isn't carried out by the FDA, as many assume. The drug companies themselves are responsible for it and sometimes contract the job out to research organizations that recruit human guinea pigs, conduct the tests, and analyze the data. Like there isn't a conflict of interest there. To make matters worse, testing is often done in places where it's cheap and far from scrutiny: abroad, especially India, on volunteers so desperate for money they may take part in several different studies at a time. This means drugs mixing within their systems like liquors in a Long Island iced tea, rendering the tests totally unreliable. At least one drug tested this way—recalled a couple of years ago—killed a dozen people.

All this, *Breaking* has cold. What it hasn't had is proof that the company, Armitage, that manufactured the bad drug knew that the testing company it used was shady.

And since Armitage was never called on the carpet, it and other drug companies continue testing their wares this way, potentially endangering the public.

"So what is it you have?" Ev asks.

"A whistleblower."

"Inside one of the testing companies or Armitage itself?"

"Inside Armitage."

"High inside?"

"High."

"Disgruntled?"

"Angry. But only about this testing issue. Not anything personal that I can see."

"How'd you get him?"

"Her," says Aviva, and Ev mentally checks herself. She hates it when she does that. And she should know better: Most whistle-blowers are women. "She called me out of the blue and said she could confirm that the company knew full well its safety tests were compromised."

Ev feels a tingle. An idea is coming to her but she doesn't want to get ahead of herself.

"But wait, there's more. They're about to bring out their contribution to the vaccine race. You know how new variants still keep popping up? At least one of them appears invulnerable to everything we currently have. Now here comes Armitage to the rescue. They missed the boat the first time around, losing out on all those juicy profits, so they've got a lot riding on this thing. But what if they've cut corners in some way? It would be catastrophic. There's our news peg."

Now Ev's mind really starts racing. With nearly 70 percent of Americans taking at least one prescription drug, the Armitage story was always going to be big. But add in this vaccine element and it becomes undeniably urgent. Potentially unsafe prescription drugs are bad enough, but an ineffective or even dangerous vaccine? It's been the greatest fear of everyone in the medical community. If even one vaccine actually turned out to be shoddy, it could undermine even *more* Americans' belief in science and scientists.

In a heartbeat, Ev puts on her executive producer hat. The story would be a perfect way to kick off sweeps, giving *Breaking* the oxygen it critically needs. If they really have Armitage cold, it would be big enough that Gareth would make Candy run an excerpt of it during *Smell the Coffee!* to promote it. And Ken Chang would probably run a teaser story on *National Report*. The network might even do promotion in some newspapers and send it to TV critics to review. If she could capitalize on the increased viewership with a few more good stories in the weeks after, it just might get her numbers going in the right direction.

"The whistleblower will go on camera?"

"I'm working on it," says Aviva. "She's nervous."

"But then why call us at all? How did she even know we were interested in this story?"

"We've been sniffing around for a long time. Word gets out. It probably took her a while to work up her nerve to talk. If she gets caught, there goes her job and who knows what else. Big Pharma plays dirty." Aviva puts down the pen. "I'm pretty sure I can get her on camera, but only with her identity hidden."

Ev nods; this is common enough. "She nails them?"

"With two hammers."

"What if someone else tries to book her?"

"Strangely but happily," Aviva says, "she only wants to work with us. She says she won't talk to anyone else."

Ev smiles at this unexpected vote of confidence from a civilian. "Who is this smart lady?"

"I can't reveal her name, but she's a former researcher now in management. I've made copies of her ID and checked her credentials. She says I can tell Legal and Standards her identity before broadcast. She understands we have to be careful. We don't want to be labeled *fake news*."

Ev rolls her eyes. "When are you talking to her again?"

"Still setting it up," says Aviva.

"I want you back out there ASAP. Rent a hotel room, book a crew. Get Bob"—Bob Wilkinson is their ace investigative correspondent—"on a plane. The minute she says yes, you do the interview."

"You want this for May sweeps, yes?"

"I want it to *lead* sweeps," Ev says.

36

"Hell, yeah." Aviva beams. This is a plum berth. "Can I get some extra help?"

"Who do you want?"

Aviva names several well-regarded editors. "Oh, and I could use Tab."

"Hmm?" Ev asks.

"She's fantastic. Conscientious. Never complains. Plus she's good at social media, which is the stuff I hate."

"You don't find her a little, I don't know . . . strange?"

"All the good ones are strange in some way," Aviva says, winking.

Ev considers. If Aviva, who's covered everything from wars to the G-20, likes Tab so much, maybe she'll try to find a way to save the girl from the layoffs. Aloud she simply says, "I'll see what I can do."

"Have I told you it was a good day when you took over *Breaking*?" Aviva asks, crossing her arms.

"Don't think so, no," Ev says with a small smile.

"I'm serious. Alan would have drawn it out, kept me guessing. He needed to *wield* his power."

There's a pause as they regard one another. Ev imagines that some men might be confused by their relationship. She and Aviva are friends, yes. They've known each other for a decade and spent many long days on the road together. But they don't gossip or have spa dates or discuss their relationships. Partnerships like theirs never seem to make it into pop culture, where women are represented as either besties or frenemies. The respectful distance between Ev and Aviva means there are no personal issues brewing, nothing that could trigger conflict, and this enables them to do very good journalism together.

"You know what this reminds me of?" Aviva asks.

"What?"

"Penobscot Moms." Aviva raises her eyebrows. "My all-time favorite story."

"This'll be bigger than that," Ev predicts. "Way bigger."

Armitage might just jump-start our little show, she wants to say. But she keeps this to herself.

Back in her office, Ev runs her eyes over the five Emmy Awards on a shelf over her desk. Each is engraved *Everleigh Page, Producer*. She picks up the one for "Penobscot Moms," her index finger tracing the letters.

She and Aviva had been working on *National Report* then. They'd gotten a tip that children of the Penobscot tribe in Maine were being ripped away from their mothers by Child Protective Services at five times the rate of non-Native kids, often for dicey reasons, and thrown into unregulated boarding schools or foster homes. The result, which seemed nothing less than intentional, was not just broken families but a slow and deliberate evisceration of Native culture as generations of children lost the connection to their heritage.

It was a gut-wrenching story that touched on a significant thread of American history, but the EP of *National Report* had not seen it that way. He'd insisted "Indians" weren't "relatable." He'd offered them a standard two-minute slot for the story on a Saturday night, a notoriously low-rated time for news.

Ev had argued but he wouldn't budge. She became angry to a degree that surprised her. Maybe because she'd spent four years— well, not quite four—at college in upstate New York, in the heart of the former Iroquois Confederacy.

In any case Ev, brimming with outrage, had stormed out of his office and, without thinking, had pulled the kind of stunt that, if it backfires, can mean kissing your career goodbye: She'd gone upstairs to Ken Chang, who was not only the anchor of the show but its managing editor—the face of the entire News Division. She blew right past his secretary and into his office that was the size of half a basketball court. Ken was impressed enough by the story to make it a sponsored three-part "event." The head of CPS in Maine lost his job and the agency underwent a complete overhaul.

After the story won a string of awards, people started calling Ev and Aviva "Thelma and Louise." Soon they moved over to *Breaking*, where Ev was promoted to senior producer. Three years later, executive producer.

Aviva topped out at senior investigative producer and Ev had wondered if her own higher rise might cause a rift between them. But Aviva seems to like nothing better than the actual work of producing, especially being out in the field. And she's terrific at training younger producers. They come back from their time with her knowing six times as much as when they went out.

So now Thelma and Louise are reteaming for another story, this one most likely even bigger than the last. But this time, she won't have to knock on Ken's door to get it on the air.

She's in charge now. She calls the shots.

FOUR

Leigh tossed the *Lawton Leader*, the school newspaper, onto the floor next to her bed. "What dreck."

"You always say that," Dilly said.

"But it is." Leigh lay back on her pillow and closed her eyes.

"Then why do you read every edition?" Dilly asked, leafing through her chemistry book.

Leigh considered. "Habit, I guess. My dad sort of made me read the paper every day."

"*Made* you?"

"He would quiz me at dinner."

"What? Why?" Dilly closed the book.

"I don't know." Leigh swiveled and put her legs up on the wall, staring at the ceiling.

"Yes, you do," Dilly said, exhaling loudly. "Look, not to offend you, but do you realize that you're super hard to get to know? We've lived together for weeks and I barely know any more about you than the day we met. You've mentioned that your mom died and it's obvious you don't like to talk about your dad. But that's about it. It's like you're afraid that *anything you say about yourself will be used against you in a court of law.*" Dilly said this last part in a jokey, TV way but it didn't help.

Leigh's face was hot-poker hot; Dilly had nailed her so completely. Yet she wasn't mad, except at herself.

"I guess I prefer observing. Watching. Listening."

"That's all good but now *I* want to listen to *you.*"

"Okay," she said. "But you'll tell me if this gets boring?"

"I will but it won't."

Leigh took a breath. "After my mom died, it was like, my dad didn't know how to talk to me. We'd have these silent dinners. Excruciating. I think the newspapers were—"

"Stop and go back," Dilly said. "Why didn't he know how to talk to you?"

Leigh fell silent. "We didn't have a great relationship," she said. "Don't have."

"Why not?"

"I don't think he quite appreciated the way I reacted to my mom's death."

"Weren't you just a kid?"

"I was eight." Leigh chewed lightly on the inside of her cheek. "But I . . ." She sighed. "I don't know."

"Yes, you do," Dilly said gently. Leigh heard Dilly strike a match and, soon after, the sound of a long, satisfied drag. Dilly came over and sat down on Leigh's bed, handing her the cigarette.

She brought it to her lips and inhaled, coughing only slightly.

The doctor had broken the news outside of her mother's hospital room. His words died away, immediately replaced by the sounds of plugs being pulled out of walls and machines being wheeled away to patients who could still make use of them. Or at least that's how it had seemed to her.

Everleigh had closed her eyes, listening to muffled voices, waiting for the world to stop lurching. She'd opened them in time to see her father follow somebody to discuss paperwork.

Paperwork became his new best friend. For the next few weeks, there was always something that needed to be read, filled out, or signed and he seemed relieved at having these tasks on which to train his focus. One night he left his study long enough to come into her room. He pulled up the small chair she'd used for tea parties when she was little and perched on it.

"I'm sorry we haven't spent much time together lately," he said, resting his elbows on his knee and looking at the floor. "But that's going to change. As soon as I finish the experiment my team's responsible for at the lab, we're going to do something fun. Take a weekend trip. Yosemite, maybe. Sound good?"

"I guess," she said. She couldn't really picture a trip without her mother, but it was nice he wanted to go.

He pulled a paperback from his back pocket and handed it to her. It was called *A Grief Observed*, by C. S. Lewis. "I found this," he said. "It's by the author of all those Narnia books, so I thought you might like it."

Everleigh turned it over in her hands and read the paragraph on the back, which said the book explored "the trauma of bereavement as well as critical questions of faith and theodicy."

After her dad patted her head goodnight, she started reading. The introduction was full of words like *concussed* and *pathos*. But she kept going because her father had thought to give it to her.

A couple of weeks later, he told her that his experiment had run into some kind of setback. The next week there was another, then another. He said it wasn't working anymore to have her at the lab in the afternoons, like her mom had done. He signed her up for after-school care.

At some point it became clear they were never going to Yosemite.

Her first meltdown came during recess. She had wanted a rubber ball to kick against the side of the building. When another girl took the last one out of the locker, Everleigh grabbed it from her with such force it split along its seam. A few days later, she deliberately circled all the wrong answers on a pop quiz, and a week after that, she told the teacher she loved, Mrs. Soames, that she hated her.

Alarmed, Mrs. Soames walked her down the hall to the school psychologist, Mr. Adams, who hauled out a box of Barbies and instructed her to use them to make a play about her feelings. But Everleigh had never played with dolls. Her parents had favored educational toys. The dolls, with their inert limbs and unseeing eyes, just reminded her of death. She burst into tears.

"Now, now," Mr. Adams said, seeming both annoyed and flustered. "These are the appropriate tools for your age group. You don't think you know better than I, do you?"

In the end, Mr. Adams escorted her to the principal, who called her father.

Anton wasn't able to come until after work. When he arrived, he looked alarmed.

"My girl, are you all right?" he asked, tilting her chin up. "It's a cold, is it?" he asked, turning to the principal.

"No, Mr. Page," the principal said. "Everleigh's having some . . . difficulties. I've asked our psychologist, Mr. Adams, to sit in."

Everleigh was instructed to wait outside. The secretary was gone for the day, so she plopped down on the floor and put her ear to the door. She could just make out her dad's perplexed voice.

"Angry? I don't understand," he said. "What does she have to be angry about? Sad, yes. But not angry, surely?"

Everleigh pressed her ear more tightly to the door, realizing that you listened a lot harder when you were trying to hear something grownups didn't want you to hear than when they sat across from you, lecturing.

Mr. Adams piped up. "It's not unusual for a child to be angry at being abandoned. It's not logical, but it can be the emotional response to this particular kind of trauma."

"I must confess, this makes no sense to me," Anton said, sighing.

"Have you met Mrs. Soames? Everleigh's teacher?" the principal asked.

"No," her father replied. "I'm afraid Greta handled school matters."

"She says Everleigh's having problems with the other children in class. She's always been a kindhearted girl, very sweet with other children, sensitive to their needs. But there seems to be some distance between her and her friends. She's had a few outbursts that have alienated them."

Mr. Adams continued the thought. "It might be that Everleigh feels isolated inside her experience of losing a parent, something no other child in her class has suffered. She may be feeling jealous of them because of this. Being around them right now may be painful for her, causing her to lash out or withdraw."

"This is all so hard to take in," Anton said. "Perhaps these episodes will subside on their own? For lack of a better word, evaporate?" He sounded hopeful.

"Feelings are real things, Mr. Page," said Mr. Adams. "They might as well be furniture."

Her father was silent for a moment, then asked a question Everleigh couldn't quite hear.

"Of course, Mr. Page," Mr. Adams said. "I'd be delighted. I'm up to date on the state's new Children's Grief Protocol. It's the latest thinking, with very encouraging results just unveiled at the most recent National Association of School Psychologists' conference where I was privileged to speak."

"This is very good to hear," Anton said. "When all else fails us, there is always science."

"Ah!" said the principal. "Speaking of which, I understand you've just been made director of the lab, Mr. Page. May I ask what you're working on? I was thinking you might be able to come in and speak to the high schoolers sometime."

Anton's voice brightened. "I'd be delighted. Do you have any students interested in particle physics?"

"Well, *that* sucks," Dilly said. "Did you have to keep going to him? The psychologist?"

Dilly lit another cigarette, and Leigh realized she'd never handed the first one back.

"For a while," Leigh said. "Eventually I managed to calm myself down and convince everyone I was okay. I figured it was easier to say nothing than to say how you were really feeling and have to defend it to all these horrified adults."

"I like horrifying adults," Dilly said, and Leigh couldn't help but laugh.

Dilly flipped over and put her legs on the wall next to Leigh's. "So then what was the deal with your dad and the newspapers?"

Leigh flexed her toes. "I never really thought about it. I guess he really only liked to talk about his work—it was even the thing that brought him and my mom together—but he had no clue how to talk about it with a child. One night when I was in middle school, he pulled out the paper and actually started reading it at the table. I was like, fine, give me the comics. He said no, if I was going to read the paper I had to start with the front page, like eating vegetables before dessert. Then he asked me questions about what I'd read, to see if I understood it. And boom, we had something to talk about. The next night, I read the entire front section before we sat down. It went on from there basically. As I got older, I realized I liked knowing what was going on in the world." She swallowed. "Fewer surprises."

"I get that," Dilly said.

Leigh flipped over onto her stomach and picked up the paper from the floor. "But we're not going to learn anything about what's going on in the world from these people. Let me read you this. It's so—"

"Not this again," Dilly said. "Look, instead of bitching, why don't you do something?"

"Like what?"

"Sign up for the paper, idiot."

The next week, after midterms, Leigh presented herself to the news editor and offered her help. He appeared unimpressed.

"Everyone else showed up at the beginning of term," he said, squinting. "And you don't have any clips."

The Leigh from the first week of school might have skulked out in defeat, but not the one who had Dilly as a best friend.

"Give me a story, any story, and see what you think," she said. In the end, she'd been given a trial assignment: five inches about a poetry reading by the lit club.

Unfortunately, the reading was boring and the students pretentious. Leigh had pulled an all-nighter, puzzling over how to approach her piece. The next morning, bleary-eyed and punchy, she handed her story to Gil Branford, the editor who supervised new reporters.

She sat across from his desk, fidgeting as his pale blue eyes flitted over her work.

"You wrote a piece about bad poetry *in* bad poetry?" Gil asked, taking her in through his John Lennon glasses.

"I wanted to accurately convey what it was like being there," she replied. He blinked. "I wanted people to *read* it," she said, turning her palms up to the ceiling. "I suspected poetry might not rate as well as the latest *lakrooz* game."

"La*crosse*," he corrected with a raised brow and the tiniest hint of a smile. "Better learn that. Kind of a religion around here." Gil went back to the piece, moving the pen slowly over it, touching down now and again.

"Unorthodox," he said when he was done, threading the pen through his fingers while studying her. "But clever. I think we do too much by rote around here. I want us to be bolder, more creative. Develop a real identity on campus." He handed back her piece and gestured at it. "Fix that stuff and put it in the bin on the copy desk."

The next week he assigned her to help with a feature on students who failed out of Lawton. The main reporter was Blair Bykova. Blair, with her spiky hair and miniskirts, was a freshman too but more established at the paper, which seemed not unconnected to the fact that she was extremely social in the newsroom. Blair was to report on how many students flunked out of school and why. Leigh was to produce a sidebar about the college's counseling center. She showed up to interview the center's administrator with three pages of questions. The interview went on for two hours and at the end, the woman put Leigh in touch with several students who'd agreed to speak on the record about their experiences. Leigh's "sidebar" mushroomed and in the end Gil recommended to the editor in chief that it become the main story. Blair's fairly straightforward rendering of statistics wound up consigned to a box at the bottom of the page.

"Nice job," Gil said, handing Leigh the first copy off the top of the stack when it arrived from the printer. "You're good at getting people to talk to you. And you're a keen observer," Gil went on. "Both important for a reporter."

Leigh felt herself flush. "Thanks," she said, trying to keep her voice steady. Out of the corner of her eye, she saw Blair take a copy for herself, her face like a mask.

FIVE

Sean bustles around her kitchen, preparing salmon in a curry sauce while Ev tosses a salad that comes out of a bag. Sean's phone rings and Ev doesn't have to ask who it is.

"'Sup?" he asks as he toasts spices in a dry skillet. "Shit. When?" He pulls the pan off the heat and leans against the counter, frowning. After several minutes of mostly silence on his end, he says, "Keep me posted. Let me know if you want me to come out." He makes some affectionate noises and hangs up.

"What's going on?" Ev asks.

"My dad fell on the stairs outside his office. They're at the hospital, seeing if he's broken a hip."

"That's terrible. I'm so sorry."

"Mom's trying to figure out if she's going to have to cancel the cruise she's surprising him with after the party." Sean slips the phone in his back pocket and starts preparing a marinade while relaying more details from the call. He pulls some lemon-infused oil he must have brought over out of a cabinet and measuring spoons out of a drawer, and it occurs to her that he knows her kitchen better than she does.

Funny to think that it was Gareth, of all people, who had brought them together. He'd convened a meeting to discuss branding for an environmental initiative the News Division was embarking on, "Green Sweep," and had brought in Sean's firm to take a crack at the logo because the in-house graphics group hadn't come up with anything he liked.

Sean and his team had shown up early and Ev went to greet them in the conference room. Sean did his artsy demographic proud, she'd thought: His deep aubergine suit was soberly hip, his eyeglasses architectural, and his leather messenger bag youthful yet professional.

"Mr. Andersen, a pleasure," Ev had said, walking up to him with her hand extended, noting the arresting combination of nut-brown skin and pottery-blue eyes.

"Call me Sean," he'd said, offering his own hand before introducing his two young assistants.

At the meeting, Gareth had addressed the room, which included EPs from the other news programs as well as a handful of the network's PR and social media people. Gareth had known what he didn't like: last year's logo, a simple green arc. What had become clear after he droned on for twenty minutes was that he had no clue what he desired instead.

Candy had been at the meeting, too. She and Ev had exchanged several pointed glances during Gareth's monologue. Ev was not a huge fan of Candy but she had to admit that there's no look as deliciously knowing as the one that passes between two women listening to a powerful man pontificate.

The room became restless. Several people coughed and shuffled papers and Ev glanced at her watch. She had another meeting coming up. The note she passed to Jeff, the snarky guy who administrated the News Division's Twitter accounts, said, *Lunch on me if you make it stop.* He rolled his eyes and shrugged. No one ever interrupted

Gareth. Absently, Jeff pushed the note off his pad, right into Sean's sight line. Ev grimaced; Sean had seen her pass the note and was now likely to conclude she was deeply unprofessional. His eyes flicked over the note, then over her.

"May I offer a suggestion?" he said a few moments later, taking advantage of the brief silence that occurred when Gareth drew breath. "I think what may be troubling you is the *position* of the arc: its points are exactly level. Forgive me saying so, but it looks like a frown."

Everyone looked at the easel. The arc did indeed look like a frown. "That's a point," Gareth said.

"What if we change the orientation?" Sean crossed to the easel and tilted the posterboard. "So that the point on the right finishes higher than the one on the left? Instead of a shape that recalls a frown we have one that resembles a rainbow. It's a slight modification that completely alters the emotion. Quite simply, it takes the arc from pessimistic to optimistic."

"*Nnnnn*," Gareth muttered, which was Gareth-speak for "decent suggestion, but I'll be damned if I show any enthusiasm."

"We could also play with the color," Sean continued. "To emphasize the rainbow idea, we could have the arc made up of multiple colors—all rich, beautiful shades of green."

Ev was about to say how much she liked this when Gareth decreed that this last bit might be "a little much." Nevertheless, the meeting was over ten minutes later, with Sean promising to deliver several mock-ups the following week. There was an exchange of business cards as everyone got up from the table, and Ev noticed that while Sean put everyone else's cards in a case designed for this purpose, he slid hers into his wallet.

The next morning he called her at the office. "I think you owe me lunch," he said.

After realizing they both lived in the Village, he suggested a tapas place on Greenwich Avenue that had just gotten a star in the *Times*. Afterward, they strolled the narrow, curving streets of the neighborhood and he confessed the relief he'd felt when she'd introduced herself in the conference room. All too often clients greeted his white assistants first, assuming one of them was the team *leader*, though they were a good ten years younger. Ev told him a similar thing happened to her at conferences sometimes, where her title plus her gender could still come as a surprise to some.

"I was psyched to get this gig with ARC," Sean admitted as they stepped around a group of tourists photographing brownstones. "I'm obsessed with news. My whole family, we're addicts. I was hoping I'd see Ken Chang. What's he like? I feel like he's a secret badass. Like he's got a mic in his hand and a knife in his sock."

Ev laughed. "I felt the same way when I started at ARC. You get over it pretty quick. But actually, Ken is a bit of a badass."

As the blocks slid by and the talk got more personal, Sean told her he'd been through a tough breakup the previous year when his girlfriend took a job in London.

"She asked me to go with her but it would have been tough with my family."

"You have children?"

"Oh, no. I mean my parents and siblings."

Ev exhaled. The last few years, most of the men she'd met were divorcés looking for an every-other-weekend nose-wiper and sandwich-maker for their kids. The children themselves hadn't bothered her half as much as the entitlement of their dads.

One thing most of the men had in common: grousing about how much Ev worked.

"Do you want kids?" she asked, trying to sound casual and not in the way of a woman desperate to have children, which she was not.

He exhaled in a way that said she might not like the answer. "It seems it's not possible for me."

"Oh?"

"I had chemo as a teenager. For Hodgkin's. That's one of the potential side effects." They stopped to admire massive Easter eggs in the window of a specialty chocolate shop.

"I'm sorry," she said. "You're okay now?"

"I'm fine. I've thought about adopting but at this point, I'm pretty used to my life the way it is. Plus my brother has three young'uns and my sister has a thirteen-year-old who's basically my mini-me. Whenever I want a kid fix, all I have to do is hit them up." He looked at her sideways. "And you?"

She shook her head with a small shrug. "I'm good," she said.

Now, post-dinner, they linger at her kitchen table. Homer arrives at her side and looks up imploringly through his curly blond fur-bangs. He knows not to beg from Sean, but she can't resist his bottomless brown eyes. She wipes the sauce off a flake of fish on her otherwise empty plate and feeds it to him.

Sean's poring over a proposal; she's going over her layoff list. Gareth says he wants a first draft of it soon, though she hopes to stall until she can show him the Armitage story.

"*Hello?*" Sean says.

"What?"

"I said your name twice." He hands her a piece of paper. She assumes he wants her to do a copyedit on his work but it's a drawing of her face, the corner of the layoff list just visible in the lower right-hand corner.

She takes it and leans back in her chair. She's flattered that he can't stop drawing her, even when he's supposed to be working. But is this really her? This frowning, joyless creature? "I look like an old hag."

"You look like a beautiful woman. Who's having a lousy day. What is that, next season's budget?"

She grunts, slides the list into her bag, and heads into the bedroom where she flings open the doors of the low cabinet that runs against the wall.

"I didn't mean to drive you from the room." Sean leans against the doorway, watching her root around, pulling out boxes and photo albums and scattering them on the floor.

"I want to show you me when I was younger."

"I've seen you when you were younger." He joins her on the floor as she flips through albums and yearbooks. First grade class picture: chubby cheeks and dimples. Third grade: expression tight, her gray eyes shiny. Her mother had died a few weeks before. The photographer had grown impatient with her stiffness and had barked at her to smile. Tears had streamed down her face, which, as she remembers it, chastened him only a little.

Junior high: pierced ears, little gold "starter studs" clashing with the silver of her braces. First year of high school: the bones of her face starting to emerge from their cocoon of baby fat. And always, whether bobbed, feathered, or long: the white-blond hair.

She stops and takes a breath. Homer lumbers in and whines softly. He drops down beside Sean, who's now sitting cross-legged, back against her bed, a large book open on his lap. Ev scoots back next to him and sees it's one of her Lawton yearbooks.

"Pretty school," Sean says. "How'd you wind up there, anyway? It's upstate. And you grew up in California."

"My dad was moving to Switzerland, so I thought going to

school on the East Coast made sense. And he liked it because it had a good physics department. Not that I ever planned on taking physics."

He pauses on a double-page spread of campus, the rotunda of the library hovering over the quad, brick paths stretching out in all directions through deep green trees.

He stops at a picture taken at the *Leader*. It shows a staff meeting: about twenty students, including her, standing together in the newsroom.

"Look at you," he says softly, running his fingertip lightly over the image. After a pause, he asks, "Who's the guy?" Even though there are several young men in the photo, it's clear whom he's asking about.

At the center of the circle of reporters is Gil. Tall and wiry with an intense gaze and a chin dimple, he'd cut quite a figure on campus. In the photo, Ev gazes at him with something like awe.

"Your boyfriend?" Sean prompts.

"My editor," she says softly. In her mind back then, it was an even loftier post. And anyway, Gil had a girlfriend at Holyoke the entire time they were at Lawton.

Sean keeps flipping and arrives at the pages dedicated to sports. A page or two each for soccer, tennis, basketball, and a few others.

"What the hell?" he says. "Nine pages for lacrosse?"

"They used to say Lawton was a lacrosse camp that happened to teach liberal arts," Ev tells him. "It was the big sport on campus."

It's an understatement. Lawton was a small school, only Division III, but prided itself out of all proportion on its lacrosse program. Lacrosse, she'd learned in a Finger Lakes history class, was the oldest sport in North America, invented by the local Native peoples in the 1600s. Back then, it had functioned as much more than a game; it was played to resolve conflicts, heal the sick, and most importantly, foster legions of skilled warriors. Early contests often mimicked war and could involve as many as a thousand players per side, storming fields that might be miles long in brutal contests that could last for days at a time.

The players of Ev's day were treated as the direct inheritors of this storied history. Girls and faculty alike stared at them as they walked by, carrying their sticks like spears. On game days, the team would gather on the quad, surrounded by hundreds of students, to chant an ominous Native war cry.

Ev can still hear it, ringing spookily across the rolling hills of campus: *Casee Kouee! Casee Kouee!*

There's an entire page dedicated to the team's star, Dan Daggett. Six-foot-four, auburn-haired, the quintessential dreamboat.

Unless you crossed him.

Ev leans over and turns the page, pretending to Sean that she's enjoying this trip down memory lane, when really she just doesn't want to look at Dan anymore.

Near the end of the book, there's a picture that's even tougher to see. It shows about a dozen girls in 1920s dress, sitting on a blanket, toasting at the camera with little teacups.

For a fraction of a second, she can't pick out who's who. In their getups, all the girls look somehow similar, as if there's a family resemblance. But May's green eyes burn through the paper, her perfect dancer's posture evident even when seated. She wears a gauzy white dress and clasps a pocket watch that supposedly had belonged to Jane Hunt, one of the organizers of the Women's Rights Convention in nearby Seneca Falls a century and a half before.

Every year, Foster House had held a suffragist theme picnic at a large clearing in the woods where local Native women were said to have brought the actual suffragists to receive the benediction of their "Great Spirit" the night before the convention began. In the picture, most of the girls appear regal but if you look closely, it's clear that she, Dilly, Tina, and Cam are wearing their vintage duds over tank tops and shorts. They'd come straight from finals and had joined the gathering in progress, giggling as they threw flapper dresses and pearls over their clothes.

If you look even closer, you might also notice that all the girls have strangely glassy stares and the color in their cheeks is unusually high, making them look feverish. But Sean doesn't mention it and she certainly isn't going to.

Ev's eyes rest briefly on Tina, the black-haired tomboy who would suffer the indignities of a drop-waist dress but vetoed any hats or jewelry. She moves onto Cam, with her heart-shaped face and wary look. Tina and Cam had been inseparable, just as Ev and Dilly had been.

Ev locks eyes with her young self: her skin unlined, her white eyebrows unplucked. Dilly's arm is around her shoulders, their heads pressed together, the pale of her own hair in stark contrast with Dilly's dark red tresses.

Looking at Dilly now, she feels such a stab of longing that she almost sucks in her breath.

"You look so . . ." Sean's voice trails off. She thinks he's going to say "cute." Or "silly." Or maybe "young."

"Clueless?" she offers.

"Happy," he says.

He kisses her on the forehead, gets up, and heads back to the kitchen.

Ev gathers the albums together and stacks them inside the cabinet. She presses the door closed until it clicks into place.

. . . . .

"What's going on?" Gareth asks.

"What do you mean?" Ev takes him off speakerphone and waves Meryl out of her office.

"You haven't been returning emails. And yesterday I called out to you as you were getting into the elevator and I'm pretty sure I heard you pressing the 'close' button frantically from inside."

"Please, Gareth. I simply didn't hear you." She scoots her chair closer to her desk. "I've had my nose to the grindstone. Isn't that what you pay me for?"

"I pay you to do what needs to be done. Where is the rest of the layoff list? You've sent me four names. Not enough. Where are the other cuts?"

Ev looks down at her desk. She has "the grid," the monthly calendar of upcoming stories, in front of her. She's been wrestling with what to put up against the competition, which stories work best in combination with others.

"I'm finalizing the list now," she says, shuffling through a stack of papers, looking for it.

"The parent company, I remind you, is getting antsy. Your show isn't doing well enough to justify your headcount. You slipped again last week and haven't won your time slot in months."

A small knot of fear twists in her gut. Is he thinking of pushing *her* out, too?

"Maybe that's because there's so little promotion," she says. "I thought we were getting some fifteen-second spots during *National Report*. But those all went to *Smell the Coffee!* What happened?"

"Candy insisted on those and she was right to. She's riding a wave and it's critical to make the most of it."

Damn that Candy. Yes, she's riding a wave but that's only because her show is the TV equivalent of empty calories. True, the morning shows are a different animal; people like a little sugar sprinkled over their news at breakfast time. But to Ev, *Smell the Coffee!* seems sillier than it has to be.

"Let me do more investigations," Ev presses. "We haven't done anything undercover in more than a year. I have a great story in the works that I want to tell you about. A whistleblower's come forward—"

"That's not what—"

"—and I'm going to be screening a rough cut for you soon. Just nailing down a key interview." Ev flings a silent prayer into the universe that Aviva's source comes through. "It's the kind of story that will have us *owning* the national conversation. Extremely promotable for sweeps."

"Investigations are hit and miss. And expensive," says Gareth. "I'd like that list today."

"I think it's important we make sure we're letting go of the right people. I've been reviewing contracts, crunching the numbers, and—"

"This is hardly a revolutionary procedure. And it doesn't take this long. Here's an idea . . . take everyone who currently has a window in their contract and exercise it."

That's ridiculous. It would mean letting go of some of her best people. And she doesn't like being strong-armed.

"And if you can't face telling them, you needn't bother."

"Hmm?"

"What do you think your number two is for? Malcolm Whatshisname? Tanaka? Make him do it. Then at your next staff meeting you blame everything on the meanies in Finance and tell everyone you saved the day by laying off far fewer people than you were supposed to. It's very simple."

"I appreciate the advice but I'm a big girl. I can fire my own employees."

"That's your choice. Just get me that list ASAP. I have a meeting upstairs next week and have to show them that we'll meet expectations."

After they hang up, Ev realizes that it's been hours since she's eaten and makes her way to the ARC commissary. She pays for her quinoa bowl and is carrying the plastic container toward the exit when she hears a loud "Ev!" and catches sight of someone waving a hand at her with the mania of a hummingbird's wing. It's Tab, at a table by herself. With an internal grimace, Ev heads over.

"Hello," she says, setting her container on the corner of Tab's table and hiking her purse more firmly onto her shoulder.

"Would you like to join me?" Tab asks.

Ev hesitates. She doesn't really want to make small talk, but Tab looks so hopeful she can't say no.

"How are you feeling?" Ev asks, sitting. "That was quite a scare the other week."

"I'm so embarrassed." Tab bumps her fist against her forehead. "I was just a little careless with my medication. Which I'll never do again. I don't want you to worry about sending me out in the field or anything."

"Important to have a handle on that stuff," says Ev, eyeing Tab's plate. She's separated out the parts of her salad so all the spinach is in one pile, mushrooms in another, cranberries in a third. If she's not mistaken, it's classic OCD behavior.

Tab stabs a stack of mushrooms with her fork and lifts them halfway to her mouth. "Can I ask you something?"

"Sure."

"How did you know you wanted to be in journalism?"

"Oh," Ev says, a little surprised. She hadn't been expecting to talk about herself. Briefly, she outlines her trajectory: how she worked at the *Daily News* where she excelled at covering politics and protests, prompting a local TV news producer to hire her during a bruising New York City mayoral campaign. After it was over, she realized she enjoyed the immediacy and visual poetry of television and decided to stay, eventually producing an award-winning series on graft in the New York City DA's office, which earned the attention of people at the network.

"But how about before all that?" Tab asks. "What made you choose journalism to begin with?"

She clears her throat. "It guess it was my college roommate," Ev admits, annoyed that Dilly is popping up in her thoughts again so soon. She looks at her watch to convey that she prefers not to elaborate.

Tab seems to get it and attempts to squeeze in another question before her boss departs. "So what about now?"

"Now?"

"What—I don't know. Any advice to share?" Tab gestures vaguely around the room. "Not many women get as far as you have. And I heard that no woman has ever been president of the News Division." This is true. ARC is the most "old boy" TV network there is, and the least diverse.

"There was a woman VP here, around ten years ago," Ev says. "She was in talent recruitment. But she only lasted a few months." She remembers it well. Eleanor Ross was a bit of a test case. Lots of fanfare when she started but she ducked out early a few times for kid-related problems during a bidding war for a hot political correspondent from another network—and that was that. The ghost of Eleanor apparently still haunts the hallways since there's never been another woman at the VP level. It's Ev's dream to get there herself one day but the way Gareth is acting lately, it's never looked less likely.

"So what's your secret then?" presses Tab.

Ev spears a slow-roasted tomato with her fork. "I guess I'd

have to say I picked a lane and it was the right one." She goes on to explain how she booked some big interviews as associate producer in the investigative unit, which got her a string of high-profile undercover assignments.

"But we don't do investigations," points out Tab.

"We used to. Other kinds of stories sell better at the moment," says Ev, toeing the company line.

"I don't believe it," Tab says, shaking her head. "I think people want an advocate . . . someone who's looking out for them. It's what my friends are getting from social media and that's ridiculous. They're depending on complete randos to help them navigate what's going on in the world." Her face turns bright red. "Sorry."

"Don't apologize," says Ev. Girls are always apologizing. "I don't take it personally."

"I think Gareth Smyter does."

"What do you mean?" Ev asks.

"I talked to him yesterday."

Ev can't even imagine how this came to pass. "Oh?"

"I think he was trying to get you to hold the elevator, but the doors closed and we got into the next one."

Ev narrows her eyes. "And?"

Tab shrugs. "I told him our crime stories are triggering. And our celebrity profiles are so fawning they're boring."

"I see." Ev wishes she'd held the elevator after all.

"Then I suggested other stuff we could be doing."

"Like?"

Tab relays her ideas: a series about children in war-torn countries who create elaborate fantasy worlds to cope, a hidden camera investigation into dangers lurking in goods from China, the founding of a transgender kibbutz. Tab's voice rises with excitement as she speaks and a few people turn to look.

When Tab describes an idea for an exposé about college administrators ignoring sexual assault on campus, Ev stiffens.

Is the girl trying to say she knows something about Ev's past?

No, that's ridiculous.

Anyway, Tab has already moved onto six other ideas that a young Ev might well have considered but boss Ev knows won't ever see air.

"And what did Gareth say to all this?"

"He mumbled something and started scrolling on his phone."

Ev almost laughs at the idea of the president of ARC News stunned into speechlessness by some upstart whose name he doesn't even know. But what's Ev supposed to do here? Management etiquette probably dictates that she act the part of Gareth's good lieutenant and defend him. But the girl's shown gumption and a willingness to challenge power.

Good instincts for a producer.

Back in her office, Ev officially pulls Tabitha from the layoff list. Another assistant producer will go instead.

Meryl pops her head in. "Aviva Abramowitz. Says it's urgent."

Ev presses the speaker button. "Hello?" she says. But the signal is faint and she hears only about every third word. "I can't make out what you're saying. Where are you?"

"Ohio," Aviva says, sounding clearer. "I only have a sec. Bad service and my battery's low."

"What's going on? Did you get the whistleblower?"

"Just met with her. She—" Her voice dies away.

Ev leans closer to the phone. "Did you get her on camera—"

"—brought internal documents, everything. But—" The line goes dead.

But? But what?

Nevertheless, a warm wave rises up through Ev the way it used to when she was on top of a big story that, for the moment, was just hers. Before broadcasting it to the world, she would imagine the evildoers going about their misdeeds with no idea there was an axe swinging just above their heads.

She knows she needs to get hold of herself, but her thoughts run away with her and she imagines this story kicking off a new era at *Breaking*. The show, roaring back in the ratings, winning its timeslot. She and Aviva accepting a Peabody Award.

They could invite the whistleblower to the ceremony. Whistle-blowers are, after all, the story-within-the-story: how and why they choose to come forward, the inherent bravery and loneliness of their mission.

But this whistleblower won't be alone. Whoever she is, Ev and Aviva will have her back.

SIX

"**D**id you know the student council is basically all guys?" Dilly asked, opening a fresh pack of cigarettes and passing them out. She, Leigh, and a few others were walking across the quad after Twenty-first Century Society, their boots sinking into the fresh snow.

"I'm the one who told you that, remember?" Leigh said, lighting up. "Though there's actually one girl, May Jessup. I interviewed her after the meeting I covered."

"Probably why the one all-girls dorm is the worst," said Carol.

"And why there's no full-time gyno at the med center," said Ann.

"What matters right now is pizza and its immediate consumption," said Hailey.

The discussion shifted to whether people wanted to go to the on-campus café or hike into town for a decent slice. Dilly walked ahead in concentrated silence.

Leigh grabbed her sleeve. "What's up?"

"When's the deadline to run for next year?"

"For student council? You had to file last week."

"Maybe I can get an extension."

Leigh looked at her friend. "Why would you want to do that?"

"Class just now," Dilly said. "When Professor Addison said the 'Year of the Woman' in politics didn't turn out to be the beginning of anything really big—I mean, since then things have basically plateaued—something clicked. It starts here, right? In college. You need women in the pipeline. And if I run, maybe some other girls will, too."

Leigh knew she shouldn't be surprised. Dilly might not be that interested in politics but, as she'd learned, her friend had strong feelings about fairness. She was the middle child of five and had long ago learned she needed to fight for her share, whether it was of her parents' attention or buttermilk biscuits. And she wasn't afraid of a fight. She'd been bullied as a child by a neighborhood boy and her older brother had counseled her not to avoid the bully but get right in his space and show no fear. Fake it till you make it.

But running for student council at the drop of a hat? Even for Dilly, it was a bit much.

"Maybe you can get an extension. But you'd still have to get like a zillion signatures. And there's a debate next week. I'm covering it and there's tons of topics. Do you know there are eight recycling proposals? Do you know what the school's current stance on admission quotas is and why it's being criticized from every side?"

Leigh went on but she could see that with every word, Dilly was only becoming more determined.

"Is anyone besides me covering the debate?" Leigh asked Gil a few days later, leaning against the conference table as the afternoon editorial meeting wrapped up.

"Didn't your roommate just announce she's running?" he asked, making a stack of all the folders in front of him. Leigh became aware that Blair was taking her time gathering up her own things so she could eavesdrop.

"Yep. Why?" she asked.

"You can't cover a debate that one of your friends is participating in. That's, um, *basic*?" Blair said.

"She's right," Gil said.

"I'm just going to report what happens," Leigh said, feeling her face flush. "Like I always do."

"I'm sure that would be your intention," Gil said. "But covering someone you're friends with constitutes what's called a conflict of interest. Meaning our readers would have every right to be concerned that you gave her favorable coverage."

"It's like you think you own the school," Blair said, under her breath. She walked away and Leigh sank back down into her seat.

Gil rolled his eyes in Blair's direction. "Ignore her. Anyway, I have something else for you this week. You're aware of what's happening Sunday?"

"Sunday."

"The game."

"Game?"

"Lacrosse? Lawton versus Middlebury? Ring any bells?"

Leigh pressed her lips together, embarrassed that she had no idea what he was talking about.

"Lawton has a chance to get to the Division III playoffs for the first time in almost ten years. If they do, it'll be thanks to Dan Daggett, our star attackman." Leigh tried not to roll her eyes at the word *attackman* as Gil continued. "This game also presents Dan with the chance to beat his father's freshman scoring record, set a generation ago. It's a huge deal. His parents and lots of big donor alumni are coming. And it's a night game, which is always more dramatic. We're sending three reporters to cover the game but I want you to do a sidebar, a "tick-tock" of the day itself as Dan—and the school—experience it. Talk to lots of people and do some visceral storytelling."

Sports was the most siloed department at the paper. "I've never done sports."

"It's not a sports piece. It's about everything around sports. The emotion, the culture. It'll be good for your portfolio."

The minute he said it, she saw the possibilities.

The only thing she didn't like was that her piece was going to be the "sidebar."

She hadn't meant to set a bomb off.

She'd called Delta Sigma Phi, the lacrosse frat, saying she'd be by the morning of the game to talk to Dan and observe his game-day routine. But when she got there, the boy who answered the door informed her that Dan didn't talk to anyone—didn't talk at all, in fact—before a game because he was "channeling his entire being" into the contest ahead.

Leigh was, however, ushered into the kitchen while the guy informed of what Dan had had for breakfast—black coffee, six eggs, an entire package of bacon, a giant bowl of red and white jellybeans (Lawton's school colors), a gallon of milk—and then, bizarrely, she was shown the bowls, dishes, cups, and glasses still on the table, like some kind of pungent shrine. Several of the brothers who moved in and out had Dan's jersey number tattooed on their biceps in what she hoped was temporary ink.

All this was a bit weird, though perhaps to be expected from the star's teammates who depended on him for their own fortunes. But the students at the spirit rally on the quad were no less intense. It was 7 a.m., almost twelve hours before the game. They should have been sleeping or nursing hangovers but here was the band playing the school's fight song and the cheerleaders brandishing pom-poms. The guys all had their faces painted while the girls sported tight T-shirts with—ugh—"DD" across the breasts.

Leigh stepped back from the scene and watched silently. There was something troubling about it, something it took a few minutes to identify. Finally, she realized: The whole thing was utterly devoid of humor. Of fun. There was little smiling and almost no laughing. The students seemed single-minded, fanatical, almost reverential of the team and Dan.

That night, the bleachers were packed. When Dan, as fearsome and self-serious as a professional athlete, took the field, everyone screamed themselves hoarse. When he broke his dad's record early in the second half, the crowd erupted with such ferocity the word *cult* popped into Leigh's head.

It popped up in her article, too, which turned into a rather unsparing examination of what could be seen as a freakishly lockstep display by college students who were supposed to be developing their independence and expanding their minds.

The *Leader*'s editor in chief, who evidently had been hoping for a giddy profile of athletes and their fans on a suspenseful day, was alarmed. But Gil said it was exactly the kind of smart, unexpected thing they should be running, and, after a tense discussion, into the paper it went.

Reaction was swift. Leigh didn't realize how many people suddenly knew who she was until she sat down for dinner at the cafeteria. Some students actually changed direction in order to walk by the table she shared with Dilly. Most just gave her dirty looks but some tossed insults like *You don't know what the fuck you're talking about* and *Who the hell do you think you are?* Leigh felt sick as she pushed overcooked ravioli around her plate.

"This is all my fault," Dilly said, shaking her head. "You wouldn't have even had to write that story if you'd been covering the debate. Which, because of me, you didn't get to. And yet you never complained, not even once."

Leigh shook her head. "I don't care about that. I actually liked doing the lacrosse piece. I feel like that stuff needed to be said. And anyway, the world needs you on the student council way more than it needed me covering a debate."

A sweaty guy with a bulging vein in his neck came up beside them and glared at Leigh.

"*Traitor*," he said.

Dilly turned toward him. "Fuck off, lemming!" she said. "Ever heard of free speech?"

The guy sidled off and from nowhere, May Jessup, with her dark, glossy hair and lifted chin, appeared with the calm of a deity. She laid a hand on Dilly's arm. "I know you're angry. But you're wasting your breath yelling at a few kids. It's about changing the culture at this school. If you win a seat on the council, we can work on that in the fall, okay?"

Dilly crossed her arms and nodded.

May turned to Leigh. "Don't you worry, either. You called it like you saw it. That always makes the establishment angry. But remember this . . . there are other people at this school, too. People who agree with what you wrote. People who support you."

The next time they saw May, it was the last week of the school year. With Leigh's help—from painting signs to editing her speeches— Dilly had won her student council race and the two of them decided to celebrate with dinner in town. Dilly was hoping a check from her mother had arrived so they could splurge, and they headed to the annex that housed the student mailboxes. May was hurrying out. She nodded at them but didn't stop to talk.

Inside their boxes, they each discovered a printed card on thick, expensive paper.

*After a period of careful thought and reflection,
the sisters of Foster House are delighted to
extend to you an invitation to join
our family and history in the fall.*

"Where the hell's Foster House?" Dilly asked.

"Off campus," Leigh said. "I saw it once. On Indian Street, I think."

There was something else she could have told Dilly about the place, but her friend would have thought she was crazy.

As Leigh turned the card over in her hands, a feeling came over her. One she could only describe as a warm chill.

SEVEN

The next night, Ev works late, poring over the latest version of the Armitage script. The magnitude of the story is setting in, just how much they're biting off by going after this powerful company. It's going to make a lot of people angry, people who will likely use social media to try to smear not just the anonymous whistleblower but Ev herself, Aviva, and all of ARC News. That's the way it goes these days; the messenger, especially if it's a woman, isn't just shot but crucified. Trolled. Doxed.

She exhales and rolls her shoulders. She uses her feet to spin slowly in her desk chair. She goes around once, twice. What can they do to circumvent this, the inevitable? How can they prove the story is driven by fact and not some kind of agenda or personal animus?

It occurs to her that they might try documenting their process. Show their math. Maybe they can find an interesting way to detail the meticulousness of their newsgathering, demonstrate to everyone how they ascertain facts and verify them. Explain what primary sources are, and—who knows—let the audience listen in on a booking phone call. Show how a news story is something like a theory, a thing you prod and test to make sure it's right.

Newsgathering, done well, is less an art than a science. One you can document.

She spins around a couple more times, looking up at the ceiling. Even though she was never interested in science as a career, she's always drawn comfort from its methods. Her mother's daughter, shaped by many afternoons at her lab. Greta, a microbiologist, would bring her there after school and set her up with little experiments using simple things like hydrogen peroxide and yeast. No matter what she tried, her mother knew exactly what was going to happen. Complicated as the world was, there was an order to it. Even if it was sometimes hidden.

One day when she was six, Greta lifted a pink-nosed rat from its cage and asked if she'd like to see how his insides worked.

"Rats and humans have the same basic physiology, so you'll get an idea what we look like inside, too. Won't that be interesting?" she asked, petting the rat. "I'm going to give him anesthesia, he won't feel a thing."

Everleigh hesitated. She loved animals—she'd been begging for a dog—and was concerned that the rat might feel something after all. Plus she wasn't at all sure she wanted to see blood and whatever else was in there. But she nodded because she knew it would make her mother happy.

Greta gave him a quick injection, laid him on a metal table, and made a small incision to show her daughter the tiny stomach and intestines, her voice tinged with wonder at the micro-miracles of biology. Everleigh had to admit it was interesting, or at least what she was able to see while watching from between two fingers.

"Would you like to see his heart?" Greta asked. "It's an incredible thing. I can show it to you, but it will mean the rat has to die."

Everleigh bit her lip. She wanted to please her mother, who had probably killed hundreds of rats without flinching. But she couldn't bear for this tiny innocent thing to die. Tears welled up in her eyes and her mother lifted her onto the lab table so they were eye-to-eye.

"What's wrong, honey?" Greta asked, searching her face.

"I don't want him to die. N-not because of me."

"Then we're going to sew him right back up," her mother said, taking the corner of her white lab coat and using it to dab her daughter's eyes. Faster than seemed possible, she threaded a tiny needle and made a series of deft stitches, closing up the rat's abdomen. Within two minutes, he was waking up, wriggling and sniffing the air. "See?" Greta said. "He's fine. Here, you hold him."

Greta handed her the rat, who seemed content to rest quietly in the small hand of his savior.

"I'm glad you stopped me," Greta had said, running her index finger over the rat's head.

"You are?"

"I think I was a little cavalier just now."

"What does that mean?"

"It means I forgot your little friend here is a living thing. And I was pretty casual about taking his life. Sometimes we have to, for science. But we shouldn't do it lightly."

Everleigh giggled as the rat burrowed into the crook of her arm. "I thought you might be mad," she said. "That you'd think if I didn't want to kill the rat, I can't be a scientist."

"Honey, you need to understand something." Greta cupped her chin. "I bring you here to get you excited about learning. Any kind of learning. This is the kind I do, but you don't have to." She took out the barrette holding her messy white-blond bun, retwisted her locks, and put the barrette back in, her hair just as messy as it was before. "You don't have to be a scientist. But I want you to know what it feels like when your brain is working, when you have a question in front of you and you try to find the answer." She gestured toward a shelf of beakers and test tubes. "You know how sometimes I'm up to my ears in these things and you have to practically kick me to get my attention and let me know it's time to go home for dinner?"

Everleigh nodded.

"That's because I get so lost in my work that I don't know what time it is. It's the best feeling in the world and I want you to know what it's like." Greta reached for a baggie of apple slices. "You want to feed him?"

Everleigh nodded again. She took a slice and held it to the rat's mouth, laughing as he began to nibble at it.

Greta touched her nose to her daughter's. "Who's my sweet girl?"

Ev twirls in her chair one more time, stretches, and looks at the clock on the wall of her office. She notes with an inward smile that it's nearly eleven and she has entirely forgotten about dinner.

EIGHT

How different move-in day was sophomore year. The previous September, Leigh had hauled her suitcases and boxes up the stairs by herself, a good seven trips, only to unpack them in an empty room. It remained empty most days and nights as Fran and Caroline partied orientation week away with their friends from home. There was a little awkward small talk with other freshmen over cracked tile in the communal bathrooms and, one night, limp pizza in the common room, but that had been pretty much it.

Now, here she stood on the wide porch of Foster House, swallowed by Dilly in a bear hug while girls she hadn't yet been introduced to cheerfully grabbed her belongings from the taxi and hauled them upstairs.

As Leigh stepped through the threshold, the house beckoned her as if into another world. Gardenias perfumed the air. Elaborately carved wooden banisters and moldings, polished to gleaming, drew her eye while thick rugs with long tassels cushioned her footfalls. Potted ferns dotted the rooms' corners and chinoiserie wallpaper depicting peacocks perched in fruit trees covered the walls.

"C'mon up," said Dilly.

She followed Dilly up the stairs, past a dozen charcoal portraits of white and Indigenous women in nineteenth-century dress. Their eyes seemed to follow her, but she knew from an art class the previous year that it was just the Mona Lisa effect.

Breathing hard, she arrived at the third floor, where the sophomores were housed.

"Ta-da!" said Dilly, pushing open a door.

Leigh blinked when she saw the room she and Dilly were to share. It was enormous, with generous closets and large windows. Cushioned window seats provided the perfect spot to enjoy the view over the sweeping backyard, some fields, and, in the distance, the verdant, beckoning edge of the woods.

"I hope you don't mind but I found these sheets and got a set for each of us."

Leigh ran her hand over a pillow. The material was deliciously soft and festooned with tiny vines and jasmine blooms. But if you looked closely, you'd see the leaves were shaped like little daggers.

Leigh laughed. "So *you*," she said.

"So *us*," Dilly replied. She headed toward the door. "I'm going downstairs to put in our order for breakfast stuff. I'll make sure they get that cereal you like. See you in a bit."

The bathroom, across the hall, was tiled in black and white, with a clawfoot tub and a fluffy bathmat the size of a door. Leigh wasted no time hanging her towels and unloading her shampoo and toothpaste onto one of the shelves next to the sink.

"Hey, neighbor." A stocky girl with a black bob, wearing a Lawton sweatshirt and a nose ring, stood in the doorway. "You must be a sophomore, too, yes?"

"Uh-huh. Leigh Page." They shook hands.

"Tina Lapinski. I was in Springfield last year. Weren't you there, too? At the beginning of the year? Then you disappeared."

"I moved into Stanley."

"Why? What happened?"

Leigh looked down. "Nothing interesting." She had no intention of sullying this place with the mention of Fran and Caroline. She zipped up her empty toiletry bag firmly. "Anyway. Who's your roommate?"

"Camilla. Last name's Overton, I think? She's in the infirmary, I don't know why, but she should be back later in the week. I was thinking of putting her stuff away but that would be weird, right?"

"Kinda."

"I want to do something to welcome her when she comes. It sucks to be sick the first week of school. May says she's super smart but she's going to be behind."

Leigh was moved by Tina's kindness toward someone she'd never met. "We could pick up her textbooks and bring them to her tomorrow. That might help her keep up. If she's well enough to study, obviously."

"I like that." Tina smiled. "Let's do it."

That evening, the entire house, minus Camilla, gathered for the traditional welcome dinner. As the girls took their seats in the formal dining room with its white tablecloth and candelabras, Iris, head of house, formally introduced her fellow seniors: Maggie, Sarah, and Georgia. Next came the juniors: May—whom Leigh had met when she'd interviewed her about the student council and then again with Dilly in the dining hall—along with Belina, Katie, and Jeffreyanne. Iris, with her reddish curls and spray of freckles, went on to give a brief rundown of the house rules. Girls cleaned their own rooms and made their own breakfasts and lunches. A housekeeper cleaned the common areas, and a part-time cook came in to prepare the evening meal.

And what a meal it was. Beef *en croute*, roasted zucchini with basil, warm baguettes with soft butter, and glasses of icy champagne in elegant flutes.

"It's not like this usually," warned Belina. Her hair was in pigtails and her brown eyes, which turned up at the corners, gave her a saucy look. "No alcohol and we eat our share of pasta and sandwiches. But Lacey, the cook, is a sweetheart."

They were just about to dig in when they heard the front door open, followed by the sound of footsteps. And suddenly, in the arched entryway to the room, a woman appeared.

She was in her midfifties, Leigh guessed, and striking. She was tall with brown skin and lustrous black hair pulled back in a high bun. She wore a tribal-looking beaded necklace, a pantsuit, and, over it, a lab coat.

It was her eyes that were most arresting. They were amber with gold flecks. But there was something different about the left one. Leigh was closest to her and when she looked hard, she realized with a shock that it had two pupils. Like tiny planets in a hazel universe, one hovered slightly above the other.

"Good evening, everyone," the woman said. "Sorry for disturbing your dinner. Things were crazy at the hospital, but I wanted to greet you at least briefly on your first night." Her voice was husky, her words clipped and precise.

Iris stood. "For our sophomores, let me introduce Dr. Tala Long. She owns this house and runs the surgery unit over at St. Francis. She lives up the hill on Catamount but has an office here, off the kitchen, so you'll see her around."

Dr. Long appraised the girls warmly. When her eyes fell on Leigh, it felt as if they lingered an extra moment.

The girls murmured their greetings.

"I hope you'll find this place a bit of an oasis from everything . . . out there. And I hope you'll feel truly at home here. But also, please respect the house as you would your own home." Her mouth twitched. "As in, please don't break anything because I *hate* dealing with handymen, okay?" She raised her arms up playfully and the girls laughed. "Now then. I need to get going, but I look forward to seeing you again and getting to know our new members very soon. Please excuse me." Dr. Long made her way back to the kitchen and could be heard laughing with the cook. A few moments later, the screen door to the back porch banged shut and she was, presumably, gone.

"Is she Native American?" asked Tina. "The necklace . . ."

"Yes," said May. "She's Seneca, one of the tribes of the original Iroquois Confederacy that's been in the area for, like, a thousand years."

Maggie spoke up as she sliced into her beef. "The house has supposedly been in her family for generations."

"Does she have a family?" asked Dilly, taking a sip of champagne.

"She's divorced, I think," said Sarah. She salted a hunk of buttered baguette. "She has a couple of adult kids. I think they live out of state. She said she was raised by her grandmother, who ran the house before her, but the grandmother died last year."

"She's supposed to be an incredible doctor," said Maggie, pushing her glasses up her nose. She helped herself to more zucchini. "She has a ton of awards in her office. Apparently, she's brought more than one person back from the dead."

Leigh wanted to ask what this meant but Katie launched into a story about how the guy she was dating barely wrote all summer and should she keep seeing him.

NINE

T he next week, Ev's in Gareth's office. After a cursory glance at her longer layoff list, Gareth renders an opinion. "I don't know if there are enough names on here."

"It's not about names, is it though, really?" Ev says, pushing her hair behind her shoulders. "It's about salaries. The bottom line. Cost savings. Which are significant."

"Ultimately, yes." Gareth puts down the piece of paper. "But the money men want to see heads roll, too. They have a direct relationship to the benefit burden on the company. You might chat with Candy. She's come up with some new trick for using freelancers on an extended basis."

Ev tries to ignore the mention of Candy. But she's starting to get paranoid that there are knives out for her show, *Breaking*, in particular. Why so much focus on cutting its staff and, at the same time, starving it of promotable, investigative stories? She tries never to take anything personally, but it's like they're trying to kill her child.

Ev does a quick mental calculation of what she can offer. Like any smart manager, she's kept a little something in reserve. Her ultimate goal remains to drag this out and then win Gareth over with Armitage. Granted, this seems less and less doable given how much pressure she's getting, but she has to try.

"I can find you two more names," she says. "Just give me till the morning to go over what their severance packages would cost."

"I'd like three. By end of day."

"I don't think—"

"You've heard Steve Henderson might be leaving Digital?" Gareth asks, cutting her off. A rumor has been going around that there will soon be an opening for VP of the booming department.

"Yes . . ."

"The parent company is very impressed with our management team on the whole. They're keenly interested in our ratings and which EPs are delivering them. But in this competitive environ-ment, they're particularly fond of cost cutters. I thought you should know that."

Ev's taken aback. Gareth has never put his cards on the table so plainly before. But it now seems that if she falls in line, there might, just possibly, be a reward.

"This will hurt, but only for a second." The nurse ties a rubber tourniquet around Ev's upper arm and swabs the inside of her elbow with antiseptic.

It's Healthy Heart Week at ARC. Everyone's supposed to get their cholesterol and blood pressure checked. Afterward, you get a little heart sticker with a thumbs-up in the middle that you wear for the rest of the day. It's not something she minds. She's in excellent health and has always had good numbers. And, thanks to regular runs with Sean and the healthy food he prepares, she feels fitter than ever.

The needle goes in and she sucks in her breath. The feeling of being pierced, it's not exactly painful but it seems like a violation. It always amazes her that skin, capable of containing bone and muscle, racing fluids and thoughts—an entire world, really—can be breached so easily.

She remembers Dr. Long, quietly and expertly extracting a few drops of everyone's blood at Foster House on Commitment night.

What was that blood for? Were they ever told? She can't remember.

The nurse presses a bandage onto her skin and sends Ev into the waiting room until her results are ready.

She sits and leans her head against the wall, eyes closed, pondering Foster House. The first time she'd laid eyes on it she'd been jogging through Lawton after dark and had gotten lost in a neighborhood of rundown houses with broken windows and wheel-less cars in their front yards. The gracious white house on the corner had stood out like a society lady among coal miners. Planning to ask for directions back to campus, she'd trotted up the steps and peeked in the bay window next to the front door. Inside, about a dozen girls her age, a couple of whom she recognized from school, all in what looked like vintage dress, were seated at a long dinner table, finishing a meal. After a few moments, they put down their napkins and stood, filing into a hallway heading toward the back of the house.

There was something eerie about the scene, palpable even through glass, and she hadn't been able to stop herself from padding around to the other side of the house to see where they were going. She arrived at the kitchen window in the back and looked inside.

No one was there. She had a view all the way back into the dining room but there was no one to be seen. There were no stairs and no doors between the dining room and the kitchen that she could see. Just a narrow passage barely lit by a single sconce. She could see the whole of it from where she was standing. And it was empty.

It was as if the girls had disappeared into thin air. As if—

"Ms. Page?" Ev's eyes snap open and the scene dematerializes. She follows the nurse into a small room where she's informed that her LDL is 195 and her blood pressure is 160/90. She's advised to come back for a consultation with a doctor and to consider whether there's anything that might be causing a higher-than-usual level of stress.

TEN

The sconce cast a soft glow on the hallway wall. May had them stop in front of a bookcase. She and Belina gripped its side and pulled with some effort. It groaned in protest, eventually giving way, revealing a hidden staircase.

Leigh, Dilly, Tina, and Cam—who'd arrived at Foster House from the infirmary just days earlier looking wan but game—made their way down to a small space surrounded by walls made of stone. May slid past them, holding a large skeleton key that she inserted into the lock on a low door, before standing aside.

"Welcome to the Lucretia Mott room," she said, "and your Commitment."

They ducked and, along with Belina, filed into a snug room where a fire crackled, framed by a plain wooden mantle. Leigh wondered who'd been down to light it; all of their housemates had been having dinner together upstairs and were still up there, clearing the table. She looked around. Low upholstered chairs and settees were flanked by burnished mahogany side tables on top of which were scattered lace doilies and small cut-glass bowls. "Have a seat and we'll bring you something to drink."

Leigh and Dilly took a settee while Tina flopped down on the chair next to it, slumping back and throwing her legs out in front of her. Cam, her short wavy brown hair revealing dazzling golden highlights in the fire's glow, perched on a tufted ottoman.

Around them hung various small portraits and still lifes. The largest work, about two by three feet, was a charcoal drawing of twelve women sitting in a circle.

"That's Elizabeth Cady Stanton on the left, along with Lucretia, Alice Paul, Jane Hunt, and several of the Iroquois Clan Mothers in this very house. Right where you're sitting, in fact," May said. The suffragists wore high-necked blouses and the Native women, fringed capes. But it was their expressions that took Leigh aback. Instead of the severe portraits that she dimly remembered from history textbooks, here they were relaxed, with smiles and twinkles in the eye, as if someone had just told a joke. "They met a few times in the upstairs drawing room, but in the summer of 1848, as they were drafting the 'Declaration of Sentiments'—basically a list of demands—for the Women's Rights Convention, they decided belowground was safer and Mr. Foster set up this parlor for them."

"Safer?" Leigh asked.

"Let's just say not all the menfolk in these parts cottoned to women's empowerment," Belina said, handing each of them a cup of an earthy, nutty tea.

In the few moments of silence that followed, Leigh gazed at the women on the wall, becoming acutely aware of the costumes May had insisted they all don for the evening. She'd explained that it was Foster tradition, on special occasions, to pay tribute to their suffragist forebears by sporting the garb of the twenties, when women finally won the right to vote and all their hard work had finally come to fruition. The four of them had done the best they could, picking through the bargain bins at the vintage store in town, and now here was Cam tugging at a knife-pleated satin skirt; Tina, who'd traded her nose ring for a tiny diamond stud, wore what looked vaguely like a tennis dress; and Dilly was in a pale lilac chemise with lace insets at the shoulders and waist. Leigh wore a black flapper dress with tassels that swirled around her knees. Only her cream high-tops, perhaps, took away from the overall effect.

May swept her eyes over them approvingly. "I think you'll agree it's a pretty special thing to be living here," she said. "You're all moved in now, so you know what a lovely house it is. But it's important to know its history. You're lucky to be part of it. And Foster House is lucky to have you, too. We know you'll do important things during your next three years on campus. And after that, great things in the world."

"Flattering, I'm sure," said Tina, batting her eyelashes in comic fashion. "But how can you know that? We could be a crop of total losers."

"We know because our alumnae tell us," May replied, "when they come back twenty years after graduation for their Recommitment ceremony. A return for Recommitment was the only request of Aurora Foster when she died, leaving behind this house to Dr. Long's great-great or great-great-great grandmother. She hoped it would one day be used by female students if Lawton ever went coed. And most alumnae, except for those who were sick or had passed away, have done it. You will, too."

"You better, or they'll have something to say about it," Belina said, winking.

"Who?" asked Cam.

Belina pointed at the painting.

Dilly squinted at her. "What are you talking about?"

"I'm not sure the ladies on that wall have entirely left the building."

"Stop it," May said, her green eyes widening as she swatted Belina's arm. "Girls, don't listen to her."

"No, keep going," Leigh said. "Unless you're kidding, that is."

May shot Belina a look and Belina folded her arms over her chest. "I think it's only fair to say something. *We* were told."

"Not till later, we weren't," May replied.

"Told what?" asked Tina.

Belina glanced at May, who exhaled and gave a reluctant nod. "Put it this way," Belina said. "Things don't go bump in the night, but . . . I don't know. Sometimes it seems like there's something here."

"*Ooh*, ghosts?" Dilly asked, hopefully. She didn't spook easily.

"No, no," said May. "I think it hits everyone a little differently, but I'd say it's more like . . . a presence."

"A scary presence?" asked Leigh before she could worry about sounding childish.

"Actually, quite the opposite," said Belina. "For me it's like a warm energy, a sense of playful curiosity. Not on my part—more as if someone's feeling that way about *me*."

"Sometimes the air will have a sort of texture to it, too, almost like liquid," May said. "It doesn't happen often or last long. I sense it mostly in the drawing room." She cleared her throat. "Anyway. Shall we get on with it?"

Without waiting for an answer, she lifted her voice. "Dr. Long, if you have everything together, would you join us please?"

"One moment," said Dr. Long, her voice coming from behind a velvet curtain on the other side of the room. The pledges looked at one another with raised eyebrows.

A few seconds later, the doctor appeared. Tonight she wore a long, starched white cotton dress with a high neck and intricate beading across the bodice. Her hair was down her back in a braid as thick as the votive candles on the mantle and she carried a tray holding several syringes and small glass vials. They clinked musically against one another as she moved. She set the tray on a side table and squinted down at it for a few moments, as if trying to make sure she had everything she needed.

"Please give me the ring finger of your right hand," she said to Cam, straightening up. She dabbed a cotton ball in some clear liquid. The sharp smell of rubbing alcohol wafted their way. "Tonight, you become part of Foster House," she said, sounding suddenly formal, as if speaking from a script. "You become part of our legacy and the continuation of the bond between our ancestors."

May gestured at the vials. "This moment marks your Commitment to Foster House, to one another—and to yourselves."

Belina seemed to want to lighten things up. "Think of it this way . . . at least you're not being forced to drink fifteen shots of vodka and run around campus in a diaper like the Greeks."

"It'll be over before you know it," said May so smoothly it made the whole thing feel quite normal.

Cam looked scared, so Tina put her arm around her shoulders and whispered into her ear, "*I know, I know. But this time it's for a good reason.*" Leigh wondered what she meant.

It was indeed over quickly and, when it was her turn, Leigh barely felt the needle, although she found it soothing to look at Dilly while it was happening. Dr. Long put each girl's droplets of blood into a separate vial encircled by a metal band with something engraved on it. She exhaled loudly as if relieved—as if, despite being a doctor, there was something nerve-wracking about what she had just done. She slid the vials into separate slots inside a wooden box, which seemed odd. Wasn't the point to mix it all together for some kind of hokey rite?

The doctor lifted the tray and disappeared behind the curtain.

"We're sisters now," said May.

Leigh leaned in close to Dilly, meaning to ask what she thought the blood was for. But before she could say anything, she became aware that May and Belina were singing. The tune, solemn and gentle, sounded like a hymn:

For she knoweth not her power;
She obeyeth but the pleading
Of her heart, and the high leading
Of her soul, unto this hour.

Another voice chimed in from behind Leigh and she turned. It was Dr. Long, eyes closed.

Slow advancing, halting, creeping,
Comes the Woman to the hour!—
She walketh veiled and sleeping,
For she knoweth not her power.

Leigh felt herself growing woozy. Maybe it was the warming tea or the late hour, but it seemed like other voices were joining in. From up high—far away—somewhere.

She looked around, searching the faces of the others to see if they heard it too, but no one seemed to.

In the end, she credited Belina, planting ideas in her head.

Gaining eleven sisters in the blink of an eye had some advantages. There was always someone to lend you stamps or quiz you before a test. There were card games and impromptu dance parties and enough people to put up a huge tent in the backyard and set up a projector inside to screen movies on the canvas.

But the house was noisy, there was little privacy, and people seemed to think nothing of helping themselves to your stuff, whether it was a candy bar you left in a reading nook or a magazine on your bed. Leigh did like all the older girls, and loved the kindly May, but spent most of her time with Dilly, Tina, and Cam.

Leigh and Tina bonded over animals. Though Tina insisted she was ecstatic to be away from her family's farm, she brought home an endless string of stray critters. Whether it was a lost puppy, a bird with a bad wing, or an abandoned litter of miniscule baby mice, all were carted into the house. Leigh often volunteered to shelter them in her room, and, for sickly animals, would join Tina in cajoling Dr. Long into helping minister to them.

Tina tried to look after Cam, too. Cam, with her wide eyes and waiflike presence, was sweet and generous but could be unpredictable and moody. Even her sleep habits were odd. Once when Leigh had gotten up in the middle of the night to get a snack, she'd seen Cam sitting at the dining room table, her eyes seeming to stare into the distance as she intently polished the silver. Another time, Cam slept almost an entire week away.

It was one thing getting to know her housemates; she wasn't nearly as prepared for them to know her. She realized this after one of their Sunday dinners when talk turned to whose turn it was to wash the dishes and was there enough hot water, of which the house sometimes ran short.

"Not if Leigh took a shower today," Iris said, and everybody chuckled.

"Seriously," Belina said. "Forty-five minutes seems to be the bare minimum."

"The bathroom's a steam room when you're done, honey," Maggie said, nudging Leigh with her elbow. "You could write *War and Peace* on the mirror."

"How much time does it take to wash a human body?" Sarah chimed in.

"Maybe *you* shouldn't judge another's desire for cleanliness," May said. "Have you done laundry once this semester?"

Everyone laughed.

Leigh felt bonfires erupting on her cheeks. She knew her showers were a little longer than the others'; the deep tub and dinner-plate showerhead made it feel luxurious and she enjoyed the daily chance for some time alone. But she hadn't realized anyone else noticed.

She rose and collected everyone else's plates to take them to the kitchen. After putting everything in the sink, she went out to the porch.

"What's wrong?" Tina asked a few moments later, pushing out through the screen door. "You're not upset, are you?"

"Wouldn't you be?" Leigh said, wrapping her arms around her middle.

"They're just teasing. Haven't you ever been teased?"

"Of course, in the third grade. Not as an adult."

"Oh, right," Tina said, exhaling and looking up at the stars, the tiny stud in her nose glinting in the dark.

"Right, what?"

"I keep forgetting you're an only child."

"That has nothing to do with it."

"Yes, it does. When you have siblings, it's all teasing, all the time. No matter what age. You learn to brush it off."

Leigh kicked at the side of the house.

"Sit with me," Tina instructed, lowering herself down on the edge of the porch. Reluctantly, Leigh followed suit. "Look, Dilly told me it's hard for you to open up to people."

Leigh shot her a look.

"Don't worry. She didn't violate your privacy or anything. Cam's the same way. We've been living together for a couple of months now and yet I'm pretty sure there are some things going on with her I don't know about. But we're all living together in this house now. It's natural for people to want to get close, and a bit of gentle teasing is part of that. It's a way of communicating, of testing boundaries. And it's completely normal."

Leigh chewed on a hangnail for a moment. "Can I tell you something?" she asked.

"Of course."

"Sometimes I don't feel like I belong here."

"Why not?"

"Everyone's so . . . together. Assured. Making their mark. They know what they want to do. You with all your community outreach stuff. Cam, despite whatever's going on with her, aces every test and half her professors want her to TA for them. And Dilly. I don't think the student council knows what hit them. I swear, that girl *walked* out of the womb."

Tina laughed. "First of all, I'm completely faking it. All the time. When I call a grown-up and ask for donations, I'm so nervous I sometimes barf in the garbage can right afterward." She shook her head. "But, hey. You're on the *Leader*. That's huge."

"Maybe from the outside. But the truth is, I'm struggling. Most of my story ideas get rejected. I have to do at least three rewrites before anything gets printed. And you know Blair Bykova?"

"I've seen her byline."

"She basically hates me. I'm pretty sure she's trying to sabotage me with Jeremy Rubin, the deputy editor in chief. Lately she's getting stories I should be getting and they're putting way more of her stuff on the front page than mine. And—" Leigh looked at Tina. "Wait, why are you smiling?"

"'Cause I'm happy you're telling me this stuff! I mean, I'm not glad it's happening to you, but it's good that you're talking about it. And I'm not worried about your *Leader* career. You're going to be a star. It's just a matter of time."

Leigh was touched by Tina's support. "Thanks."

Tina leaned over, pressing her shoulder into Leigh's. "And about what happened before. The fact that they're teasing you is actually a *good* thing. They've seen your flaws and love you anyway. That's pretty awesome, isn't it?"

Leigh had to nod.

"Next time, just dish it right back to them. Laugh it off, or give 'em a little kick in the butt."

Leigh looked up at the night sky. "I.e., don't run out of the room like a baby?"

"I doubt they noticed. They've moved on to ragging on Jeffreyanne for letting her boyfriend sneak his laundry in with ours."

Leigh smiled and stood. "Guess I'll get started on the dishes."

"I'll help you," Tina said, rising also. "If there's any hot water left."

Leigh gave her a little kick in the butt.

Enough time had gone by that the uproar from Leigh's article about lacrosse culture at Lawton had finally died down. She wasn't allowed anywhere near the sports beat, of course, which was fine with her. She'd almost forgotten the whole thing, but the night she, Dilly, and Cam tagged along with some other girls to a party, she felt her heart lurch when she realized they were standing outside Delta Sigma Phi.

The game-day seriousness was gone, replaced by loud, proud debauchery. The music was deafening, the smell of alcohol and pot heavy in the air. Leigh hesitated at the threshold but Dilly and Cam were already disappearing into the crowd.

As she prowled warily, she wondered if any of the boys would recognize her and say something, but most didn't seem sober enough. They were fresh from yet another victory, pink-faced and high-fiving.

She began to relax, unbuttoning her jacket and accepting a drink from one of the brothers. But she stayed on the room's perimeter, her back pressed against a wall. Guys weren't high on her agenda right now. She'd done enough messing around back home to last quite a while.

It was weird the way she'd gone boy crazy; she hadn't seen it coming. But in eighth grade, when guys' glances started to linger, she found herself dressing to encourage their attentions. When their hands wandered during a slow dance, she pressed herself closer. The first time a boy kissed her, in ninth grade, over their history homework, she felt not so much an erotic thrill as a sense of relief. At being chosen. Wanted.

The feeling turned out to be a gateway drug. She lost her virginity on Valentine's Day of sophomore year to a boy who gave her a tiny stuffed teddy bear from the drugstore. Others followed. She always had a place to take a guy since Anton was at the lab until late most evenings. Usually, she picked loners. She related to them and could be reasonably sure they wouldn't brag about their conquest in some locker room.

But, like with any other drug, it took ever more to get her "high," to achieve the rush of being desired. Maybe because of this, senior year she broke her rule and went home with the defensive captain of the football team. His eyes on her had somehow been both dead and hungry at the same time. It was only after he began undressing her that she realized he hadn't once kissed her. The thrill of being singled out disappeared and she only went through with it because she was scared of what he might do if she tried to back out.

After that, physical intimacy had lost some of its appeal.

A tall, lanky brother asked her to dance and she did, closing her eyes and feeling the bass come up through her feet as if the house itself were partying along with them.

Sometime later, she ran into Dilly by the bathroom and they realized they hadn't seen Cam since they'd arrived. Leigh felt a trickle of worry. Cam didn't go out much and she sometimes had a weird response to alcohol, passing out cold after a single drink.

"Let's try upstairs," she said. They threaded their way up, searched the second- and third-floor hallways, poking their heads into rooms, but Cam was nowhere to be seen.

"Do they have a basement?" Dilly asked.

There was a set of stairs next to the kitchen. They couldn't find the light so they held the banister tightly as they descended, feeling the temperature drop with every step.

ELEVEN

Aviva welcomes her into the darkened edit suite to screen a rough cut of the Armitage story.

"You look a little grim considering your coup," Ev says, taking a chair across from her.

Aviva punches some buttons on the Avid machine to cue up the story. "Stuff's happening."

Ev frowns. When Aviva returned to New York after the interview, she warned that Armitage might be onto them, though she hadn't shared many details. It was the *but* she had been getting to when their phone call was cut off.

"What exactly?"

"The whistleblower is getting calls at weird hours, hang-ups. She thinks her email may have been hacked, so no more emails or texts—not even on her personal account." The whirring of the machine stops with a click. "In short, she's pretty sure somebody knows—or suspects—what she's up to."

"Yet she went on camera."

"She did."

"You think she might try to back out after the fact?" Though the whistleblower has already given the interview, she could ask them not to air it. And if her safety or livelihood were at stake, it would be difficult to deny her.

"I don't know. She's rattled, and getting another job could be tough if Armitage figures out her identity and blackballs her. Or comes after her legally. But like I told you before, she wants to tell her story and tell it to us only." Aviva takes a deep breath. "Anyway. You remember that we're disguising her, right? And I've run her voice through the changer software already."

"Got it."

"And we'll give her a fake name, obviously. I personally am thinking of her as 'Whitney.'"

"Because why?"

"Whitney Whistleblower. Action figure sold separately."

"Nice," says Ev.

"Here we go. Still missing most of the B-roll and music, but you'll get the idea." She hits play and the monitor comes alive with bars and tone followed by a ten-second countdown. Ev turns her chair toward the screen and balances a notepad on her lap.

The voice of Bob Wilkinson, the correspondent, fills the room. Aviva begins the story well. She's telling it through people, which is the best way to get into any issue. Sweet, family-oriented, attractive Americans who developed mysterious symptoms, several of whom suffered painful deaths. What they all had in common: Liquex, a drug subsequently pulled from the market. Then, in the next "act" that will follow the first commercial break, a primer on how the bad drug made it to market: It was tested by an outside company hired by Armitage. This brings up the first problem, according to experts Aviva has interviewed. The companies that take on this kind of work are gripped by an inherent conflict; if the drug fails, drug makers would be unhappy and might not give them more drugs to test.

The story then follows the company's trail to India, where it tested the drug far from government oversight on poor locals paid to take part, a scenario rife with problems. This section isn't working as well. It's too abstract, too full of stats and not enough people. Ev wants the Indian population to come alive in this section as well as in the American one, through the voices of individuals. They are victims, too.

The next act raises the question of whether Armitage knew, or should have known, what the testing company was—and currently is—up to. Armitage executives, in previous interviews on the topic, say no and outline layers of communications systems that complicated the matter and contracts that the testing company signed assuming complete responsibility for their testing. There's plausible deniability there and the execs know it. They speak of their "sympathy" for victims' families and only wish there was something they could have done.

Just when you think that's where the story will be left, with this "he said, she said" stalemate so typical in news, along comes Whitney. She is in silhouette, in three-quarter profile. Her head is neat, her movements controlled. Her voice as rendered by the software is slightly gravelly but both assured and passionate.

Whitney says Armitage knew exactly what was going on. She talks about meetings she went to and presents a series of internal memos. She also raises suspicions about the all-important question of how the company has been testing its new vaccine—the part that makes this story so timely and potentially alarming. But somehow it doesn't all come together clearly enough to create a compelling case. This part of the story still needs work.

The piece ends with a black hole where they'll put Armitage's response to the whistleblower's claim, when they contact the company for it. Which won't be for a while yet; you don't tip your hand to a giant corporation with rooms full of lawyers any earlier than you have to.

"It's very strong," Ev says. "I'm amazed at what you've put together in such a short time."

"But?"

"But I think a couple of the acts aren't working as well as they could. I'd like to take another whack at the script, play with the structure a little."

"That's fine," says Aviva. "I'm too close to it now to see what's working and what isn't anyway."

"Now we have to talk about Richard. We're going to have to loop him in sooner rather than later," Ev says, shifting in her seat. Richard Torres is the new legal counsel for the network, installed by the parent company. He costs a fortune but apparently will save millions in jury awards. It's his job to vet anything that could spark a lawsuit by making sure all facts are checked and that the highest standards of fairness are observed.

At the mention of his name, Aviva rolls her eyes.

"Now, now," says Ev. "We have to keep him on our side. In any case, I don't see anything here that should trigger him too badly." She stands, buoyant. "It's an important story and well done. I'm very proud of you."

"Be proud of Whitney, too," says Aviva. "She's taking a real chance."

"All right then," Ev replies. "I'm proud of you—and Whitney."

She's proud, yes. But grateful, too. Because god knows not every encounter with a potential source goes this well.

TWELVE

One spring morning junior year, Leigh spied Dr. Long out back. She wore a large floppy sunhat and gardening gloves as she meticulously tended to the rosebushes that ran along a high stone wall.

Leigh stepped closer to the window, watching. She found the doctor intriguing. Most of the time, she seemed serious, driven, much like Leigh's own mother. Dr. Long was clearly invested in her career, like Greta—who was also in medicine. The doctor had a shelf of awards in her little office, just as Maggie had said, and when she stopped by the house, she was almost always in scrubs, as if she were perpetually coming from, or hurrying off to, the hospital.

Although she hadn't talked much about her heritage, she seemed committed to upholding its legacy, at least a little. Once a semester, she'd gather the girls for a traditional Seneca feast. She'd prepare rabbit or partridge, squash, and an array of beans in shapes and colors Leigh had never seen. While the housekeeper came like clockwork twice a week, Dr. Long insisted on caring for the portraits of the suffragists and Clan Mothers herself, carefully massaging a homemade oil into their frames. When the girls had the flu or an infection, it was rarely aspirin or antibiotics she doled out. Instead she'd consult a small notebook, grind some leaves, mash some roots, and create an elixir by boiling them over the firepit in the yard.

But she had another side, too, a funny, almost silly one. She could be comically absent-minded—again, much like Greta. She'd miss appointments with plumbers and electricians, smacking herself in the forehead in an exaggerated way when she realized. Or she'd walk into a room only to announce to the ceiling that she had no idea what she'd come in for.

Despite a fastidiousness about Foster House's appearance, her car seemed like little more than a receptacle for candy and fast-food wrappers. And on sunny afternoons, she'd bring over a friend or two to loll on chaises by the pond, smoke her pipe, and comb through a stack of supermarket gossip magazines. Recently, on the spur of the moment, she'd invited Leigh to join her instead. Far from the dinners with Leigh's father and *The San Francisco Chronicle* quizzes, this was actually fun. Their legs dangling in the cool water, they took turns reading aloud about the shenanigans of celebrities and space aliens, alternating between bursts of outrage and laughter.

Now, Leigh observed as Dr. Long deadheaded some wilted blossoms. Studying could wait.

"Can I help?" she asked, striding across the grass, using her hand to shade her eyes from the sun.

Dr. Long smiled. "Thanks, but I think I'm about done." She straightened up and rubbed her lower back before stacking her shears and trowels into a large woven basket. "I could use you for another little chore, though, while I'm here."

They faced one another across a long table on the patio. Leigh no longer needed to sneak peeks at the doctor's left eye. In the beginning, she'd wondered if its two pupils ever moved in relationship to one another, but that was stupid. Normal pupils didn't migrate around the iris, did they? Sure enough, they'd remained where they were, just as she had first seen them: separated by about a millimeter, one slightly higher than the other. She wondered if the doctor saw double or somehow saw *more* of things. But there was no way she was asking.

Dr. Long pulled out her pipe, lit up, and took a long drag, sending a perfect smoke ring heavenward.

"*Ooh*, that's good," she said. "Please don't comment on the hypocrisy of a doctor smoking. I've heard it all." She winked at Leigh and proceeded to unspool a leather roll full of knives. They were simple yet well-made with antler and bone handles.

"Circa 1740," she said, holding one up. "I inherited these along with the house. They should probably be in a museum but I can't bear to part with them. I actually use them sometimes."

"On patients?" asked Leigh with a giggle.

"I've been tempted with some of them, but . . . so far, no," said Dr. Long with a small smirk. "When I was a teenager, I used to gut deer after a hunt but these days it's mostly skinning potatoes and carving birds. They still work remarkably well. But they need sharpening and the handles could use a polish. Care to try?"

Leigh accepted a paring knife, a cloth, and a tub of a white substance that looked like lard. Dr. Long mimicked how to rub the stuff into the handle in small, even circles, and Leigh began.

Working on the Iroquois knife, she remembered May saying that the doctor's tribal ancestors had been in the area a thousand years.

"Do you know a lot about your ancestors?" Leigh asked. "Someone mentioned them at the welcome dinner."

"Ah, the women of my nation," Dr. Long said wryly. "The one topic guaranteed to make me feel I'm not living up to my potential."

She took another drag off her pipe and began sharpening a cleaver on a flat black stone. "Women were the *real* bosses of the Iroquois tribes. We were the ones who hired and fired clan leaders. We controlled the food and supplies. It was women who began wars—and ended them."

"You're kidding. In, what, the 1800s?"

"Oh, no. This goes back at least to the 1600s. Probably far beyond."

"How did they get all this power?"

"Negotiation."

"With the men? But how do you negotiate with the person who holds all the cards?"

"You find your own, I guess."

"What did the women use for leverage?" Leigh pushed, nonplussed.

"Well, first, the classic *Lysistratic nonaction*. You know it?"

"From the Greek play?"

"Correct. They went on a sex strike. And 'withheld' childbearing, too. It worked like a charm because Iroquois men believed that their women were the only ones who knew the 'secret' of birth." Dr. Long raised her eyebrows in a manner that said, *Men can be so clueless*, and Leigh laughed. "Second, as I said, women minded the tribe's stores—everything from corn to moccasins—so they threatened to restrict the men's access until things changed. It's more complicated than that but eventually they got the world that they wanted." Dr. Long checked her teeth in the reflection of the cleaver. "They say it was the first feminist rebellion in the United States."

"And white suffragists saw all this and were like, *hmm, maybe patriarchy isn't the only way*, huh?"

"Correct. How could they not have been inspired? But they wanted nuts-and-bolts information, too. My grandmother told me the suffragists invited Native women to speak at their events, to advise them about how to push their own society toward equality. The Native women gave them the ammunition they needed and, boom, America changed. Or started changing, anyway."

"How did the suffragists even *meet* these women?"

"From what I understand, journalists who spent time among the Iroquois wrote about Native women's empowerment in newspapers and it caught the attention of white women," Dr. Long said, scraping a scimitar-shaped knife hard against the stone. "Lucretia Mott arranged to spend a month at the Cattaraugus Reservation and watched as Native women helped reorganize the Seneca government. Soon after, she met Elizabeth Cady Stanton, and together with other white women like Alice Paul, as well as Wolf, Bear, and Turtle Clan Mothers, they organized the Women's Rights Convention. There's a picture of them meeting in the downstairs parlor," she said, gesturing in the direction of the house. "You saw it at Commitment."

Leigh's mind was racing. What a tale! She was trying to pitch more stories at the *Leader* these days and hadn't been having much luck. But local Indigenous women helping the world's most famous suffragists win American women the right to vote—all right under the roof of Lawton student housing? This could make one heck of a feature. In her mind, the conversation had just become an interview.

"I learned about this stuff in middle school, but honestly, it was kind of boring," she admitted.

"The suffragists were hardly boring. They were fierce. I mean, they *set fire* to the president of the United States."

"What?"

"Alice Paul burned President Wilson in effigy—right in front of the White House."

"I can't even imagine it," Leigh said, shaking her head.

"Why not?" Dr. Long asked, looking up.

"The portraits of them. With their corsets and bonnets. Can't really see them raging."

"What you see in the paintings is not always what they wore."

"No?"

"Many dumped their corsets and skirts after seeing Native women in tunics and leg coverings made of animal skin. Several of the white women adopted something similar—bloomers, they called them."

"How did that go over, I wonder," Leigh mused.

"Probably about as well as your lacrosse article," said Dr. Long, raising one eyebrow.

"You *read* that?" Leigh asked.

"May shared it with me when she suggested you for membership." Dr. Long exhaled loudly. "Anyone who ventures outside the lines, especially if they're a woman, comes in for a fight. Take it from me—surgery is still a boy's club. Foster House has seen its share of strong women over the last twenty-five years. They've done everything from protest apartheid to pushing the administration to rename some campus buildings for women. For this, they faced ridicule and threats. Sometimes they'd run in the front door here and lock it behind them. But they were on the right side of history and so . . ."

Leigh tuned out for a moment. She was too busy fantasizing about the article she could write. At sports-crazy Lawton, the paper's pages were often dominated by boys. This could be a rare moment for the girls—if only Dr. Long would agree to go on the record.

"So about your great-great grandmother. Did she know the suffragists personally? Help them maybe?" This would make the story more resonant.

"Unfortunately, a lot of my family's personal connections have been lost to time, as our oral traditions have mostly died out. I know my great-great-great-*great* grandmother was given this home by Aurora Foster, but I don't know why or what else may have happened between them." She sighed, putting down the knife she was working on. "I admit that sometimes I'm tempted to move on. Sell this place and travel. It's a lot of work to keep it up. So much to stay on top of. I forgot to send a tax check one quarter and you would have thought I'd killed someone. But I promised my grandmother, who promised her mother. Who may have promised *her* mother, for all I know."

"What about your own mother?" Leigh asked.

"She died when I was young." She paused, searching Leigh's eyes. "Yours too, yes?"

Leigh was startled. "How did you know?"

The doctor shrugged. "It's just something I recognize. The tribe no one wants to belong to."

Leigh chewed the inside of her mouth, feeling an equal mix of discomfort and gratitude at being so effortlessly understood on a deeper level.

Dr. Long looked up at the house. "Anyway. For some reason, they all agreed to do what they could for Lawton's female students. Over the years, some of the girls have even been Indigenous, which made it more meaningful. And so I said I'd do my part. But since my grandmother passed and *I* took on the work, I've learned exactly what it requires." Here, her voice dropped almost to a whisper as she seemed to mutter to herself. "I'm dreading June. I'm just not sure I can manage it . . ."

What is she talking about? Leigh wondered. Granted, running a house for twelve undergrads could take up precious time. But Dr. Long could always farm it out. Between the girls' room and board payments and her head-of-surgery money, surely she could afford help. And what did June have to do with anything? Wasn't that when the girls moved out?

Leigh let a beat go by, not quite knowing what to say. She doubted she should ask her next question, but it would be amazing for the article.

"Belina said something about the House being . . . haunted? With the spirits of suffragists or maybe even . . ." She couldn't bring herself to say *your family*.

Leigh pressed her lips together as she noticed Dr. Long observing her closely. Something told her not to fidget, to try to look composed. To look as open as possible to anything Dr. Long might say.

Several long moments of silence went by before an almost imperceptible shake of the woman's head. "Leigh. You're a great girl. *But come on.*"

Dr. Long took the paring knife from her, slid it back into its pocket, and rerolled the leather bag.

The "interview" was over.

THIRTEEN

A wet snout in her ear wakes her up. She opens one eye. It's not even 8 a.m., way too early for a Saturday. She pushes herself up to a sitting position and Homer wags his tail.

Sean is in Chicago visiting his parents. He's helping clear gutters and other chores Erik isn't well enough to do after his fall. He was planning to send Homer to stay with the dog walker, but Ev volunteered to stay at Sean's and take care of the dog herself.

She heads into the kitchen. Despite reading the instructions, it takes a good ten minutes to figure how to use Sean's Italian coffeemaker. She gives up on the gadget that steams the milk and pours it in cold. She takes a seat at the small breakfast bar, looking warily at the toaster that has about a dozen dials and buttons.

The Andersens are obsessed with all things food and drink. She found this out firsthand in the winter, when Erik and Carmen had visited New York. They'd asked Sean's siblings, Peter, who also lives in Chicago, and Annette, who'd recently moved to Westchester County, north of New York City, and their families, to join them. The whole brood had set up camp in a Harlem townhouse that belonged to a friend of Carmen's who was on sabbatical.

Erik had flung open the door with such zest that Ev had found it hard to believe he was in his late seventies. He'd put his hands on the sides of Sean's face for an extremely long moment, sharing a wry smile that seemed to hint at some previous tension, now resolved, between them. Then he turned to Ev.

"Here she is at last," he said, before pulling her into a bear hug without so much as a handshake first. "We've been so looking forward to meeting you." He smelled like eucalyptus and had two pens in his breast pocket that pressed into her cheek.

Carmen, standing a few feet behind her husband, was less handsy. She waved a dish towel in the air, bidding them into the farmhouse-style kitchen where she introduced Ev to Peter, who looked like a taller, lankier version of Sean, and his wife, Jasmin. Each gave her a kiss on the cheek, murmuring that it was good to finally meet her.

On the far side of the room, by the pantry, stood a petite woman with dark skin and beautifully arched eyebrows, like Carmen. Sean guided Ev over.

"Here's Annette," Sean said. "My baby sis."

Annette did not smile at her as they shook hands. At the time, Ev tried not to take it personally; Annette's husband, Jamel, had recently left for a year in Qatar on a consultancy and Sean had confided that she was struggling to care for their son, Zach, by herself.

Annette grabbed Sean's arm. "You'll help me later, right?" She pouted like Ev imagined only a little sister could. "You promised."

"With your spreadsheet? You got it." Sean looked around the room. "Where's my nephew?"

"Field trip. His class is sleeping on the *Intrepid*," Annette said, referring to the aircraft carrier docked on Manhattan's West Side.

"Does he want to come over tomorrow morning?" Sean asked. "Ev and I could pick him up at the pier and he could come over and play with Homer." Homer had actually been Zach's dog, but Annette had asked Sean to take him after discovering she was allergic. "We could take him out to brunch and bring him up here afterward," Sean continued. The references to "we" seemed to get Annette's attention and not in a good way.

"I'll text him and see," Annette had said, looking Ev up and down.

Ev, too, was surprised. Partly because they hadn't discussed any of this beforehand and partly because she hadn't realized that Sean was quite so Zach-interested. True, he'd gone up to New Rochelle to see his sister and nephew on weekends when Ev had to work, but for some reason she had assumed he was mostly just yielding to a sister who insisted that her son have two adults present at all soccer games and school events.

The next thing she knew, Sean plopped down on the floor to crawl around after three tots who had materialized from behind Jasmin's legs. She realized she must have been staring when Erik waved a hand in front of her face.

"Join me?" he asked, holding up a bottle of red. "We can watch the peasants do the work."

"Nice way to get out of helping, Dad," Peter said. "Entertaining the pretty lady."

"Let him relax," Carmen said, winking at her husband. "He works hard." She handed Peter a bowl of raw shrimp. "I need you to get on deveining these."

Ev and Erik perched atop stools as everyone else plunged into various cooking tasks assigned by Carmen. Even though it was someone else's house, the Andersens so filled the space that it felt as if it were their actual home. NPR droned from somewhere; stacks of papers waiting to be graded and candy-colored plastic toys were strewn everywhere. There was constant touching, shorthand references to things that had happened in the past, and endless private jokes.

Each member of the family took turns unpacking, in detail, the various dramas of their lives, all offered up for thorough inspection. Peter and Jasmin detailed a playground incident that had happened to Berit, their five-year-old. She appeared to have been tripped by another child though it wasn't clear whether it was on purpose. Both sets of parents had met with the playground monitor, a meeting that must have taken hours judging by how long it took to describe. Nevertheless, Jasmin said they weren't satisfied that they had learned the truth. Carmen and Erik spent several minutes looking at Berit's knee. It didn't seem to have a mark on it, but they still offered to put in a call to the school's principal.

Sean talked about a situation with a seemingly unsatisfiable client whom he had recently complained to Ev about. Erik and Peter extracted every last aspect of the devolving relationship before pelting Sean with suggestions for tactics he might try to get it back on track.

Then Annette started in. "Um, you guys have no idea," she announced, laying down the knife she was using. "Let me tell you about *my* week. Started with PTA, where Zach's science teacher told me he needs a biology tutor. So I had to interview tutors. Then I had to get him checked for ADHD because, since Jamel left, he's been having trouble concentrating in class. The doctor said he's only borderline, and that we should retest in six months. But I'm not waiting for that, so yesterday I repainted his room mushroom because it's supposed to be soothing." She took a sip of wine. "I've been reading all about color therapy. This awesome book, *The Healing Home* . . . I think it would make for a great business. I could work out of the house and still be available to Zach whenever he needs me."

"Let's talk about this," Carmen said, snipping a fistful of scallions into a giant pot. "First off, I know a great adolescent psychologist here in New York. I'll get you his number. Someone find my phone. But—have you thought about going back to sports marketing? You were just starting to get somewhere with that and I think—"

"*Mom*—" Annette cut in.

Ev excused herself to the bathroom. She leaned against the sink, thinking. It was lovely, of course, how the Andersens looked out for one another. But for someone used to living alone, it was all a bit . . . tiring.

When the food was ready, the two smallest children, a baby and a toddler, were strapped into highchairs and everyone took their seats.

"I saved you a place next to me," Annette had said to Sean, pulling him to the opposite side of the table from where Eric had pulled a chair out for Ev.

Everyone held hands while Peter gave a warm, apparently improvised prayer. Ev was next to Carmen, whose hand was large and pleasantly cool. After the prayer, Carmen asked everyone to pass their bowls and she served the gumbo, which was delicate, if a little too spicy, with several layers of flavor that revealed themselves one after the other.

"Sean speaks so much about you, Ev," Erik began. "We have always been devourers of news in our house and he says that thanks to you, we need not fear that journalism is dying." Erik raised his glass in her general direction before continuing. "He also might have let slip that you are the most scintillating woman he's ever met. It's not a very Sean word, but I believe that's the one he used." He took a sip of wine and looked at Sean, who was rolling his eyes. "And so, I'm very much afraid . . . we want to know everything."

Ev felt a light sweat break out under the collective family lens.

At least her story didn't take long to tell: She was born in the Bay Area. When she was a child, her mother had been diagnosed with adenoid cystic cancer, a rare and unpredictable cancer of the glands.

Slow-growing at first, it could and did suddenly turn aggressive and relentless. Though Greta had tried every treatment, both accepted and experimental, none did more than briefly stave off the inevitable.

Just before Ev entered college, her father, a physicist, had been selected to work on the landmark particle acceleration project at the CERN lab outside of Geneva. He was supposed to be there only a year but he'd fallen for a Swiss physicist with two daughters whom he'd married. He'd re-upped with CERN and he and his wife had gone on to have a daughter of their own. Ev had contact with her father via email but hadn't seen him and his other family in several years.

Not the happiest tale, but others had lived through far worse. Anyway, the truth was that Ev, child of scientists that she was, had met these challenges rather analytically, and though she'd never admit it to anyone else, she had discovered something of a silver lining.

Not having family meant freedom from lots of life's intractable struggles. Many of her contemporaries had spent their youths coping with their parents' bitter divorces; she had not. For them, holidays often meant traveling great distances only to continue battles going back decades. And nowadays, her generation was coping with parents' mounting infirmities, contending with dementia and trying to find affordable assisted living.

While many of her contemporaries spent hours dealing with the stress of all this, Ev was able to expend her energy on the world around her, her focus directed outward, on work. The kind of work she liked to think she did well, the kind of work that helped others.

As she finished her story, Ev realized a silence had fallen over the table. The Andersens wore stricken expressions, as if her fate were unspeakably sad.

"You poor dear," Erik said in a low voice, shaking his head. "Is there hope for you and your father? A chance that you could become close again?"

Ev was thrown by the question. Her parents had been in their late twenties when they'd met working in different areas of the same lab. Not long after, they'd had her and, as joyful as her mother was, maybe her dad simply hadn't been as excited or even ready, because—when he'd suddenly been left to parent alone—he'd been utterly out of his depth. Or frustrated. Or scared.

Whichever it was, he hadn't been there when she needed him most, so why would he be now? Especially when he had a whole other family a world away.

Ev stabbed at a large shrimp with her fork, trying to wrestle it out of its shell.

Perhaps Carmen realized it was a sensitive subject, because she rested her hand lightly on Ev's forearm. "My father left when I was in middle school," she said. "Probably what made me determined to find a good man." She looked at her husband before continuing. "But when I was a child, I was sure I was the only one this had ever happened to. It wasn't until I got to college and met other girls, staying up all night and talking, that I realized everyone had something painful in their past. And that his leaving was not my fault." Her tone grew wistful. "To this day, those women are my best friends."

Ev nodded, projecting knowing agreement as best she could. If she'd told the Andersens what really happened with her college friends, they'd have cried right there at the table.

. . . . .

Ev shakes off the memory with the Andersens, drains her coffee, and gets dressed. Her plan was to do some work but Homer has planted himself by the front door like he does when he wants out, so she decides to take him to Central Park. She flags down a cab and the dog sits at her feet with his chin on her knee, drooling and watching the buildings and trees go by.

Ev heads for a dog-friendly lawn north of the Sheep Meadow and puts down a beach towel. She fans out sections of the Saturday paper while Homer rolls over on his back and starts wriggling. Ev gives his stomach a rub. "Good boy," she says.

She picks up the Arts section but her eyes keep sliding off the page. A couple nearby is blowing bubbles that their lurching toddler tries to snatch from the air. Some teens play catch with a football while old folks practice tai chi.

She rolls over on her stomach. The sun on her shoulders is like a warm hand and her eyelids flutter. She can feel herself drifting off, her mind alighting on a series of illogical, gossamer thoughts as it often does just before she falls asleep.

A burst of laughter erupts from somewhere, startling her awake. She squints into the near distance. A group of young women is circling a patch of grass, checking for stones and twigs before unfolding a large blanket. They appear to be in their early twenties and favor the combination of copious tattoos paired with delicate sundresses. They place their sandals on the perimeter of the blanket and unpack several large bags of food. Laughter and the aroma of pot drift her way.

Homer materializes in front of her, panting. Ev fishes out his plastic travel bowl and pours in some water. He drinks lustily, then flops down next to her.

Ev rests her head on his side, feeling it go up and down with his breath as she continues to watch the women.

FOURTEEN

The picnic was to be at a clearing deep in the woods somewhere between campus and Foster House. May had drawn a detailed map and told the sophomores to join the older girls there as soon as their finals were over. Each of their tests had ended at a different time, but Leigh, Dilly, Tina, and Cam had wanted to wait until all four of them were finished so they could make the hike together. It was late afternoon by the time the four of them set off, the heat rising as they trekked over hills and creek beds.

The mood was buoyant. Even Cam, who'd been in a funk for weeks, suddenly seemed to hum with energy. Usually when the four of them went anywhere, Leigh and Dilly were well in front, with Tina and Cam bringing up the rear. But on this day, Cam was ahead, teasing the rest of them for not keeping up. Her brown eyes, which turned down at the outer corners, sometimes giving her a doleful expression, actually sparkled. Leigh watched her skipping along, thinking she must have aced her test.

Tina, who was strong but not agile, had been doing her best to keep up, puffing along a few feet behind them, accepting Leigh's hand to scramble up some of the rockier spots. But she, too, was upbeat, talking about a concert in Albany she wanted them all to go to.

Dilly was chatting about her summer plans: working at her uncle's law firm in New Orleans on a big case. He was even going to take her to London to help do research.

Leigh herself was quiet. She would be spending the summer in Europe too, and knew she should be excited, but the invitation from her dad made her uneasy.

"Ronja and I are living together now," he'd said breathlessly during their last phone call. "Her daughters are adorable. Sweethearts. They're four and six, and they don't speak English yet. I've found a language lab in Geneva where you can take Tourist French in the afternoons . . ."

Leigh wasn't particularly interested in taking "Tourist French," whatever that was, but it didn't seem to be up for debate.

"I can't wait to be there," she'd said to Anton, trying to feel positive. Maybe the visit would mark a fresh start.

"You know, I've learned something this year," Anton said. Leigh had perked up, thinking he was about to say how much he missed her. "I've learned that I don't do well without a woman. I'm not very good at social situations and the like. I could never pick out a birthday present or tie without your mother's help. So I'm extremely lucky to have found Ronja. In fact, I've never been happier."

The statement had stung like a slap.

It felt just as acute as she replayed it on the hiking trail. As they crossed a small footbridge and paused to admire the view, Dilly seemed to read Leigh's mind.

"Why don't you visit me in London?" she said.

"What?"

"There's a tunnel now that connects England and France, so it would be super easy. Captain and Teacup are going to come over and would love to see you, they told me so." Dilly's dad was known as Captain and her mother, for some reason, Teacup. They'd visited for Dilly's birthday and taken both girls out to dinner. "They think you're a good influence on me, making me more respectful."

"I'm sure that's not possible," Leigh said, but she was happy about the invitation.

Dilly grabbed Leigh's waist and pulled, bumping their sides together. "I'll come visit you, too. You shouldn't have to watch your dad and the Swiss Miss paw each other by yourself."

Leigh smiled and bumped back, propelled by a burst of optimism.

Half an hour later, they arrived at the clearing, which was well off the main path and on the edge of a steep escarpment. They could hear what sounded like a small waterfall nearby. Leigh had expected to find May, Belina, and the others talking and laughing as they would at a Foster House dinner. Instead, they were sitting silently, facing each other in a circle, their backs propped against their rucksacks.

"Hello, all," Dilly called out. The girls looked up vaguely, little smiles playing on their lips.

"Hey there," said Georgia softly, beckoning them over. She was sitting under a tree about twenty feet apart from the others, reading a book.

"What's going on?" Leigh asked as they all sat down.

"Shh," Georgia said. "What took you guys so long?"

"My test started late," Tina said. "What are they, hypnotized?"

"*Salvia divinorum*," said Georgia, holding up a quilted bag. From inside, she drew a long, narrow pipe.

"Is that a fancy name for weed?" Tina asked.

"It's an herb Native Americans use. Dr. Long shares it from her stash," Georgia said, poking at the charred contents of the pipe with a wooden match.

"What does it do?" asked Leigh, wondering why the girls seemed so spaced-out.

"Induces 'divine intoxication,'" Georgia said. "Basically, it puts you in a deep meditative state. Legend says Iroquois women picked some here in the woods for the suffragists and it spurred them to greatness at the convention. Dr. Long says it reveals what you need to know. Take that however you wish."

"*Magical Mystery Tour*," Dilly said, smiling.

"The other day, someone asked me about magic at Foster House," Cam said, stretching out her legs and crossing them in front of her. "Well, not magic really, but if weird stuff ever happens there."

"Like what?" asked Georgia.

"Like, if it's haunted," Cam said, suddenly looking embarrassed.

Leigh thought back to Belina's and May's comments during Commitment. And how Dr. Long had clammed up when she mentioned this same thing.

"I've had people ask me, too," Dilly said. "They want to know if silverware ever goes floating by at dinner."

"Boo!" Tina yelled, flinging her fingertips wide.

"Will you keep it down?" Georgia hissed. "I've never seen anything weird, but FYI, you'll probably hear lots more questions like that."

"Why? What do you mean?" Leigh asked.

"We're an all-woman house. But we're not a sorority, defined by a relationship with some frat. We stand on our own. Some people don't like that."

Just as Dr. Long had cautioned her.

"I don't get why they'd think Foster is haunted, though," Cam said.

Georgia put her elbows on her knees and leaned forward. "Women on their own have a certain kind of power. Other people can sense it, even if they don't understand it. So they start rumors that we're part of some kind of lesbian cult. *Evil wiccans, practicing the dark arts* . . . stuff like that."

"Lame," Dilly said, shaking her head.

"The important thing to remember is," Georgia said, "when someone comes for one of us, they come for all of us."

Before anyone could say anything, May's hand rose slowly up into the air.

"I think she wants you," Cam said, nudging Leigh.

Leigh stood, made her way over to May, and sat down. She wasn't completely surprised at being summoned this way; ever since she'd mentioned her mother's death during a late-night study session, May had singled her out, whether it was to suggest a walk into town or to ask if there was something special she'd like for dinner.

May reached for a lock of Leigh's long white hair and began to braid it, looking at her fingers from time to time as if the hair was made of a wonderful substance that might rub off.

A pair of hawks circled above. Crickets chirped. Somewhere, the waterfall whooshed. Leigh's scalp tingled pleasantly.

"*Look*," May said.

Leigh followed her gaze but saw nothing but a small pile of dirt. "Beautiful, isn't it?"

Gradually, the older girls started to come back to the world, blinking and stretching. They stood docilely and followed Georgia's instructions about folding blankets and emptying water glasses, though it seemed to take a lot longer than it should.

May struggled to heave her backpack onto her back and Leigh helped her, guiding her arms through the loops. May hugged her and whispered in her ear. It sounded like: *Who's my sweet girl?*

Leigh looked at her in surprise. She tried to search May's face but she was already turning toward the path, Belina reaching for her hand to help her step over a tree limb that had fallen to the ground.

After the last of the older girls had disappeared into the trees, Leigh, Dilly, Tina, and Cam plunked down along the edge of the escarpment, their feet dangling, nibbling at the last of the cheese and fruit. The shadows had grown long and there was a softness to everything before them, as if the objects around them were blurring into one another.

Dilly reached for the pipe and looked at the others. "Georgia says it comes on fast."

"It's okay. I'll be on guard," Leigh said.

"You're doing it, too," Dilly replied.

"No." Leigh shook her head. "She said someone should act as sitter."

"I'll be the sitter," Cam said. "I don't think I'm supposed to do this kind of thing anyway." No one quite knew what she meant but she looked genuinely uneasy.

"No sitter," Dilly said.

"But—" Leigh started.

Dilly dipped her chin and looked up into Leigh's eyes. "I'm not doing this without you."

"All for one and drugs for all," Tina said, giggling and tipping backward.

They passed the pipe around. Afterward, Leigh clasped her hands around her knees and waited. Nothing happened. Maybe she was too analytical—

A squirrel hopped over to a tree, then froze, its face watchful. He looked like a little old man. Leigh tried to point him out to the others but got distracted by her hand. As she moved it through space, it emitted faint rainbow-colored tracers in the air. From the corner of her eye she saw Tina and Cam rise and follow a laughing butterfly.

Dilly gripped her arm. "Listen."

Leigh held still to take in the sounds around her. "To what?"

"The waterfall."

"What about it?" Leigh asked.

"It's getting louder. Like the water is coming closer." Dilly's eyes were glassy. Her face went pale. "It's flood season. How could we have forgotten?"

To Leigh the waterfall sounded the same as ever. She felt her eyes slide back to the squirrel. He was trying to tell her something. Dilly gripped her forearm harder and Leigh willed her mind back to her friend. She looked deeply into her face.

Dilly, who wasn't afraid of anything, was scared.

"We're going to drown. I *know* it," Dilly said. She flipped onto all fours and began to scramble, her fingers clawing at the dirt and dead leaves. Her legs, kicking, loosened some rocks at the edge of the cliff and she started to slide toward the yawning green void.

"No!" Leigh threw her arms around Dilly's waist and tried to pull, forcing herself to concentrate on what was happening. "Tina! Cam!" she shouted. She pressed her cheek into Dilly's back, feeling the warmth of her skin and her quick, shallow breaths. "It's okay, it's okay," she repeated. "The water's no threat to us. We're going to be fine."

Suddenly she felt something fall on her from above. Rotund and furry—a bear cub. *Dear god.* Then Leigh realized it was just Tina, trying to help by pinning them. But her relief was short-lived as Dilly's elbow came up, hitting Tina in the eye. Tina rolled off, howling.

Dilly continued to struggle, sending more rocks and dirt flying, her lower half now dangling in empty air.

"Help me!" Leigh said to Cam, who had finally appeared although she was now made of rainbow.

"I'll take one arm, you take the other!" Cam yelled back, the bright colors pulsating in her face.

Leigh raised herself onto her knees and grasped Dilly's left arm. Cam grabbed the right one and together they pulled. But Dilly continued to slip, her legs kicking away the very ground that could have saved her. She was going to go over.

Tina recovered herself. She scrambled over and flung herself on top of Dilly, anchoring her just as she was about to fall. Leigh, blinking fast, saw what needed to be done. Trusting Cam and Tina to keep Dilly in place, she crawled up to the edge and then over it so that her rib cage hung against the rockface. She reached out for Dilly's flailing left leg. It slipped her grasp once, twice . . . and then she had it. Holding tight, she tried to wriggle her way backward, loose earth crumbling underneath her with every movement, threatening to send her over as well.

She felt a yank on her ankle so hard it took her breath away. It was wispy little rainbow Cam, pulling with the strength of ten Cams. Leigh could feel her stomach scraping along the dirt and leaves and cried out in pain. But she held on to Dilly's leg and finally all four of them found themselves on solid ground. Panting, they lay in a heap, their breath slowly synchronizing.

Minutes or hours later, Leigh felt someone move. She wasn't sure who it was until Dilly's face appeared next to hers. Dilly pulled Leigh in close, their eyes just inches apart. Dilly blew lightly and Leigh felt her friend's breath slide past her cheeks and up through her eyelashes.

The four pushed themselves up to a seated position. They

made a circle, sitting cross-legged, knees touching. They put their arms around one another and leaned in, four damp foreheads meeting in the middle.

"Thank you," Dilly said at last, hoarsely.

"No, no," the others murmured. They pulled back and fell silent, mesmerized, their eyes caressing one another. They sat like that for a century, an eon. Civilizations rose and fell but they didn't move.

"Is there any food left? I'm famished." It was Tina who spoke and stood first. She reached down and helped Cam up. Leigh did the same for Dilly. They stood like Mount Rushmore, shoulder to shoulder, gazing down at the treetops surrounding the clearing. The mighty pines came up only to their knees. Leigh reached down and buzzed them with her palm. Dilly picked up a boulder and rolled it between her fingers. The cliff was no higher than a curb.

Moments later, a roaring sound signaled that the water had indeed breeched its banks. It rushed in around them, wave after wave, but it barely reached their ankles. They laughed and splashed like children at the beach as an enormous pink sun slid down toward the horizon.

FIFTEEN

"Next time, we're going to talk about attribution," Ev says, turning off the PowerPoint. "We have to characterize our sources, especially anonymous ones, in ways that let our viewers know how to assess what those sources are saying." She sweeps her gaze over the seven associate and assistant producers sitting around the table in her office. Very few are good writers but it's hardly their fault. These days, young people are expected to shoot and edit and upload and download because tech is seen as a natural fit for them and because networks can use them to save money on union employees. The downside for the kids is that they don't get enough exposure to basic storytelling, which they're going to need in their careers. They may not stay at ARC; they may well take the skills she teaches them and get a job elsewhere. Even so, they make such little money that she feels it's the least she can do for them. "Okay, everybody. See you next week."

The kids murmur their thanks, pick up their scripts and phones, and file out.

"Tab, may I have a word?" Ev asks.

Tab follows Ev to her desk and sits, her right leg bouncing.

"I know you're on three stories right now, but I'd like you to work with Aviva on something."

"Is it the story that has her here around the clock? Nobody seems to know what it is."

"Yes," says Ev. "It's exclusive and exciting and, for now, top secret. It's going to lead sweeps. We've kept the team purposely small. But now she's polishing a cut to screen for Gareth and Richard, and I want it to have the best possible B-roll, graphics, music, everything. Can you tell her we've spoken and that you're available to get her whatever she needs?"

Tab rises. "I'll go find her."

"Thanks."

Tab hesitates in the doorway in her wide-wale corduroy overall dress, looking much younger than her years. "May I say something?" She keeps her gaze trained on the floor.

"Sure."

"I know I'm a little . . ." Tab clears her throat. "Different, I guess? I just want you to know I know that." Her cheeks redden. "Anyway . . . thanks."

As Tab walks away, her gait bouncy and hopeful, Ev realizes she's more self-aware than she appears. Another good trait for a journalist.

"An underarm protector? Is that a real thing?" Ev asks, strolling the aisle of the sporting goods store. She and Sean have Zach for the day and Annette has tasked them with buying him equipment for a fencing camp he's attending this summer.

"It's close to the heart, so I would say yes," Sean replies, consulting a printout of Annette's exhaustive email. He holds up something that looks like a T-shirt cut in half from collar to hem. Then he glances at his watch. "We're gonna be late. Let's see how he's coming along."

They wander over to the changing rooms where a figure in full regalia—jacket, gloves, and mask—turns in front of a three-way mirror while pointing a foil, a practice sword with a button on the point, at his reflection.

"That you in there?" Sean asks.

"*Allez*," comes Zach's voice from behind the mesh. In the getup, he looks tall and lean. The mask covers his face and Ev almost forgets there's a thirteen-year-old boy in there.

"That's not the jacket we sent you in with," says Sean.

"This one's cooler," Zach says, running a gloved finger along black piping. "And more comfortable."

"It's hard to talk this way," Sean says, moving his head this way and that, trying to see through the mesh. "Would you take the hat off?"

"Mask."

"Take it off," Sean says.

Instead, Zach spins back toward the mirror, doing some approximation of a lunge.

"Your mom was very specific about what I'm supposed to get you," Sean insists, waving the list.

This prompts Ev to wonder why Annette wants Sean to deal with this. Then again, last month Sean told her that Jamel, Annette's husband, met another woman in Doha and is planning to stay there. Maybe she just can't get out of bed.

Anyway, Ev's met him a few times now and has to say Zach isn't the worst kid in the world. He's occasionally sulky and curiously helpless, like many teens today. The children of the playdate generation, slathered in hand sanitizer, with all their time scheduled for them, don't seem to be able to figure things out for themselves.

Breaking has actually done stories about this phenomenon. Ev herself has even had parents try to barge into her office with their twentysomethings to take part in a job interview or negotiate a raise. The Andersens aren't this bad, but they do tend to be overly cautious with their next generation and resistant to asking too much of this perfectly capable child.

Zach seems to be his happiest self around Sean, especially when they discuss drawing, with which Zach is obsessed. Sean is deeply fond of his nephew, too, and it's clearly important to him that Ev and Zach forge some kind of relationship. So here she is, riding shotgun for the day.

"The nylon jacket looks weird on," Zach says, lunging again. "And it's scratchy."

"This one is too tight," Sean responds. "You're not going to have room for your plastrons."

Ev can't help but wonder if this will really matter for a beginner. Is there any chance of Zach actually getting hurt? These blades are so flexible they're practically Slinkys.

"Let him get what he wants," she says.

Sean looks at her in surprise and even Zach turns his masked face in her direction.

"He's the one who's going to have to wear it for two weeks," she says, shrugging. As Zach turns back to the mirror, she leans in to Sean and whispers, "Give him a break. He's going through a lot, right?"

Sean gives her a smile that says he's pleased she's taking an interest. "Yeah," he says. "Good call." He grabs her hand and gives it a squeeze.

. . . . .

At the Met they drop Zach off at the American Wing for "Saturday Sketching," a program where kids get to draw works of art under the guidance of an artist-instructor. Ev and Sean explore the Greek and Egyptian galleries and play hide-and-seek in the Temple of Dendur before deciding to get coffee while they wait for Zach to be done.

"There's a café near his class," Sean says, consulting a museum guide.

"Roof Bar is nicer."

"But how will he find us?"

"Um, text him?" she says, widening her eyes. "And let him use a map. Like we are."

Sean is concerned that Zach might have trouble with this, despite the fact that the kid probably has a million GPS apps on his phone, so they wind up at the American Wing cafeteria. They order two cappuccinos at the counter and settle in at one of the white Spartan tables near the windows overlooking a narrow slice of Central Park. Sean's phone goes off and he pulls it from his jacket pocket, looking at the number.

"Work," he says. "Sorry."

Ev does a brushing motion with her fingers to let him know it's fine for him to get it. He answers and his brow knits, either in concern or because he can't hear what the person's saying. He stands and starts pacing. After a few moments he points at the door, indicating that he needs to take it outside. It's probably his high-maintenance client.

Ev takes out her own phone and surfs some news sites, emailing a few stories to her managing editor, Malcolm, to look into in the week ahead in case they'll work for *Breaking*.

A shadow falls across the table and she looks up to see Zach, sketchpad under his arm. He resembles Sean with his high forehead and long lashes. But his eyes are caramel brown instead of blue and he has a smattering of freckles across his cheeks.

"Hey," Ev says. "How was it?"

"Okay," he says, looking around.

"Sean had to take a call," she says.

Zach nods but doesn't sit down.

"How about something to eat?" Ev asks.

"Do they have grilled cheese?" he asks.

"No idea." She gestures toward the line, which is now considerably shorter. "Why don't you go see?"

Zach looks confused, as if venturing across a large room to order lunch by himself is something only astronauts do. But she's determined to do something good for him, even if it makes him uncomfortable.

"Here," she says, handing him a twenty. "Go to town."

He takes the money but doesn't meet her eye. He mutters something that might or might not be "thanks," hesitates for a few moments, and heads off.

When he comes back, he sits, placing his tray kitty-corner across the table from her. He takes a sip of soda and unwraps his sandwich. Before he takes a bite, he reaches into the front pocket of his jean jacket and pulls out a few wrinkled singles, which he hands to her.

"Oh—keep it," Ev says, nevertheless appreciating that he thought to offer her the change. "Can I see what you did in class?"

Zach wipes the grease off his hands with a paper napkin before reaching for his sketchpad. He flips through it, touching only the very edges of the paper, till he finds a pencil drawing and hands it to her. She wipes her hands on her jeans and accepts it.

At first she doesn't know what it is. The class met in the sculpture court but he hasn't drawn a sculpture. Then she realizes he's sketched a section of the lead-glass windows in the ceiling, the shafts of light coming through them and hitting the wall. The picture is abstract and yet organic, the light and shadow rendered almost as well as a work of Sean's.

"This is good," she says.

He shrugs.

"Interesting choice to sketch the space itself."

Zach shrugs again. It's his favorite rejoinder to most questions and observations.

She tries to elicit more about the class and when that doesn't work, she asks if he's excited about fencing camp.

"I guess," he says, pulling his sandwich apart and watching the strings of cheese lengthen. "At least I'll be out of the house."

Ev nods. "Tough with your dad gone," she says.

Zach says nothing.

"Same thing happened to me. Sort of."

"Your dad went to Doha?" Zach asks with his mouth full.

"No." Ev runs her finger along the cold foam on the rim of her cup and brings it to her mouth. "He went to Europe. Switzerland, a year's sabbatical it was supposed to be."

Zach doesn't say anything but she can tell she has his attention.

"I was older than you, it was the summer before I left for college. But suddenly I had to do everything myself. I had to pack my stuff, buy my plane ticket, even write the tuition check."

"Where was your mom?" It's the first personal question Zach has ever asked her.

"She died when I was eight."

Silently, Zach dips a French fry in a tiny pool of ketchup he's made on the tray.

Ev pushes her cup away. "What sucks is that moment when you realize that the temporary is permanent."

"What do you mean?" Zach asks.

"When you understand that they're not coming back."

"You didn't know that's what death meant?" Zach looks disbelieving.

"No, I mean my dad," she says. "He met this woman and said he couldn't bear to leave her. And I remember thinking, *Why? Why couldn't you keep your head down, do your job, and come back at the end of the year like you were supposed to?*" The pain of it comes back quickly, the memories more insidious than Ev had realized. She grows lost in thought, almost forgetting Zach is there. "I know now how naïve that was. People live life wherever they go. They dig in, no matter how shallow the dirt. They grow roots and sprout leaves. And children. Eventually, you realize they've set up a new life and it doesn't necessarily have much room for you." She sighs, bringing her focus back to Zach. "The only silver lining was that my mother wasn't around for it. I can only imagine what this is like for your mom."

Zach puts his French fry down. "My dad's coming back, though." He says this with an assurance tinged by sudden doubt, as if he's just assembled some seemingly unrelated puzzle pieces in his head.

"Oh." It hits Ev that Annette hasn't told Zach what's going on. Of course she hasn't. If he needs a bulletproof vest for fencing camp and can't be asked to find his way around a museum, he certainly can't be allowed to face the fact that life, as he knows it, is over. "I'm sure he is," she says, but she knows it's not convincing.

Zach pushes his chair away from the table and stares out the window. It's at this moment that Sean reappears. He puts his hand on Zach's shoulder. "Hey, kiddo—" he starts, but Zach jerks away. "What's wrong?" Sean asks.

"What's going on with Dad? Did he meet someone else? Is he staying in Doha?"

Sean looks at Ev.

"It was an accident," she says, swallowing. "I—I didn't realize."

"Shit," Sean says, closing his eyes. He rubs his chin. "Shit-shit-shit. Give us a minute, okay?"

Part of Ev wants to stay. She wants to shout that the Andersens' idea of "protecting" Zach is only going to wind up hurting him. Sean may have grown up in a functional family, but Zach is not and he needs someone to talk him through it, to meet him where he is, not where they wish he was. And she, Ev, would be happy to do it if they would only ask.

But she can see from Sean's stricken face that that's the last thing that's going to happen. She nods and heads toward the door, temples throbbing.

Out on the sidewalk, Sean says he thinks it's best if she sleeps at her place, so he and Zach can talk. He doesn't seem angry with her but he's clearly distressed over Zach's reaction and how to tell Annette about what's happened. She says it's fine and kisses him goodbye. She tries to give Zach a sympathetic look, but he keeps his eyes averted.

Once home, Ev sets herself up for an evening on the couch with a blanket and some scripts that need reworking. She's too tired to do much and, the later it gets, the more her thoughts stray to Zach and the odyssey ahead of him.

She closes her eyes, the warmth of the reading lamp on her lids, and allows herself to slide into sleep.

She's in a car, the window open. Streets go by. Buildings. Bridges. The wind caresses her skin.

It's strange, going somewhere but having no idea where. She senses that if she turns and looks at the driver, she'll immediately know their destination. But she doesn't want to know quite yet.

They pick up speed. She smells flowers, though there are none that she can see. The buildings start to look different, as if they've entered another country. The car radio is on, a news anchor speaking in a language she doesn't understand.

She turns her head a fraction. There's something hanging from the rearview mirror. A watch. But the time shown is earlier than when they left.

She turns a fraction more and the knee of the driver comes into view. It's bare, between the hem of a dress and the top of a leather boot.

Greta.

Of course.

Greta keeps her eyes straight ahead but on the sky, not the road. Her expression is soft, her hair wrapped in a silk scarf. One white strand escapes and whips near her cheek.

She's talking but her lips aren't moving.

Ev looks down at her hands and realizes that she's not a child anymore.

How could she not have understood that her mother is still alive? Why didn't she think to pick up a phone? How much time has been wasted, time they could have been together? Why didn't she *know*?

"No one knows anything," Greta says, silently. They keep driving, now going up a long, steep hill. Ev wonders what's on the other side.

Greta takes her daughter's hand, which is now small and fits perfectly inside her own. "And you know what? It's better this way. Because this way we never bump up against the end. You see? There's always room. Look at all this room . . ." Greta takes her other hand off the wheel and gestures at the world around them. The car reaches the top of the hill. She's going to see what's on the other side and—

Ev jerks awake and blinks, pen rolling off her chest, papers all over the floor. Her heart is beating fast and Greta's voice echoes inside her ears. She cups her hands around them, trying to keep the sound in, trying to hold on to it just a little bit longer.

It takes several moments to register where she is and she ponders why her living room looks so foreign. A chill makes her pull the blanket more tightly around her and she closes her eyes again, trying to get back. Back into the car. Back with Greta.

But she can't.

SIXTEEN

They're in the screening room, the lights low. They sit around a long oval table, Aviva separated from everyone else by several empty seats. Ev can tell Aviva's anxious, despite her many years of experience. All producers are in this situation. You're showing your work to the toughest of audiences, your most senior colleagues.

Today's screening is small—just Ev, Aviva, Gareth, and Richard in the room—but Gareth's presence means the stakes are higher than normal. Generally speaking, he's far too busy to see *Breaking* stories before they air, even though he'd surely like to. But Ev has called for this special private screening because this story targets a major corporation.

She won't deny that she wants more face time with her boss. She can't stop thinking about his casual reference to the VP job opening up. He mentioned it in the context of cost cutters but surely a true bombshell of a story will count for something, too. She hopes so, because she has reason to believe there's someone else Gareth is considering besides her.

The other day, as she sat waiting to go into his office, Candy came out, laughing and tossing her red hair like a show pony's mane. Word is, they've been spending more time together lately. It's very possible he's considering this cost-slicing, ratings-generating, legacy hire for the Digital VP slot. Ev wants to remind him about her journalism chops—and her ability to generate important but buzz-worthy stories—before he makes any big decisions.

Maybe she's being petty here. An outsider would likely think so. But an outsider wouldn't understand just how little ground there is in this world that's earmarked for women. There's just not enough to share. Even more important, given the events in the world today, ARC News needs real journalists in upper management. And because Candy works in the stunts-laden world of *Smell the Coffee!*, she hasn't exercised those muscles in years.

As the story unfolds on the large screen on the opposite wall, Ev feels a wave of satisfaction. Aviva has assembled an overwhelming case and Ev's structure wrings the most out of each moment in such a way that a less-sophisticated viewer will understand what is going on, but a news junkie will not be bored. She's also incorporated an account of *Breaking*'s journalistic efforts with an ingenious parallel structure: Even as they tell the story, they weave in their news-gathering methods, right down to their fact-checking. It's humble, surprising, and somehow doesn't take away from the story's forward momentum.

Tab, too, has risen to the occasion, finding the perfect B-roll to illustrate every moment. Her close-ups of Liquex's oval white pills, half in shadow, are practically poetic. They almost become a character in the piece, staring with unseeing eyes at the moral catastrophe in their midst.

Ev glances at Gareth. He sits, as usual, sphinxlike. And you can't look for clues on his pad of paper; he never writes anything down. Not only is he the best in the business at analyzing the strengths and weaknesses of a story, he has an astounding memory and can recite a detailed critique of an hour's worth of programming without a single note.

Ev shifts her attention to Richard. She needs his support, too. It's his job to make sure if Armitage sues ARC over this story that ARC wins the suit. Richard is in his midfifties, with salt-and-pepper hair, cut primly like a schoolboy's. His eyes are so dark you can't see where the irises and pupils separate, which makes him difficult to read.

Today, Ev expects his attitude to resemble a bloodhound on the trail of a bunny. And during the first couple of acts, he did scrawl several things on his pad, as he usually does. But now he's actually sitting back, watching like a viewer at home. She knows that what she and Aviva have produced is good, but this is a special kind of validation.

They're about to watch act six, the final one, which belongs to Whitney alone and her allegations about possible problems with Armitage's vaccine. And it's here that Ev has tried something unusual: nearly four minutes of Whitney speaking in her spirited yet dignified way, with no interruption by the correspondent track. It's risky, unorthodox. Everyone is so used to quick cuts now. But what Whitney is saying is powerful, and somehow, even with all the trickery to hide her identity, her essential integrity reveals itself. If she were the protagonist of a novel, you'd be with her from page one.

Of course, they're not just relying on Whitney's word. She's provided classified paperwork, including memos and emails, which is, granted, cryptic if you see only one entry, but taken together, everything is spelled out quite clearly. Maybe not 100 percent, but very close.

"Are you a hero?" asks Bob, the correspondent.

"No," replies Whitney. "I'm just a person with a choice to make.

We all have choices to make. My choice is to tell you what I know. Whether it does any good is out of my hands. But I'd like to think I'm helping, even if it's just one person." She says this with great emotion, as if it's a particular person she's speaking about.

The screen fades to black. Aviva hits rewind and slides the dimmer switch up, lifting the room back to its customary brightness. Ev feels lit up as well. She's always pleased with what she puts on the air but not often is she this proud.

Gareth and Richard exchange a look that she can't decipher.

"Very nice," says Gareth, finally. He seems to mean it but there's something odd about his tone. A few moments of awkward silence go by, and Aviva looks like she's about to burst from the tension. "Richard," says Gareth finally. "I think you can leave us."

Now it's Ev and Aviva's turn to look at one another, this time in confusion.

But Richard clearly understands something they do not. He rises. "Nice to see you, as always," he says to Ev. He picks up his pad, nods in Aviva's direction, and departs.

Next, Gareth turns to Aviva. "Probably best if you go now, too."

Aviva's eyebrows betray her surprise. "Is there a problem?"

"No," says Gareth.

"If there are any issues with this story, I feel very strongly that I should be here to hear them."

"I appreciate that, but this is something I need to discuss with Ev alone." Gareth says this with steely finality.

"With all due respect, I prefer to stay."

Gareth blinks. It's probably not every day he faces this kind of pushback. "I'm not going to explain this to you any further. Now, *if you please . . .*" He lifts his chin in the direction of the door.

Whatever Aviva was hoping would happen at this screening, this is not it. She turns to Ev, clearly expecting her to intervene.

Ev looks at them both. She knows what she'd like to say. Thelma is supposed to side with Louise.

"Aviva, why don't you grab lunch and I'll catch up with you later?"

Aviva's expression hardens. She seems to think this is some kind of betrayal, but it's not. Whatever Gareth is about to say, Ev will pass on to her. So what if she gets the information twenty minutes from now?

Aviva glares at them, gathers her script, and walks out.

"I wish I'd known what you were planning to show us today," says Gareth.

"I told you it had to do with a drug company. I told you it was big," says Ev. "That's why I wanted you to see it now. So we can make plans. I think both *National Report* and *Smell the Coffee!* need to run some spots—"

"Big, yes. But this is Armitage and that's too big."

Ev rubs her palms over her armrests. "What do you mean?"

Gareth's phone vibrates and he glances at it, grimacing. "They just moved up the affiliates' meeting. I've got to run."

"You can't go without telling me what's going on."

"It's going to have to wait," he says, standing. "We'll talk this afternoon. Come to my office." He leaves the room.

Ev stares at the doorway through which her boss just disappeared.

Who's ever heard of a story that's too big?

The ensuing hours are brutal. Ev tries to distract herself with the Mac 'n' Cheese Channel but a pot of bubbling Fontina being poured over gluten-free gemelli isn't working its usual magic. She goes for a walk, threading her way through the hordes of midtown tourists.

While she's out, Aviva texts her twice to ask what's happening. She texts back that she doesn't know. Back at the office, Ev reads some scripts, though she keeps getting interrupted by more texts from Aviva. Eventually, she turns off her phone. At last, Gareth's assistant, Colleen, calls to say he's ready for her.

She takes a seat across from his desk and endures an agonizing few more minutes waiting for him to get off the phone.

Finally he hangs up and looks at her. "For openers, Armitage accounts for nearly a fifth of the ads that run during *National Report*."

"I didn't know it was that much," Ev says. It's not her job to keep track of who advertises during news programming. And anyway, there's supposed to be a church-and-state-style separation between news and the advertising that sponsors it. "But surely you're not saying that Armitage buying airtime on ARC inoculates them against being investigated?"

"No, but there's another problem. We've had a new directive from above," Gareth says with the tiniest hint of a sigh. "It's part of what Richard was brought in to oversee."

"What kind of directive?"

"As far as the News Division goes, I'd characterize it as a lack of appetite. For a fight."

"But if there's a fight with Armitage, we'll win. I'm telling you, this story is solid. If Richard had asked any questions, we could have made that clear."

"Richard didn't ask any questions because he knew there wasn't any point."

"What are you talking about?"

"He knows this story isn't going to air."

"You can't be serious." Ev feels her voice go up and wills herself to keep it low. "We'll make whatever changes are necessary to satisfy Legal and Standards and get this thing into airable shape."

"It's pretty close to airable shape now. I'm fairly sure even Richard would admit that. This is an award winner. Your sections detailing journalistic work methods are inspired. I think we should try doing that with some of our other controversial stories." He clears his throat. "But *this* is not airing."

"It's up there with any other investigative story we've done."

"Yes—under our old guidelines. Under those, the standard was, if we can beat a potential lawsuit, we air it."

"Right," Ev says uncertainly.

"Now, under our new parent company, unless a story is impossible to ignore, with every other network in hot pursuit, we've been advised to avoid airing anything that will even *trigger* a suit."

"Even *trigger* a suit? That's insane."

"The parent company doesn't want the expense. Or the publicity. They're reeling from a labor lawsuit in Indonesia and penalties for some kind of environmental infractions in Europe. They've got tentacles all over the globe and half of them are on fire."

"We don't *know* Armitage will sue," Ev says, grasping at any straw. But as a litigious, deep-pocketed multinational, of course it will. She roots around for another argument and finds it. "Look, I think you may be missing something about the journalistic moment we're in. We need to help restore people's faith in us by doing our best work. If Armitage's vaccine is in any way substandard, that could spell big trouble for Americans' faith in medical science, and there couldn't be a worse time for that. If we air this, we could stop the first domino from falling. And what about this: If we don't air this story and one of our competitors does—and it leaks that we killed it—we're going to look terrible. We'll have our heads handed to us and we'll deserve it."

But even this, Gareth has thought of, or believes he has; she can see it in his eyes. None of it matters. What it all comes down to is that it's the parent company that ultimately decides everything.

"Couldn't I just speak to . . ." Ev begins. But she doesn't even know whom at the parent company she'd have to consult. The CEO, Frank Marchant, is rumored to have an office somewhere in this building, but she's never seen him and has little idea what he even looks like. "Whoever it is who could override this directive? Make them see that awards will be showered on us? Which will only burnish ARC's reputation, which in turn bolsters their bottom line?"

Gareth shakes his head sadly. "I've tried that. Not regarding Armitage, obviously, but other contentious stories. I've fought them over most of their policies since they bought a majority stake." He looks out the window, his brow knitted. "And when I'm not fighting with them, I'm fighting with the West Coast to give us more airtime for news programming so we can prove how 'valuable' we are." He sighs. "It's all . . . fighting."

Ev is taken aback. She's never seen Gareth in anything less than utter command. But now, suddenly, he appears deflated. Contrary to what she's always assumed, this extremely wealthy, supremely self-assured man is frustrated. Tired. Now she understands his reaction to Aviva's prodding, which had seemed uncharacteristically thin-skinned. He battles everyone above him; maybe he no longer has the time or energy to battle those below.

"Look," he says. "Armitage is a good story. An important story. I want you to understand that I know that. But it's not going to air."

Ev swallows hard. It takes several long moments to digest what he's said. It takes a few more to fathom that the news business, once again, has transformed itself beneath her feet. She wonders wildly if there's any point to being part of it anymore, if she even *wants* to rise further within its ranks, but bats away the thought before it can take root. "I'll explain to Aviva."

"Thank you," Gareth says. "But no sharing any details."

"Why not?"

"We can't let this kind of information go too far down the food chain. If producers find out how absurd things are getting, they might get indignant and blab to some paper or blog." He raises an eyebrow as if to remind her that she herself blabbed recently to Channel Surf. "In fact, I probably shouldn't have told you. But I felt under these circumstances, you had a right to know."

"I appreciate it," says Ev. She can't quite believe she's thanking him for this god-awful information, but he didn't have to tell her. He could have made something up or gotten Richard to poke so many "holes" in the story that he could have justified not running it. She rises to her feet. "Consider Armitage dead."

Gareth studies her carefully. He nods. Not to her, it seems, but to himself.

Aviva's not in her office. She texts Ev that she's at the ARC gym.

"Hi." Ev places her hand on the side of the elliptical.

Aviva stops, pink and puffing. "I couldn't just sit at my desk," she says.

"Understood," says Ev.

"So what's going on?"

"Not here."

Aviva steps off the machine and grabs her towel. They head for a small alcove where there's a drinking fountain next to a low bench. It affords privacy but forces them to sit a little too close together.

"They're not running it," Ev says. Better to cut to the chase. "It's Richard. He's not comfortable with Whitney's hidden identity."

"That's absurd."

"I know."

"We've done millions of stories with people who can't or won't go public."

"I know."

"I'll sit down with him and talk him through her credentials and share the entire transcript of our interview. I can *make* him comfortable."

"You can't. There's more to it."

"What do you mean?"

"CBS." Ev swallows. "CBS almost aired a story recently that involved a whistleblower. Who turned out to be disgruntled and lying. The parent company got wind of it somehow. Now they're spooked and they're just not up for the risk." Ev is amazed how quickly this story that she thought up in the elevator has taken on a life of its own. She almost believes it herself.

"This is outrageous. One has absolutely nothing to do with the other."

"I know."

"Why don't I go talk to Richard?"

"It's out of Richard's hands."

"Then I'll talk to Gareth. I'll go up there right now."

"Don't even think about it."

Aviva doesn't look convinced. "Then you talk to him."

"I did. It's what I've been doing all afternoon, pushing him."

"Push some more! This is going to set a terrible precedent."

"There's no point."

"I can't believe this," says Aviva, shaking. "You don't even seem mad." Ev can see that Aviva's disbelief is transforming into anger. "What's going on? You used to be a fighter. You went to Ken fucking Chang for the Penobscot Moms. Everyone thought it was crazy but you did and—"

"Aviva—"

"People could even *threaten* you and it didn't matter."

"Threaten me?" This brings Ev up short. "What are you talking about?"

"You don't remember? That story you told me?"

"What story?"

"About what happened to you in college? When you wrote for the paper?"

"That's—" Ev can't believe she ever talked about that. It must have been a late night with too many drinks.

"So I repeat: What's happened to you?"

"Don't make this personal," Ev says. "I'm not. We're two small cogs in a giant machine. We've known this for years. We just have to keep plugging. Find the next story, one they'll air."

Aviva crosses her arms. "The next story? What am I supposed to tell Whitney about *this* story? She put her career on the line for us. She reached out to me personally. Do you want to explain this to her? How about I put you two on the phone together?"

Ev softens her tone. "Why don't you take a couple of weeks off? Hang out with the family. Take James and Michaela and go up to the country. You're angry and tired and not thinking clearly. You'll feel better after a break and we'll find you a new, even better story."

"We both know that's a load of crap."

"Aviva."

The one person in the choppy waters of TV news that she's ever considered a real friend is looking at her as if she doesn't know her. There's a punishing silence and then Aviva says, "I hope whatever you're getting out of this is worth it."

Ev wants to tell her that she isn't getting anything out of it, not a thing. But Aviva is already gone.

SEVENTEEN

The staff of the *Leader* was at Quittin' Time, a dive bar in town, on a beautiful September evening, toasting Gil, who had just been named editor in chief. After a couple of rounds, he asked Leigh to join him in a back booth.

"As you may or may not know," he began, sliding in. "This fall will mark a quarter century since Lawton went co-ed."

Leigh nodded; May had mentioned it at a recent Sunday dinner because, of course, it was Foster House's anniversary as a home for the college's women. The very first co-eds to attend Lawton actually had *had* to live at Foster because no dorms had yet been built to accommodate them.

"So it got me thinking," Gil said, "maybe this is a good moment to take stock. What is it like for women at this school that barely admitted their own mothers? What do they think of Lawton as a place to live and learn?"

"Are you asking me?"

"I'm giving you an assignment, if you're up for it. I'd like you to report a survey series. Women, speaking out on academics, sports, dating—everything. Every month, a different topic. We can call it 'Ladies of Lawton.'"

Leigh rolled her eyes.

"Okay, okay, not that," Gil said, laughing. "But what do you think?"

Leigh took a sip of her beer and felt a tingle rise from the soles of her feet and travel up her body. An entire series, all to herself? And the topic couldn't be better. Women—their lives, their experiences at the school—didn't command much attention at Lawton. And she never did get to do the story of Native American women helping the suffragists at Foster House.

It was time for the school's female student body to have their say.

A big challenge for a lone reporter. Was she up to it?

It was a rainy late afternoon, fat drops rhythmically plopping against the leaves on the trees outside. Everyone had gone out to a voter registration drive and then a movie in town, but Leigh had a cold. She'd told Dilly to go on without her and set herself up with tissues, books, and a quilt on some large pillows in front of the enormous hearth in the drawing room. Dr. Long had a shift at the hospital, but before departing made Leigh some broth with a small bulb from some plant bobbing around inside the mug.

"This should help with the congestion and allow you to rest," she'd said, resting her palm lightly on Leigh's forehead for a moment.

Leigh had thanked her and taken a sip of the dark green liquid, which was pleasant in a mossy kind of way. After finishing the broth, she tried to go back to studying, but her eyes kept being drawn to the fireplace and its dancing flames. Eventually, she drifted off.

When she awoke, it was nearly dark and the fire had gone out. The wood was charred to deepest black, surrounded by little tufts of ash. It was chilly. She sat up and looked around, gathering the quilt around her shoulders. Something was different. The room felt like it was hovering around her, expectant. The air seemed heavy, almost viscous. She squinted through the dim. It took a few moments for her eyes to adjust. When they did, her hand flew to her mouth.

The room's twelve chairs—which had been scattered haphazardly around the perimeter—were now pulled around her in a small perfect circle.

"Hello?" she called, rising to her feet and looking around.

No one answered. She took three slow, deep breaths.

There was an energy within the circle. Like a pulse, it was steady and insistent, though she detected nothing threatening about it. She closed her eyes, trying to follow the energy, to ride it. It was taking her somewhere, trying to tell her something. But what? She—

A great crashing noise erupted from the fireplace. Leigh's eyes flew open as the dormant fire burst back to life. In seconds, flames filled the huge hearth, so bright she had to look away, the heat so intense she had to take a step back. The roar filled her ears as sparks flew out and cascaded around her.

And then, as quickly as it had exploded into being, the fire died away again, leaving behind a few slender trails of smoke and the soft sounds of logs popping and crackling.

Leigh stood still, heart beating fast, for several moments. Shaking, she made her way over to one of the chairs and sat.

It was warm.

The first two installments of her series, on academics and clubs, went pretty much as expected. Aside from a small dispute over whether women TAs were paid less than the male ones, which the administration denied, her reporting, while solid, hadn't uncovered anything particularly eye-opening.

But when she started interviewing girls about their social lives, she noticed something that made her whiskers twitch. First was Margaret, a sophomore.

"My parents would never have let me go to a 'party' school," she said, running her hands through corkscrew curls. "But Lawton is way wilder than I expected. Between the campus events, like the Harvest Bonfire and the Spring Fling, and all the dorm parties, it seems like there's something going on practically every night. Freshman year I went way overboard, but now I'm cutting back."

"Hard to do?" Leigh had asked. "Lotsa temptation?"

"The easiest thing to do was cut out frat parties." Margaret looked away. "They can get kind of crazy anyway."

"Crazy?"

"Well, they're off-campus. So—you know." Margaret checked her watch, started sliding things into her backpack, and stood. "Gotta run."

Next it was a girl named Kasha who was telling her about the past weekend's exploits. "I had dinner in town, then went to meet a friend at Alpha Tau Omega. But after twenty minutes, when I couldn't find her, I left. You don't hang around those places alone."

"What places? The frats?" Leigh asked.

Kasha nodded.

"Why not?"

Kasha shrugged, looking uncomfortable. "You hear things. Let's just leave it there, okay?"

Next came Cherie, who said she herself didn't go out much. She started telling Leigh about her roommate, a girl who'd been obsessed with avoiding the "freshman fifteen" but was now eating everything in sight.

"Why do you think that is?"

"I don't know," Cherie said. "But I can tell you that the first time she binged, it was a Sunday. She'd gone out with some basket-ball player the night before and come home at, like, five in the morning. When the cafeteria opened, I'll never forget it. She got, like, six stacks of pancakes. And she's been at it ever since."

It was at this point that Leigh decided to talk to Gil. She sat down across from him in the newsroom and flipped through her notes, relating what she'd been hearing.

"It's like each girl thinks she's saying something so obvious that it doesn't require further explanation. Or something so incendiary that it can't be uttered. Or both."

"And that thing is?" Gil asked.

"Sexual activity, or attempted sexual contact, that they didn't want. Has to be, right?"

Gil nodded. "I'd say that's fair speculation. So why did you come to me?"

"I wanted to know what you think."

"I think you can guess."

"You think I should go back and get them to talk."

"Immediately."

"But if they wanted to talk, wouldn't they have done that in the first place?"

Gil leaned forward, his blue eyes boring into hers. "What happened to my favorite hard-charging reporter?"

"Pushing them on this would just feel . . . pushy. Gross."

He rubbed his chin. "Look, it really doesn't matter what they want."

"It doesn't?"

"If they're talking about what you think they're talking about, and this is a fact of life on this campus that no one's discussing— maybe one that the administration doesn't even know about—then it's a story."

Leigh knew he was right but still felt uneasy. Until now, she'd only interviewed subjects who wanted to talk. For this, she was going to have to convince people to reveal something intensely private and painful when clearly every instinct was telling them not to. And what if nothing good came of it? How would she explain that to them?

"I think these girls opened up to you, to the extent they did, for a reason," Gil said. "You're a great interviewer and people trust you, but they also may have cracked the door open, hoping you'd walk through it. And anyway, what about the guys involved? You want them to keep getting away with whatever they're getting away with?"

Leigh shook her head. Of course she didn't.

"You can do this," he said. "I can help."

Over the next hour, he gave her a crash course in attribution so that she and her sources could come to an agreement on how much of their identities would be revealed, if any, and how much of what they told her would be published. Everything they said would be deemed "on the record," "on background," "on deep background," or "off the record."

Her hand was beginning to ache from all the notes she was taking when Gil suddenly stopped and laid his hands flat on the desk.

"I want you to understand something," he said. "This story might be nothing. It might go nowhere. But if these girls are talking about what you think they're talking about and they're willing to open up to you, this won't be part of the series."

"It won't?"

"It'll be bigger than that. It'll be a stand-alone, front-page piece," he said. "The kind of thing the *Patriot* might even pick up."

The *Patriot* was the town's local paper. It had a circulation of fifteen thousand.

Leigh's eyes widened. If she'd ever doubted that journalism was what she wanted to do with her life, her quickening pulse at this moment made things crystal clear.

She was a reporter. She was a seeker of truth. And if that landed her name on the front page, well, it would deserve to be there.

Ev is in her apartment's tiny laundry room, stuffing jeans into the washing machine, when she gets an idea.

In her haste, she dumps in too much detergent, slams the door closed, and heads to the kitchen. Her laptop is on the table and she types in *"Lawton Leader,"* "archives," and her senior year. She's not sure the *Leader* even has online archives, but in a few moments results pop up. She clicks on a series of links and seconds later, her past materializes.

LAWTON WOMEN DESCRIBE CULTURE OF SEXUAL ASSAULT

By Everleigh Page

In a series of in-depth interviews, women of every class at Lawton College, speaking anonymously, detailed more than a dozen instances of unwanted sexual contact by fellow students. Most of them did not report it, some not even realizing it was worth reporting.

Is there any rush in the world greater than your first big story? Ev sits back in her chair, feeling the thrill all over again. Her name had been in the paper many times before this, of course, and her series on the women of Lawton had guaranteed her a quarter page each month. But that was deep inside the paper and, while prestigious, couldn't compare with the lead story on the front page, right under the masthead.

> Even more troubling, what Lawton women described, often in harrowing detail, was far from the "man in the bushes" scenario so many associate with rape. In fact, the encounters involved almost exclusively students who were at least casual acquaintances and, very often friends or even dates.
>
> To make matters worse, many of those who did report the alleged attacks say that, far from supporting them, Dean of Students Sheldon Sykes became accusatory, asking what they were wearing and how much they'd had to drink. Dean Sykes is so far refusing to comment. . . .

The concepts of date rape and campus rape weren't nationally understood back then, and for many, this was the first they were hearing about any of it.

The story exploded on their quiet campus. The Take Back the Night people came up from New York for a rally, and there was a series of emergency faculty meetings. Her reporting came under fire by the administration and many male students, but it was solid. Gil had pushed her to include at least ten girls, not the five or six she'd initially found, so it would have real weight.

Getting their accounts had been grueling. She'd started by approaching the girls who'd made the original ambiguous statements. Suddenly, they didn't know what she was talking about. *Did I say that? I didn't mean anything by it.* Wildly, she'd thought of Marianne Becker, Dilly's first roommate. Had the girl left school so suddenly because she'd been attacked, and if so, could she track her down? But she'd decided the idea was unworkable and gone back to prodding girls on campus, gently but firmly. Some had wanted to pass the buck, saying that it was actually "a friend of a friend of a friend" who'd found trouble. But she'd kept at it, and finally, after promising that everything they said would be "on background"—directly quoted but with no name attached—she'd succeeded.

Ev blinks once or twice with emotion. The attention she'd gotten had been exciting enough, but the piece had had a healing effect on her as well. After so many years of feeling isolated inside her child-hood grief, she'd discovered that others hurt, too. By telling their stories she was helping them.

And it felt good.

A week after the story came out, Gil took her back to Quittin' Time.

"We have to keep working this," he said.

"I agree." Leigh twisted on the barstool next to him. She, too, had felt that the story wasn't done but wasn't sure how to take it any further.

"It's had an impact," he said. "But it's going to blow over, espe-cially if Dean Sykes keeps stonewalling. He's hoping this will all go away. So we have to push. And I think there's something we could try, though it might be tough." Gil waved at the bartender, signaling for two more beers.

"What?"

"Getting a name."

"A name."

"Of one of the guys. We need one of the victims to name her

attacker." Gil tapped the bar with his index finger. "The only way this thing is going to feel real is if one of these guys is exposed. More than one, if possible. Right now the whole issue is kind of abstract."

He had a point. Unless the administration went on the record, admitting and vowing to address the problem—and right now no one was even returning calls—how was this story going to advance? And if it didn't advance, how were things going to change?

But she wasn't at all sure she could get the goods. None of the victims had mentioned a name voluntarily. Several claimed they didn't even know who'd assaulted them; they were too drunk or names had never been exchanged. But of those who did know their attackers, would any be willing to point the finger?

"On it," she said, before taking a long sip of beer. She'd find a way.

"You realize if you get a name, you'll have to contact the guy and ask for a response."

"Of course." She hadn't realized this at all.

"And I think you should do something else, too. Or at least try."

"What?"

"If a girl names a guy, see if she'd be willing to go public with her own name as well. I know, I know," he said, holding a hand up as she looked at him in alarm. "Revealing the names of sex crime victims isn't done. It's not like being mugged. And you promised them everything was 'on background.' But think. If a girl accuses some guy publicly while herself remaining anonymous, imagine how easy it will be for people to dismiss her. I know how guys think, okay? They'll be skeptical. They'll accuse her of lying. And they'll feel sorry for the accused, out there on his own while she gets to hide. The last thing these guys need is sympathy."

Leigh exhaled in a short, sharp burst. She saw his logic. But it was way too much to ask. No girl was going to go public.

She grabbed some cold popcorn from one of the small bowls on the bar and looked out the window. In the glow cast by a street-lamp, she could see snow wafting down.

Well, there might be *one* girl who'd be willing.

No one else at Foster House knew what had happened to Cam. She still hadn't opened up much about herself. It seemed like there was some kind of sadness or worry inside of her being kept back by an invisible dam, and that Cam was afraid that if she let even a little water over it, a torrent would come flooding out.

So she'd been surprised when Cam had knocked on her door one night and come right out with it.

"It happened to me," she'd said quickly.

"What do you mean?" Leigh had asked, standing aside to let Cam in.

"I was assaulted."

She closed the door and pulled Cam over to the bed, where they sat, facing one another. "When was this?"

"At the beginning of school," Cam said, picking at a loose thread on the arm of the fisherman's sweater that dwarfed her small frame.

"This year?"

"Freshman year. Orientation week."

"Oh my god." She put her hand on Cam's knee. "Are you okay?"

"Mostly. Sometimes I forget about it for a while and feel kind of okay. Happy, even. I mean, it was three years ago. But then there'll be a couple of weeks when it's all I think about and everything is just, I don't know. Black."

Leigh reached for Cam's hand and squeezed it, but Cam didn't squeeze back. "Does Tina know?"

"No."

"Why are you telling me?"

Cam shrugged. "I hear you trying to convince girls to talk to you on the house phone. I see you at the dining room table with your notes spread out, trying to write a story without any new information. I just . . . wanted to help." She smiled an odd, flat smile. "I'd like to use the dining room table myself once in a while."

They had done the interview that night, Cam hesitant at first but growing stronger as she went. By the end, she'd appeared more angry than sad, and the experience of telling her story seemed to work as a kind of therapy. Afterward, they'd hugged, Leigh feeling grateful for Cam's help and happy that they were now much closer friends.

Telling her story anonymously was one thing, though. Would Cam be brave enough to go public?

Part of her thought Cam would embrace the idea, that she'd draw strength from owning her truth. But there was that secretive side of Cam, not to mention her mood swings.

No, she thought, Cam had done enough for her and the girls of Lawton already. She wasn't going to push for more.

She was about to tell Gil that it was going to be impossible to do what he wanted when he squinted at her thoughtfully.

"So what are your plans after graduation?" he asked.

"None yet."

"I'm about to start interviewing. You know that, right?"

She nodded. Gil was a fifth-year senior who'd worked various jobs on campus in exchange for financial aid. So while they'd graduate at the same time, he was a year older and, apparently, much more prepared. "I've got interviews at papers from Albany to Chicago to Boston. Trying to save money by doing them all during one or two trips. Anyway, I thought wherever I wind up, I could put in a good word for you. If you wanted."

"That," she said, looking down at her beer and trying to sound casual, "would be incredible."

. . . . .

She'd been right that the girls she'd interviewed wanted no part of coming forward publicly. She couldn't help but think nothing was going to change on campus and that, as Gil feared, the whole issue was going to die away.

And so, she reasoned, there was no harm in just asking Cam.

She made some hot chocolate and invited her outside to the porch swing overlooking the snow-covered backyard.

"I need to tell you something," Leigh began.

"Shoot," Cam replied, pulling a handful of mini marshmallows from the bag and dropping them into her mug.

"We've gotten a lot of letters at the *Leader*. And they're going to publish some."

"What kind of letters?"

"People are skeptical about the rape stories. They don't believe them. Don't think we should have printed them." This was completely true.

"I know a lot of guys don't."

"Girls, either," Leigh said. "Most of whom would prefer to think this stuff isn't going on. It scares them. And anonymous victims just don't feel real. They're disembodied. They could be anyone. Or no one. One of the deans is even accusing the *Leader* of making it all up." Leigh couldn't imagine anyone would believe such a thing, but some apparently did. "I know it wouldn't be easy, but you could change all that."

"Me personally?"

"Yes. If you came forward publicly."

Cam made a small snorting sound of disbelief.

"I know. It sounds crazy. But what you could do is nothing less than prove this whole thing is legit," Leigh said. "If you're a real person, it'll make everyone else more real and more believable. Maybe you'd embolden others to go public, too. Which would help everyone."

"Why not try one of the others?"

"I have. Believe me, I did not want to ask this of you." Leigh kicked at the ice that encroached on the deck. "Look," she continued. "I know victims are accused of being sluts and lying and all kinds of other things. That's one reason why they're not named in the press. People try to discredit them, pore through their pasts looking for dirt. But the only way to change things is to refuse to be ashamed. *You* did nothing wrong. And you're one of Lawton's best, beyond reproach. Dean's list every semester. You don't smoke, you barely drink." The truth was, Cam hardly socialized at all, unless she, Dilly, or Tina dragged her out. "And of course," Leigh said, lifting her arms towards the house. "You're a member of Foster House."

Cam regarded her. "As are you."

"Yes. But that's not the reason to do this," Leigh said quickly. As Foster girls, they were supposed to be there for one another, but she didn't want Cam to think she'd trade on sisterhood that way.

"Aren't you not supposed to report on friends?" Cam asked. "Didn't you have to recuse yourself from student council coverage because of Dilly?"

"Yes. But I think this is very different. I think it's reasonable that someone who's been through what you have would *only* talk to a friend. You could argue that there's no other way a story like this is going to be told." Leigh took a sip from her mug. "But I'll be clearing it with Gil, just in case."

Cam put her drink down. "Can I think about it?"

"Of course," Leigh said, rearranging the blanket she'd brought out so it covered them better. "There's one other thing, though. But this part's easier."

161

"What's that?"

"If you go public, it's important that you name the guy as well. I know you didn't want to before. But that's what this is really all about. Whoever he is, he's the villain. And everyone needs to know it."

Cam said nothing. Leigh followed her gaze across the yard and up into the bare trees. A blackbird was watching them from a high branch, its feathers gleaming in the harsh sunlight. Leigh remembered Dr. Long once saying that her people believed that blackbirds carried messages. The trick was to decipher them.

Ev clicks on the next story.

LACROSSE STAR DAN DAGGETT ACCUSED OF RAPE

VICTIM GOES PUBLIC

By Everleigh Page

Lawton senior Dan Daggett, a three-time All State starting attackman for the Lawton Leopards lacrosse team, sexually assaulted a freshman girl three years ago at the Harvest Bonfire, according to the alleged victim.

Camilla Overton, who initially gave her account to the Leader anonymously, is now making her alleged attacker's name public as well as her own and is offering her story in greater detail.

She says it all began when Daggett asked her to dance at the annual freshman event at Klyber Field. Overton agreed, she says, feeling flattered that he had noticed her. She says after one or two songs, he began to spin her off in a jokey, ballroom dancing kind of way, farther and farther from the crowd gathered around the flames.

The two wound up in the pitch-black woods where she says he pushed her down into a pile of leaves. . . .

Through Coach Martinson, Daggett proclaimed his innocence . . .

The rush of this story was different. Somber, in a minor key. Hard-won in a very different way than the first. Shared, of course, with Cam. The whistleblower.

But there was nothing minor about its effect.

The student council held an emergency session, there was a call to boycott all lacrosse games, and Coach Martinson as well as the team's other top staff were seen entering Crowley Hall, the building that held the higher levels of the administration, where the two groups were said to have huddled for hours on end.

Eyes followed Leigh everywhere she went. There were dirty looks and snide comments. But there were also encouraging words, mostly from girls but not exclusively. She'd heard from some faculty, too. Professor Addison, who taught Twentieth Century Society, with his skullcap of salt and pepper hair and wrinkled corduroy jacket, had stopped her on the quad and pulled her into a brief, surprising hug.

"Important work you're doing," he'd said.

"Thank you," she'd replied, flushing at this show of support from a professor in public.

"Any trouble with Dean Sykes?" Addison peered closely at her as he said this.

Leigh shook her head with conviction. What could he do to her, for telling the truth?

. . . . .

A sudden headache creases Ev's brain. She presses on her temples and takes a few deep breaths. She knows full well there's no point in scrolling further to find her next story.

There isn't one.

The Dan Daggett story was the last she ever wrote for the *Leader*.

Because days later, Cam took it all back.

EIGHTEEN

Ev is at Sean's, sitting cross-legged on a chair by the window, playing tug with Homer. Sean is splayed on the couch, his computer on his stomach, in a Zoom with his family, which they do every Sunday afternoon. While she gazes out onto the neighboring rooftops, with their satellite dishes and water tanks, Ev half-listens to their chatter about a brewing battle over budget cuts within Carmen's department at Northwestern and Zach's latest art project.

"That one is really good," Sean says to Zach about a sketch the boy has drawn on his iPad. "You got the shading on the underside of the skateboard just right. What I would do is accentuate the wood grain a bit."

"Zach, you're not skateboarding without your helmet, are you?" Carmen asks. "And kneepads?"

"No, Mawmaw," the kid says. "How do I do wood grain stuff?" Zach asks Sean.

"Brush tool," Sean says, and then goes into a lengthy description of how it works before Zach signs off to do homework.

Erik pipes up. "Is Ev there with you?"

Sean beckons and Ev pushes herself out of the chair and approaches the computer.

"Hi there," she says, perching next to Sean. She exchanges pleasantries with Carmen and Erik, keeping her answers friendly but short because they have a concert up at Lincoln Center and she wants to shower before they leave.

"Dad, how are you feeling?" Sean asks. Erik, though he did not break his hip, has still not recovered from his fall.

"As if he'd tell you anything close to the truth," says Carmen, pretending to elbow her husband in the ribs. Carmen summarizes the experience of Erik's latest doctor's appointment while Erik complains that the whole thing was a bore with an exorbitant co-pay.

Ev excuses herself and grabs a fresh towel from the hallway closet.

After her shower, she wraps it around herself and heads down the hall toward Sean's bedroom. He's still talking to his parents but Carmen's hushed tone draws her attention. She pauses to listen.

"I know how much you care for her, baby. But isn't she a bit . . . closed off?"

"Mom," Sean says, sounding frustrated but clearly trying to keep his voice low. "We've talked about this."

"Yes, but as you two go along, I'm worried you're going to get hurt. She just seems to have such a hard shell."

"I know. You've said that before. But as I've told you, I see a whole other side of her. Has she got a few walls up? Yes. Is it any wonder? Lost her mom young, dad on the other side of the world with another family. After almost fifty years of marriage, can either of you even *imagine* that life? And don't forget she works in TV. It's dog-eat-dog over there. So give her a break."

"I understand all that," said Carmen. "And I feel for Ev, I do. But do you have to be the one to help her with all this? Ever since you were sick, it's like you need to 'save' anyone else with a problem. But it's a lot of responsibility. Maybe a therapist could—"

"I talked to her about therapy once. No dice. She was practically frog-marched to the school psychologist when she was a kid. I think she's still scarred from it. I think in time, the armor will come off. It already has, from time to time. I feel like I'm the one person she can let her guard down with and—"

"But she's in her forties, yes?" Carmen cuts in. "How much more change do you think you're going to see?"

"Just say it. You don't like her."

This is followed by a painful silence.

Ev retreats to Sean's room to dress. By the time she comes out, his parents are gone but he's back on with Zach.

Ev begins to clear their brunch cups and plates off the coffee table, hoping Sean will get the hint that it's time to get going.

"You're coming Tuesday, right?" Zach asks.

"I'll be there," says Sean.

Ev isn't sure what they're talking about. It might be a chat with Zach's guidance counselor. He's been having trouble in school lately.

"Where's Homer?" Zach asks, and Sean tilts the computer toward the floor, where the dog is gnawing on a rawhide.

Ev carries everything into the kitchen. Moments later, she hears Annette join the conversation. She peeks out and sees Sean's sister holding two lamps up to the screen for Sean's perusal. After failing to find even one client for her color therapy business, she's decided to widen her scope to general home decorating. Her plan is to use her own house as the basis for a portfolio.

"Which do you prefer? For the foyer table?" Annette asks Sean.

He peers at the choices.

Ev sighs. It's good that Sean's sister has ambition and goals. But she left the working world when she had Zach and now is counting on jumping back into it with a cool job for which she has no relevant experience.

Ev clears her throat. The concert starts in half an hour. Of course, there's a warm-up act they can miss, but Ev hates arriving after everyone is seated and having to step over their feet and purses, mumbling apologies. Unfortunately, Sean misses her signal and is now enthusiastically embroiled in Annette's questions.

Ev heads to the bathroom to brush her teeth and then grabs the dressy coat she leaves at Sean's. She comes back into the living room, holding it.

"Oh—hi," says Annette, and Ev realizes she's stepped into view of the camera. "I didn't know you were there." She doesn't even try to fake a cordial tone.

Ev raises a hand in greeting. "Yup. We're actually heading out. Jazz quartet uptown."

Sean shoots her a look telling her . . . something. Was she a bit abrupt?

Annette puts down the lamps. "Glad you're taking a break. Sounds like you work every weekend."

As in *you're a bad girlfriend*, thinks Ev. "Sweeps coming up," she replies. "Have to command the troops."

Things with Annette were never great, but they took their first icy turn several months ago when Ev and Sean went up to Westchester to see Zach in his school play. An hour and twenty minutes in a rental car to see a bunch of middle schoolers take on *Twelve Angry Men*.

"I thought you were coming on your own," Ev had heard Annette whisper to Sean when they'd kissed hello. "I was hoping you'd stay over." She'd given Ev a forced smile and a dead-fish handshake before taking her seat and pulling out her phone to shoot video.

Unfortunately, there had been a tsunami warning for the West Coast that ARC was keeping an eye on. So, yes, Ev had to take a few calls during the performance, the low buzz of her phone at one point coming during one of Zach's monologues. But Ev always left the room to speak. Okay, yes, once, on her way out of the auditorium, she'd jostled Annette's phone, messing up the video. And yes, the network had decided to do a live update at 11:00 p.m. and because Ev is one of the few EPs with control room experience, she had to go in, and yes, Sean left the show early to drive her back to the city instead of dropping her at the train as Annette had suggested.

"How's Zach going to feel if you abandon him in the middle of the play?" Annette had hissed to Sean as they squeezed past her. "He'll be crushed."

Sean had hugged her and promised to call the next morning and explain it all to him.

"You'd think I planned this whole thing," Ev had said, once they were in the car.

"I know, I know," Sean had replied. "But Annette's feeling freaked out and vulnerable these days. You can understand that."

"I can," Ev had said, looking out the window at the suburban darkness. She could understand.

"And she's used to having me to lean on."

"She's used to having you to herself."

There was a pause before Sean replied. "That's fair," he'd said, reaching for her hand. "She might be a little, um, threatened by you. Your place in my life. Your big job. But when life is normal, she's the best, I swear. She'll get over all this. I promise."

But Annette hadn't gotten over it. And the incident at the Met had just made things worse. Annette's apparently livid that Zach heard about his parents' breakup from Ev and now thinks it's not "safe" for Zach to be around Ev. Annette even asked Sean to consider keeping them apart, an idea he called a nonstarter.

"Ev's got a major story coming up," Sean says now. "I should have told Mom about it, actually. About this drug company—"

"Sean." Ev says this too quietly and Sean keeps right on talking. "*Sean.*"

He stops and looks at her quizzically.

"Can you not?" she says.

"What's wrong?"

"We're not airing it," she says in a low voice.

"What?"

Ev tilts her head toward the computer; she doesn't want to go into it in front of Annette. But Sean ignores her.

"What do you mean?" he prods. "You've been working on it for months."

She didn't want to tell Sean about this until after she'd figured out how to spin it. "I'll tell you everything after the show, but for now—can we go?"

They are late and incur grumbles from everyone in their row as they thread their way in. Ev barely hears a note; she keeps replaying Sean's conversation with his parents while trying to figure how to explain to him about killing Armitage.

"Want to get a drink? Talk?" he asks out on the sidewalk after the show.

"I'm tired," she says.

She braces for his protest but he only shakes his head and hails a cab. Back at his place, he takes Homer for a walk and then parks himself in the kitchen, making overnight oats for the morning.

She pulls out a nightgown from one of the drawers Sean set aside for her and shrugs it on. She lies down on the bed but her brain is churning. She skims one of Sean's trade magazines, which usually acts as a prescription-level sedative. Half an hour later, it has yet to work.

"I'm going to stay up and work for a while," Sean says from the doorway.

"Right," she says.

But he doesn't leave. "Look, I can't help wondering . . ." He hesitates, looking around the room.

"Wondering . . ." she says, sitting up.

"Why it's always a struggle."

"What is?" she asks.

"To get in there. With you."

Ev presses the pad of her index finger hard against the center of her forehead. This is their issue. Every relationship has one, doesn't it? She read an article once arguing that there's a sensitive subject humming in the background for every couple, a fundamental rift that both parties silently agree to leave undisturbed until one of them just can't take it anymore, at which point it bursts briefly to the surface. Then it sinks gently back down again. Hopefully, anyway.

"You are in there with me," she says. It's not completely true, of course. But it's truer of him than anyone else.

Later, when he comes to bed, she pretends to be asleep. She feels the gentle tug of the sheet across her waist as he pulls it over himself. Usually this is when he rests a hand on her hip. But not tonight. Within minutes, he's asleep.

She isn't so lucky.

She still can't believe Armitage won't air and forces herself to follow the ramifications of the new edict Gareth told her about. She's going to have to look through every story she's approved in the last six months and see if anything will present a problem. And any new pitches that come her way treading on this kind of ground, which is the kind of ground she wants to cover, will have to be shot down, without telling producers why.

That's going to be fun.

She puts a pillow over her head to block out the sound of the grandfather clock and Homer padding around the apartment, but more unhelpful thoughts crowd in.

Should she leave ARC? Go to another network newsmagazine? There aren't many left and they all have lines out the door. And she's not going to cable or streaming.

Hours later, it seems, she finally falls asleep. But she has that dream again.

She's on campus, walking a stone path. It's nighttime. On the left is a large low building with no windows, on the right, a solid line of trees. The path is lit but one of the lamps up ahead is out and a dark space looms. The moment she steps into the darkness she knows it's a mistake.

A twig snaps; someone is behind her. She turns but can't see anyone.

"*Leigh*," a voice whispers.

Her body convulses. She opens her eyes and pushes the pillow away, gulping for air.

Sean's arm reaches around her.

Ev's flooded with relief and turns toward him. She wants to relate the dream but only regular breathing, a sound just below a snore, comes back at her through the dark. "Sean?" she says.

He pulls her closer but doesn't answer. She says his name again but there's no response. Somehow he's offering her comfort despite being sound asleep, as if his subconscious can sense trouble in hers.

She presses herself into his chest, wanting, for once, to talk. But he continues to sleep, even as he lightly strokes her arm.

. . . . .

The next week, a note from May arrives at ARC pressing her, again, to attend Recommitment. It ends with "While I can't tell you what you want to know, I can tell you this: It literally won't work without you."

What does that even mean? May doesn't strike her as the kind of person who would use "literally" incorrectly even though everyone else does these days.

She opens a new tab on her computer and enters "Foster House," "Lawton College," and "Recommitment." There isn't much, barely a page's worth of results. First is the Foster House website, which didn't exist back in her day but of course now does. The homepage features striking shots of the house and grounds, and an overview:

> Foster House in Lawton, New York, was the childhood home of local suffragist Aurora Foster. In the days after the Women's Rights Convention in nearby Seneca Falls, she, just a teenager, along with other activists including Elizabeth Cady Stanton and Lucretia Mott, took up Lawton College's refusal to admit women as a pet cause. They believed that one day the school would become co-ed but also knew that the first women who arrived on campus would need a nurturing environment, some "rooms of their own."

> When Lawton did finally open its doors to women in the 1970s, Foster's home became theirs. Meanwhile, funds Aurora Foster left behind had grown large enough to provide for most of its upkeep and to endow two scholarships per year.

Foster House encourages activism in its students and takes a strong role in Lawton College politics. From helping impoverished local communities to fighting for the rights of female and minority students, Foster has never shied from confrontation, becoming, at times, a proud thorn in the side of those sometimes behind the curve of history.

Foster House, over the decades, has nurtured hundreds of young women who have gone on to important careers, including award-winning writers, doctors, lawyers, Fortune 500 business leaders, as well as three representatives in the US Congress.

Ev hunts around the site and finds a button labeled "Post-College Foster." She clicks on it and up come details about career counseling services for alumnae and group trips to places like the Galapagos, hosted by Lawton professors. At the end it says, "And of course, twenty years after leaving Foster House, every sister experiences Recommitment." It offers no further explanation.

Ev goes back to her search results. There are a couple of Facebook mentions by women who say they are "off to Recommitment." Others tell their sisters, "See you at Foster!"

There are a few posts that seem to be from afterward. A woman named Rebecca Artis reaches out to two of her former housemates. "WTF?! Need to discuss. Not over phone or email. When/where can we meet?"

Someone named Sarah Klein, a doctor, writes about coming home from Recommitment inspired to finally follow through with an idea for needle-free diabetes care that she'd long ago written off as hopeless. Within a year, she'd manufactured her invention. She'd just taken her company public and was now a multimillionaire.

Two others, Joelle McNamara and Francine DuBois, best friends since rooming together at Foster, post about quitting their corporate jobs and departing for Ethiopia, to work with orphans. They say that post-Recommitment, they've realized this is their "true calling." There are a few photos of them with young children, in which they look blissfully happy.

The last entry is a blog post from several years back by a woman in Texas. She writes, "We wish to note the passing of Betty Ann Marks, who took her own life on Sunday. Betty Ann had a thriving career in finance. She was one of the early adopters of mortgage-backed security instruments here in Houston. Despite the market collapse and the ensuing chaos, she was promoted and poised for even bigger things. Days before her death she had returned from her twentieth college reunion in Lawton, New York, about which she had been extremely excited, especially seeing friends at her off-campus dorm, Foster House. It is with great puzzlement and pain that her family and friends ponder what could have caused . . ."

Ev sighs and looks out the window. It appears there are no answers to be had, not even on the mighty internet. She clicks the tab closed and pulls out a script. It needs a lot of work, but after reading the first page four times without taking in a single word, she gives up.

"Nice to see everyone," Ev says, lifting her voice so those in the back can hear. The hundred or so staffers of *Breaking* are gathered at one end of the large bright newsroom. Their faces are turned toward her, expectant and slightly nervous. They don't have regular staff meetings because everyone hates them. So when she calls one, no doubt some worry something's wrong. And something is, in the sense that layoffs are coming as soon as Gareth approves her final list. But she's not going to talk about that today. No sense scaring everyone. Today it's all about galvanizing the troops for the battle of the moment.

"So we're halfway through sweeps," she begins. "And I just want to reiterate how important a time this is for us." Ev begins to pace back and forth. "It's no secret we're enjoying our new lead-in," she says sarcastically.

General groans follow.

"I know, I know," she assures them. *Chill!* is every bit the disaster she'd feared it would be. Somehow, *Breaking* is holding its own against the shows on the other networks, but it's not winning, and surely the parent company is aware of every ad revenue penny being sacrificed. "We can't control what the network gives us. But we can control our response. So I want us all to give a bit more thought to our next couple of shows. *Chill!* is skewing differently than *Interrogation Room*. The audience is quirky. It's not the one we're used to."

Someone asks her what exactly they know about the viewers *Chill!* is delivering to them and she shares what the research department has gleaned: that their new viewers are younger and more urban. In short, not as used to getting their news from TV.

"The audience is different," she continues, "so *we* can be different. Let's open ourselves up journalistically, try something bold. But still in keeping with our sky-high standards, the ones we're known for. Now. I'd like everyone who has a story airing to think about different ways of getting into it. See if there's a way to make it more compelling, more visceral. And everyone who's sitting on a pitch for a story because they think we won't green-light it, please submit it for tomorrow's meeting. We're up for *anything*. So shake it up! Let's play for keeps the next two weeks. And beyond."

There's an outbreak of chatter and a couple of the interns clap, obviously keyed up.

"Okay," Ev says. "Thanks, everyone—"

"*Please*," comes a voice from the back.

Ev doesn't have to look to know who it is. "Problem?" she replies, trying to sound unruffled as Aviva threads her way to the front.

"Why are you saying this?" Aviva asks. Her large dark eyes are narrowed, her arms crossed over her chest. "People might believe you."

The entire room freezes. *Breaking* is full of hard-hitting journalists but, at the office, the atmosphere is collegial. People treat one another with respect, even when there's a terrorist attack an hour before airtime and everyone's hair is on fire. Public confrontations like this do not happen.

"Let's take this in my office," Ev says, straightening her jacket.

"Let's not," says Aviva. "Everyone should hear it. Because after what you just said, people might think if they come to you with a significant story that you might, you know, air it. And that's not true."

Ev's cheeks burn. She knows Aviva is angry about Armitage but this kind of public disloyalty is beyond the pale.

"I don't know what's going on with you," Ev says in a low voice, feeling the eyes of everyone on her. "But this is not the place."

"I think it *is* the place," Aviva returns. "Everyone needs to know what's happening. Because *Breaking* is not the show we like it to think it is. And ARC is not the network it used to be."

"That's enough," says Ev. "You don't know what you're talking about." She clears her throat and addresses the staff. "Sorry about this, folks. Aviva has had a disappointment and she's upset. But she's extrapolating in a way that's completely unfair to all of us."

Her gaze falls on Tab, who looks aghast. Ev hasn't yet told Tab that Armitage isn't airing and, from her expression, Aviva hasn't, either. But Tab's smart enough that she can probably guess.

Ev claps her hands smartly, twice. "This meeting is over," she says. "Back to work, please."

The ARC gym is packed. She's been coming often lately, trying to squeeze in more cardio as per the doctor so that maybe she can stop taking the beta-blockers he's prescribed, which sometimes make her woozy. She's also hoping to become a better partner for Sean on their weekly runs so he doesn't have to stop every few blocks and wait for her.

Ev takes the only free treadmill, down at the far end by the window. She starts at a light jog, turning over Aviva's stunt again and again in her mind. It's one thing to be upset over Armitage. Ev herself is still angry. But to embarrass her boss publicly? To cast aspersions on *Breaking* as a show, as well as the network?

The guy next to her revs up into a full-out sprint for several minutes and finishes. He leans heavily on the console, catching his breath. He departs without wiping down the equipment. A few minutes later a woman steps up onto the machine and starts to punch in her speed and incline. Ev is about to inform her about its less-than-hygienic state when their eyes meet and she sees who it is: Candy Wallace.

"Hey, girl," Candy says with the overly intimate tone of one of her morning show anchors. "What a day! Am I right?" Candy radiates fizzy energy as she starts pounding away, her red ponytail swinging behind her.

Ev keeps her eyes forward but notices that Candy is at level fourteen while she's at level five. She pushes the "up" arrow and goes to eight. After a minute, her thighs start to burn.

Gradually she realizes that Candy is talking to her.

"This shaman I've been working with says I have to try to tune into their 'particular frequency.' But have you met those guys up there? Totally disorganized . . ."

"Sorry, what?" she asks, cocking her head in Candy's direction.

"Those guys at Specials."

"What about them?" Ev asks, feeling a stitch in her side.

"Have you spent any time up there? It's bonkers."

"Mmmm," Ev replies. She doesn't really know anyone at Specials. They produce high-profile planned news events like political debates, conventions, and town halls but don't often mix with the rest of the News Division.

"What were you even doing there?" Ev asks, massaging her abdomen.

"Oh," Candy says. "I thought Gareth had told everyone."

"Told everyone what?" Ev asks sharply.

"I'm moving over there," she says.

"To Specials?"

"Yes." Candy bumps her level up to sixteen.

"As EP?" Ev asks.

"God no," Candy says, flying along. "VP."

Ev almost doubles over. Sweeps haven't even ended yet. She didn't get her full shot to show what she could do. And now Candy is getting the promotion? *The* promotion, as in singular. Because when it comes to women, there can be only one at a time. Gareth may be more evolved than some men out there. But at sixty-five or so, he's still a member of a different generation and there's no way he's giving vice presidencies to two women at once.

So he dangled the prospect of the Digital VP slot in front of Ev for what? What kind of game is he playing? She's done everything he's asked, from killing a major story without a fuss to earmarking some of her best employees for layoffs, and she has absolutely nothing to show for it.

But Candy, just because she's "ARC through and through" thanks to her dad and somehow convincing celebrities to bounce on trampolines while talking about their love lives at 8:16 in the morning, gets the brass ring? Ev tries to remind herself that Candy is plenty smart and actually a nice person, but the thought just makes her more irritated.

Ev pushes her level up to eleven and feels the soles of her feet sting as they slap the belt. She wishes she were running for real, on an actual road that would take her away from here. She wishes—

Candy is yelling.

"What?" Ev yells back.

"I said, you all right?"

Ev punches the "down" arrow to slow the speed but the world is going swirly and she winds up making it go faster.

"Stand on the edges!" Candy says.

Ev tries to move her feet to the sides of the belt but it's impossible with it moving so fast.

The next thing she knows, she's zooming backward, slamming to the floor and landing hard on her butt. Moments later, a couple of gym attendants are by her side, looking thoroughly freaked out. Coughing, she rejects their offer to help her up. She closes her eyes and tries to ignore the throbbing in her tailbone.

She feels something cold bump lightly against her shoulder. "Here ya go, honey."

Ev opens her eyes to see a plastic cup of water. It's being held by Candy, who gazes down at her with grave concern from so high above.

NINETEEN

E v starts to reapply her lipstick with the tiny brush that she scrapes across the tube—the way she does when she has to be "on"—then decides Gareth's not worth it. He's gone over her final layoff list and has informed her that they need to meet, surely so he can lodge another complaint. But after everything he's demanded of her and finding out that it's Candy who's getting promoted, he doesn't deserve her best self.

On the way out of her office, Meryl hands Ev a few printed sheets containing *Breaking*'s budget in case she needs to refer to it during the meeting. Ev didn't ask for this; it's the kind of thing Meryl does on her own.

"Thanks," says Ev.

Colleen stands when Ev approaches. "He's waiting for you," she says. "Upstairs."

"Upstairs?"

"In the parent company dining room. You've been there before?"

Ev has not. You have to be a senior vice president or higher at ARC to get in. Or, apparently, to be invited by someone of that level.

Colleen gives brief directions and the code for a special elevator, and a few minutes later, Ev is dozens of floors up, entering a chic square room with a dignified neutral palette and a commanding view of Central Park.

"Yes?" says a steward, appearing out of nowhere.

"I'm here for—"

"Ev." Gareth stands beside a window table, beckoning her over. The place is as hushed as a library and the two dozen or so other diners look up from their plates as she moves through. All are men and each seems to be in a $2,000 suit, sporting a sun-kissed glow though summer's not even here yet. Ev's walk is unsteady. She hadn't expected to be in this rarified place today, much less to be the object of stares by folks so high up in the parent company that she doesn't even know who they are. She wishes she'd brushed her hair and worn a nicer dress today. Gareth clasps both her hands, an old-fashioned gesture that feels like they're courting.

They sit and, since paperwork would look awkward on the elegantly minimalist table, Ev slides it under her thighs, where it scratches slightly against her skin. They toast with a dry Riesling Gareth has chosen and Ev nods when he suggests they get herb salads and the Dover sole *à deux*.

"The layoff list is excellent," Gareth says, tearing off a piece of a miniscule triangular roll. "You have a keen eye for slicing the beast while preserving the organs."

Ev exhales, relieved.

He spends several minutes praising her skillful choices and detailing why he's so confident about *Breaking*'s financial health going forward. Ev thought she'd have to defend at least something.

The salads arrive, a dozen carefully curated leaves, lightly glistening from a spritz of dressing. They eat for a moment or two before Gareth speaks again.

"I'm afraid, though, that we need a couple more cuts." He takes a sip of mineral water. "A tweak or two."

Ev puts her fork down.

"Yesterday, the finance people asked for another 1.5 percent. Just sprung it on us. China is devaluing its currency and apparently it affects the company adversely. I've put the word out to the other shows that they each need to come up with another name or two. For you, one level four and one level one should do it."

When ARC was purchased by the parent company, it adopted its corporate structure. The company divides all employees into levels, which indicate a range of experience and pay. It took months to translate these levels, which were created for factory workers in places like Malaysia, to journalists. Ev can't stand this stuff and makes a point of not retaining it. Now her mind races trying to remember. A level four would be a producer or an associate producer, she thinks, and a level one would be an assistant producer.

"All right." Two more jobs is not "tweaking," but she'll have to suck it up. "Let me take another look." She allows just a little irritation to slip into her tone.

"I thought we'd split this little chore. I pick one and you pick one."

"Oh?"

"One less thing for you to feel guilty about."

"How thoughtful." She hadn't realized he'd detected her pangs.

"My pleasure."

He doesn't offer specifics, so she has to ask. "Whom, may I ask, have you chosen?"

"Tabitha Morales."

Ev almost smiles, a natural reaction to what seems like teasing. Yet Gareth's face is absolutely straight.

"You reached down from your lofty perch into the junior levels of my staff roster, which contain almost exclusively names you don't know, and specifically chose her? Why, if I may ask?"

"She's in the first window of her contract, as I'm sure you know. And a few people have spoken to me about her. In confidence, of course. They don't feel she quite fits in. Inappropriate behavior. What's the word they're using today? *Spectrum-y*? Don't quote me, of course. Americans with Disabilities Act blah, blah, blah."

This is nonsense. Nobody in their right mind thinks Tab has autism. Even if she did, it wouldn't mean she couldn't do her job. Anyway, Ev's pretty sure she would know autistic behavior if she saw it. One thing she's realized over the years is that there's a decent chance her own father has a touch of Asperger's. It would explain a lot, like his obsessive interest in one topic—science—and his difficulty in expressing empathy.

And anyway, no one is running around complaining to the head of the News Division about an assistant producer who keeps her head down and works hard. In fact, Aviva went out of her way to mention her excellent work on Armitage before they killed it.

Then it hits her. Tab's story from weeks ago about running into Gareth in the elevator and challenging him to let *Breaking* do more serious programming. He's made it clear he's sick of "fighting" everyone around him. Could he have been so affronted as to go after her in this way?

And why has he brought Ev here for all this, anyway? Why has he invited her to the parent company's inner sanctum, which seems designed to celebrate multimillion-dollar mergers? Does he think it will intimidate her?

"Can we talk about this? Tab's an important part of the *Breaking* team. Nobody is more conscientious. And her social skills are fine."

The server, in a navy vest and slacks with white shirt and red tie, comes to remove the salad plates.

"I understand your desire to fight for your people. You're their leader, their shepherd." Gareth sips the pale yellow wine thought-fully. "But I'm *your* leader. Don't forget that."

Despite her annoyance, Ev has to admire Gareth's comfort with power. He's not embarrassed enough to come up with more excuses for why Tab should take the fall. He does not like her and wants her out.

It's so simple if you think of it like that.

"Your turn," he says.

She starts to tell him that she'll need time. Then she realizes she doesn't.

"Aviva," she says. "Aviva Abramowitz." The name catches in her throat and she coughs softly.

Gareth nods as if this is a test she's just aced. "Your thinking?"

"Based on our recent screening, I'm concerned that her work may be going in a different direction than what we'll be undertaking around here in general." She feels like a robot speaking what's been programmed.

"That's a keen assessment." Gareth's tone says, *Now you're get-ting it.*

The waiter returns and tops off their wine and water glasses. Ev stares at the bobbing ice cubes. Has she actually done this? Can she change her mind, take it back, without sounding like an idiot?

Ev realizes Gareth is trying to get her attention. "Sorry?" she says.

"I was asking about your social skills," Gareth says.

"*My* social skills?" She narrows her eyes. "Don't tell me I'm 'spectrum-y,' too."

"Social as in *social media.*" Gareth shakes his head as if he doesn't know where's she's been the last minute or so. "You were supposed to work on your tweeting and posting for the *Breaking* brand."

"I have been," Ev lies. Is he really going to interrogate her about this now, after everything else?

"Glad to hear it. It will come in handy over at the Social Media unit."

"The Social Media unit?"

"It's good if the VP has a clue what the kids are doing over there. They all grew up on this stuff and run circles around us."

"VP."

"Yes."

"Me?"

"You."

Ev sucks in her breath as silently as she can. *A vice presidency.* Social Media's not part of broadcast like Specials is, but it's not bad. Like Digital—which, it turns out, Steve Henderson isn't leaving after all—it's a growth area. And here she was, assuming Gareth would never promote two women at once. She tries to hold it together. "Interesting."

Gareth observes her closely and she watches him back. She never knows quite what he thinks of her. Once or twice, when dancing together at a party, she thought he might have been holding her a little too closely. Other times, he can seem almost fatherly, like when he proudly recounts her rise within the network to some media journalist or mucky-muck. And on rare occasions, he can be as dismissive of her as he no doubt is of the man who shines his shoes down in the lobby, some fifty floors beneath where they're sitting.

"It's flattering," she continues carefully. "Only I'm not sure Social is my forte."

"You'll pick it up. I'll have a couple smart folks get you up to speed on our strategy. The young people do most of the work anyway."

"But why me?" Ev doesn't want to sound ungrateful, but she can't help but ask. "What makes you think I'd be good at Social Media?"

Gareth smiles. "You won't be there long."

The server appears yet again, rolling a dainty cart. On it rests the fish, looking like a golden parsley-strewn sacrifice. The server begins to fillet it using delicate silver implements. It's a complicated process, taking the top half off while preserving the tiny bones, which are then lifted off in a perfect sheet. The fish is plated with a rich butter sauce ladled over the top. Tiny new potatoes that are exactly the same size, as if carved with a melon baller, come next, followed by shafts of roasted white asparagus that are precisely the same length.

"Anything else, Mr. Smyter?" the server asks.

Ev almost squirms in her seat, waiting for the guy to depart so Gareth can continue. Gareth shakes his head.

"Bon appétit," says the server, and wheels the cart away.

Despite the exquisite presentation and the mouth-watering smell, Ev doesn't make a move toward the food. Neither does Gareth.

"Why won't I be there long?" she asks.

Gareth lifts his wineglass. "How do you like this?"

"It's—nice," says Ev.

"Not too acidic?" he asks.

"I suppose it is a bit acidic," offers Ev, wondering why the hell they are talking about this now. Gareth is famous for his palate, but is it so sharp as to distract him in the middle of whatever he's brought her here to say?

"I'm taking over a small vineyard," he says, as if this is the kind of thing people say. "I've got a rare opportunity, some decent backing, and I've decided this will be my next act. Suzanne loves California and it's what she wants, too."

Ev nods slowly.

"In six months or so, after thirty-four years, eleven as president, I will be leaving ARC News."

Gareth leaving? He *is* ARC News. She tries to absorb the idea. "I see," she replies.

Gareth puts the wine down. "I want to leave it in good hands."

"Of course."

"Your hands."

"My hands," she repeats, not sure if it came out sounding like a statement or a question.

"Yes."

He can't be saying what she thinks he's saying.

"You want me to be president of News?"

"Yes."

"What about Candy? Or Fritz?" she asks before she can stop herself. Fritz is the EP of *National Report*. He has a much higher profile than she and an Ivy League pedigree to boot, while Ev—she prays no one realizes—never got a degree.

"They do their jobs well," says Gareth. "But they're not game changers."

"And I am?"

"Remember what I said on the plane back from Rome? After the pope died?"

She remembers. It was years ago, back when the network would still send dozens of people halfway around the world to cover such a story. Ev had been a new producer then. She and Gareth were the only ARC people on their flight home and he'd used his own miles to bump her up to business class.

"You said that you'd watched me all week," Ev says. "That you saw yourself in me." It was a half-empty flight, those around them asleep, the two of them drinking and playing gin rummy. She couldn't believe she was sitting with the president of the News Division. "But it sounded like a line from an old movie," Ev says. "*I've got big plans for you, kid.* I thought you'd had too many Manhattans."

Gareth laughs. "I was quite serious. I saw how you operated. Did you trust anyone else to do anything that whole week? I don't think so. You scouted locations, you booked guests. I think it was you who booked Cardinal McKenna, wasn't it? You wrote sharp copy. I thought you were going to yank the mic out of the correspondent's hand and report the story yourself." He shakes his head. "Since then, you've only grown as a journalist. Your idea to add some behind-the-scenes-of-newsgathering material to the Armitage story, as I told you, was brilliant. If anyone can confront this 'fake news' nonsense, it's you. Meanwhile, you've developed into a strategic manager. You do more with less money than anyone I've seen. And as you proved with the layoffs, you're a good soldier. Fritz threw a tantrum in my office for hours on end, demanding we save as many jobs as possible."

Ev's mind churns. Was she supposed to fight harder for her staff? Clearly not, or she and Gareth wouldn't be having this conversation.

Yet a tiny gnawing feeling persists for a few seconds, until she once again picks up the thread of what her boss is saying.

"ARC News is in good shape. But the years ahead are going to bring enormous challenges and I think you're the best one to steer the ship when that happens." Gareth pops a potato into his mouth. "And never tell HR I said this, but your, ah, *tidy* personal life, without the distractions so many other women contend with, will make it easier for you to give everything to this job. Which it will take, believe me."

Ev can't miss the stealthy sexism here. It's not fair to expect women to do it all, to penalize them for having kids and reward them when they don't. But if you wait for the expectations of the world to become completely fair, you'll be dead. Besides, no one gets ahead by standing on principle, do they? Someone else just steps in to fill the void. In this case, it would surely be another man.

Ev tries to fathom what Gareth is offering and as she does so she detects a flaw in the plan. "Let me get this straight," she says. "I'm going to do Social Media for a few months and then, boom, I become president?"

Gareth nods.

"People will see right through it. Fritz and the others will stamp their feet and everyone else will put together that I was made head of a department I wasn't fit for just so I'd have a VP title under my belt so I could persuasively become president. They'll scream bloody murder. Or laugh themselves silly."

"I could not care less," says Gareth with a casual wave of his hand. "Chalk it up to the freedom of leaving."

"But I'll be the one left behind to deal with it all."

"You can handle it. That I know." Gareth leans forward and lowers his voice. "Look, it's high time a woman was in charge of our News Division. At this rate, we'll have a woman *president* before a woman president of ARC News."

Ev can't believe what she's hearing. She's said the same thing a million times but she would never have uttered it in front of Gareth.

"You are by far the most qualified, but I'd be lying if I said I didn't want ARC News to have a woman at the top," Gareth says, putting down his knife and fork. "I want to be the one to appoint that woman. And I want that woman to be you. Besides everything else I'd like to think I've done for this place, I want that—I want you—to be my legacy."

He leans back.

It starts to sink in. He means it. This is going to happen.

. . . . .

Ev practically skips into her apartment and goes straight to the iPad. She clicks on her dance playlist. Soon music is blasting. She opens the windows and dances in front of them. She pulls out her chignon and kicks off her shoes, singing along despite not knowing the words.

The phone rings but she keeps dancing. Her blouse begins to stick to her neck and she takes it off, letting it fall on the polished floor the housekeeper cleaned earlier in the day. She pours a glass of red, but dancing without spilling is impossible so she puts it down. Song after song rises, fills the space, and dies away again before she's tired.

Collapsing on the couch, puffing, she relives the lunch, reveling in the power she'll have. She'll be able to do what she wants, steer coverage of world events the way she sees fit. Presidential elections, Davos, the Olympics—all reportage will bear her stamp. She'll show the boys of the old boys' network what's what.

Maybe she'll go back to the executive dining room and order Dover sole *à deux* just for herself.

She pours another glass of wine. She wants to scream the news out the window but that would be silly. She'll tell Sean at dinner tonight. It just so happens that there was a cancelation at Epoch, a place he's been waiting months to get into, so the setting will be perfect for her big announcement.

Anyone else she can share it with? The former colleagues she's friends with are now at other networks. She can't tell the competition before the folks at ARC find out.

And that's kind of it.

She sits up and takes a sip of wine. Her father. They don't have a great phone relationship. When they try it, it's awkward. Either

191

neither of them is saying anything or they talk over one another. Living in Europe, he doesn't watch ARC anyway. But he'll still care. He'll get that this is a big deal. She decides to email him later.

She has time for a quick shower before meeting Sean. She passes by the answering machine and sees the message light blinking.

"Me again." It's May. Ev's finger hovers above the "delete" button as she listens. "No answer on your cell so I'm trying you at home, hoping you'll change your mind." She clears her throat. "I still can't tell you what happens, but I've been trying to come up with a way of explaining why it's so important that you come in a way you'll understand. The older I get, the more I realize there's something to this idea of a woman coming back to herself. Coming back to the person she was before she started playing the game, before she decided the game was worth playing and that she might be good at it. You know?"

What is she babbling about? Ev wonders.

She hesitates just for a moment, then hits "delete."

No one looks better than Sean in candlelight. He appears burnished, like an oil painting. He looks so good Ev actually nudges one of her shoes off and brushes his ankle with her toes. He's conferring with the sommelier for a second time. He nudges her foot with his own, the silliness below contrasting with his solemn demeanor above, which makes her giggle.

She told him the news as soon as they'd ordered their drinks. He'd shaken his head slowly like he was too blown away to speak. He got up, came around the table, and kissed her, causing people to stare. The sommelier had arrived with their bottle but Sean had sent it back before he even opened it, saying they needed something infinitely more special.

Now the new bottle is open and they each have a glass.

"You're going to make history," says Sean, toasting her. "They're going to write stories about you."

Ev hadn't thought that far ahead. Of course, the first woman to finally run the News Division at the most old-fashioned network will be a news story itself, at least for those who write about media.

"Tell me everything," says Sean. "Did Gareth get down on one knee?"

"Hardly," says Ev. She tells him how Gareth pretended he was only offering her the VP of Social Media job and then, when she wasn't looking, revealed what he was really up to.

"Sounds like he had fun pushing you around the dial," observes Sean, and Ev can't argue with him. She wonders if she'll ever be as good as Gareth at power games.

"You don't know the half of it," she says. "You wouldn't believe how he started the meeting." Ev sets the scene, explaining how Gareth praised her layoff list before insisting on yet more cuts to her staff.

"That's terrible," he says.

"So terrible," she replies, straightening her face to appear appropriately sober.

"You must have been pissed."

"Furious," she assures him.

"So who are you going to send packing?" he asks. "I thought you'd already hit rock bottom."

She tells him, the sting pretty much out of it now. In fact, the more she's thought about it post-lunch, the better she's felt about Aviva leaving.

Aviva has always been a bit of a wildcard. Yes, that's part of what makes her a good producer. But she's never learned how to lose the attitude she has in the field when she comes back to the mothership. That's why Ev was the one who went to Ken Chang for Penobscot Moms. That's why she was the one who got promoted into management. Anyway, Aviva can easily find another job.

But Tab? That one she feels truly bad about.

"Aviva?" Sean asks. "Your partner in crime? Thelma to your Louise?"

"Not exactly," says Ev.

"The woman who went with us to the Emmys. With her husband—what was his name?"

"James."

"Aviva, who sat in the ladies' room with you for half an hour while you practiced your speech?"

"I think you're exaggerating."

"You told me you wanted to promote her."

"I did?" Ev doesn't remember telling him this, but concedes that it's possible. Must have been months ago, though.

"You don't seem very broken up about her going."

Ev squints with one eye, feeling a headache coming on. "Can we talk about something else?" This celebration is starting to feel more like an inquisition.

Sean exhales and lowers his shoulders. "Of course," he says. "I'm sorry." But instead of starting a new topic, he stares at the delicate arrangement of miniature driftwood on the table between them.

"So anyway—" says Ev.

"Sorry—" says Sean at the same time. "Just one more question."

"Sure."

"How did Aviva take it? Have you told her yet?"

"She's been told," she says carefully.

"What do you mean, *been told*?"

"She, Tab, and all the others have been informed."

"By whom? Wasn't it you?"

Ev feels herself redden. She folds and unfolds the cloth napkin in front of her.

"It was Malcolm," she admits. This sounds bad, Ev realizes. But as she and Gareth got up from lunch, he'd told her that everyone had to be let go by end of day. Though she'd been stunned, she'd been ready to get on with it. But Gareth said he had more to discuss with her back at his office and anyway, it was time she got used to delegating. So she called Malcolm and told him he had three hours to fire all eleven people on her list. She reasoned that this chore was making him a better manager because he's too nice. He'll likely be the one to inherit her job, and if so, he'll need to know how to do dirty work on a moment's notice.

The charcuterie board arrives and the waitress spends several moments moving the driftwood and their glasses out of the way to make room for it on the small table. After she departs, Ev reaches straight for a whisper-thin slice of prosciutto, layers it onto a crostini, and takes a large bite. She's hungrier than she realized but then again, she and Gareth had talked so much she'd barely touched her lunch.

For the first time ever, Sean seems uninterested in food. "You didn't tell them yourself?" he asks.

"I didn't have time. Gareth wanted me—"

"Let's stay on you. How could you not look these people in the eye before kicking them out into the street?"

"Don't be so dramatic. They're getting amazing severance packages." She thinks they are, anyway.

Sean shakes his head and exhales. "It's Invasion of the Manager Snatchers. You get anointed by Gareth and thirty seconds later, you're one of them. Your soul, left behind to shrivel and die somewhere or whatever the hell happened in that movie."

"Would you stop?" Ev says. "You have no idea what it is to be a boss."

"True," he says, nodding. "But I do know a little bit about what it is to be a human being."

Ev falls back in her seat as if pushed. Sean looks away. He's still not eating and this bothers her almost more than anything else. She retorts by digging in, reaching for disk after disk of salami and capicola.

"I wonder if Aviva will go to the press," Sean says.

"About what?" she asks, swallowing.

"About Armitage." Sean adjusts himself in his seat, recrossing his legs. "Maybe *she* becomes the whistleblower now, exposing ARC for covering up an important story."

If Ev weren't as seasoned as she is, Sean might have her on this one. There have been one or two fired journalists who took their stories to a competing outlet. But their stories were in print. In TV, the network owns the footage, not the producer. So Aviva can't tell the Armitage story somewhere else, at least not anytime soon. And Ev seriously doubts Aviva will go running to Page Six or Channel Surf about it being killed at ARC. After all, Aviva doesn't know the real reasons why it happened. She just thinks the network is spooked by a bad experience at CBS and that's defensible—therefore probably not enough of a "wow" to trigger much interest.

And anyway, even if Aviva did know the truth, it's highly unlikely she'd tell anyone. There'd be something . . . tacky about it. Not to mention the fact that she'd almost certainly never work at a network again.

Ev looks across the table and a new question supplants the others: Why is Sean ruining her promotion?

The promotion. That's the problem right there, of course. Why didn't she see it coming? Sean is wildly talented, but he's never risen into management. True, he insists that's his choice, that he prefers creating artwork to managing others who do it. But maybe that's just what he tells himself. And now, here she is, making, in a small way, history. He said it himself, she'll be written about. It's the first thing he thought of, the fact that she'll be a little bit famous. Not to mention she'll be making more money. She already makes more than he does but now it'll be way, way more.

"Men always say they're fine with a woman who's more successful than they are . . ." she says, crossing her arms.

"Yeah, that's it," Sean replies, pushing his untouched plate away. "My mom's not exactly a slouch, you know. Way higher on the totem pole than my dad. It's not a problem in my family. So add that to all the other stories you tell yourself. About me. About the world." He shakes his head. "You could open a library by now."

Ev blinks at how casually and unfairly he's analyzed her. She wants to ask him if this is how he spends his spare time, but the waitress comes to take the now-empty board. Ev watches as she lifts it and uses a little brush to deftly sweep away the crumbs that surround only Ev's plate.

She contemplates the rest of the meal still to come. Either she's already full, or she's lost her appetite.

This gathering has way better catering than usual and Ev wonders if Gareth is personally subsidizing it. He's certainly chosen the wine, of which there are several varieties, all of a quality much higher than you find at your typical work party in a conference room.

"To Everleigh Page and the future of Social Media at ARC," says Gareth, holding up a glass.

There's a smattering of applause, though there is more cheer from the Social side than the *Breaking* folks. Ev would like to think it's because Social is gaining her and *Breaking* is losing her.

But that may not be it. There's a distinct lack of enthusiasm among her staff since the layoffs. When she'd gotten back from Gareth's office the day he'd told her of the promotion, Malcolm had been ashen-faced and the empty desks in the newsroom had stood like silent witnesses to an execution. Everyone seemed to take the whole thing so personally. So much so that she called another staff meeting the next day to buck them up. She told them what they needed to hear: that the axe had swung all over ARC. *Breaking* wasn't being asked to give more than anyone else. She wasn't exactly sure this was true, but it would make them feel better. She told them they were a fantastic crew, that everyone in the room was among the best in the business. She started to tell them all the things they had yet to do together, then stopped as she remembered she'd be leaving them soon.

She heads over to the bar for a refill. She comes up behind three *Breaking* associate producers who are turned into a tight circle, their heads close together. She overhears snatches of their conversation as the bartender fills her glass. It seems they recently had drinks with those who were let go.

"So sad," says one of them, shaking her head.

"Nice that Malcolm came. And bought the first two rounds ..."

"Tab told me she's having a problem getting her COBRA ..."

"Did you notice that she and Aviva stayed behind together after everyone left? Wonder what they were talking about ..."

Ev can just imagine. Armitage, Armitage, Armitage. How awful she was for letting Gareth kill it. How evil she is for firing them. She wants to defend herself but she can't very well admit to eavesdropping.

Gareth waves her over to where he stands with a small group from the parent company. He introduces her to, among others, the chief technology officer, the senior vice president of Strategic Development, and someone called the brand integration evangelist. These are high-level folks, too high to care about meeting a little VP in the News Division. Ev wonders whether Gareth has tipped his hand that he is leaving and that Ev will be his replacement. Either way, they make a fuss over her. They raise their glasses and talk about ways that, under her leadership, Social can better integrate with some random division of the company she's never heard of.

Ev mentions something about the latest crop of college interns. Samantha Archer, who's in talent management and sports a copious amount of museum store jewelry, nods politely and inquires where Ev went to school.

"Lawton College," she replies.

"So did my younger sister," says Samantha, smiling. "What year did you graduate?"

Ev hesitates. She takes a long sip of champagne, stalling. This kind of thing is checkable, if Samantha has a mind to.

"Lawton College," says Gareth, leaning slightly into the space between them. "You know, I hear they're starting to do decent things with their TV station. Pouring real money into it, finally. Too many schools have been crying poor when it comes to broadcast journalism. Did anyone see that piece in the *Times*?"

Ev grips her glass. Gareth knows, she can feel it. She never presented a résumé at ARC, coming in the way she did from local news. She was hired based on her reel, not a piece of paper. But somehow, he seems to know she never graduated. Maybe he thought to look into it. Either way, he's rescued her. He may not represent crusading journalism anymore, but he does understand loyalty.

The others laugh at something Gareth says and nod at her approvingly. She looks at them more closely and realizes that she's seen several of these people over the years at company-wide, town hall–style meetings, usually on a dais or behind a lectern.

This time, they see her.

I promise this is the last time you'll hear
from me.

The text pops up, momentarily obscuring the article Ev's reading. She's in a taxi, snaking its way through Times Square on a rainy night. Horns are honking and low Middle Eastern music emanates from the front of the car.

I apologize if I've made you feel
uncomfortable.

I completely understand why you wouldn't
want to come back to Foster. I've learned
more about the circumstances that led to
your leaving school. I can only say that I'm
sorry I wasn't there to help you.

It's May. Again.

So now she understands. Ev wonders whom she's been talking to, who's explained everything. The pulsing dots at the bottom of the screen indicate that another text is forthcoming, but it takes the better part of a minute to come through.

Someone's reached out to me.

Ev narrows her eyes, waiting for the next part of the message. She sees from the dots that May's still typing but no words appear.

The driver slams on the brakes and Ev is thrown forward. She hears the swoosh of water underneath the wheels as they narrowly avoid hitting a truck. The driver swears in what sounds like Urdu.

The words materialize.

Dilly wants to see you.

Pause. Pulsing dots.

She has something to say.

Ev looks out the window at the colored lights refracted in the water droplets sliding down the glass.

Dilly has something to say?

She wonders what prompted this desire to connect. Maybe Dilly's run up enormous credit card debt and needs financial help. Maybe she's dying, ravaged by a disfiguring disease.

Whatever she wants to say, surely it includes an apology. After two decades, maybe she's had enough time to realize the enormity of her betrayal.

Ev closes her eyes and sees Dilly's short henna-red hair, swept forward over her ears, so stark against the white of her cheeks.

She sees Dilly in their freshman dorm room, pouring out her breakfast cereal at night because she had an early class and didn't want to wake her.

She sees Dilly buying beers for everyone at Quittin' Time, when Ev got her first byline.

She doesn't see the duplicity, of course. Because that happened behind her back.

TWENTY

These are Sean's friends and where is he? He has mild social anxiety and usually sticks by her side at social events, but she hasn't seen him for a good half hour.

Arms crossed in front of her, hip-hop pulsing in her ears, Ev takes another trip around the perimeter of the packed gallery. Headless teddy bears. Headless dolls. Even, a bid at a visual pun perhaps, headless nails. Between the paintings hang large mirrors that make the room look enormous. The paintings belong to Kelly Todd, who went to Rhode Island School of Design with Sean. She's lately found some success, and every time she has a show in New York, even in Flatbush where they are tonight, Sean shows up. Ev does, too, even when she should be engaging with viewers on social media about tonight's show.

Things with Sean haven't quite returned to normal since the dinner at Epoch, not that a casual observer would notice. They slept in their own apartments that night, but he called, sounding tired, to apologize the next morning. She apologized, too. She wanted—needed—peace, and that's pretty much what they have. They see each other just as often, sleep over the usual three to four nights a week, and text throughout the day. To the naked eye, he's as attentive as ever. But it feels as if 10 percent of his heart is MIA. There's a little less warmth in his touch, a little less laughing in the dark. The reason isn't clear. It could be that he's disappointed in her over what she revealed is going on at ARC. Or it could be he's distracted by Erik's health problems, which are ongoing and the source of which is still a mystery.

Ev stops by a large painting to take a closer look at the brush-strokes. A movement across the room catches her eye. Blond hair. White-blond. Down past the shoulder blades, hanging loose. A black dress, paired with what looked like sneakers. It's the woman she saw on the subway. She feels it. Once again, there's just a flash of the hair before she disappears into the crowd. Pulled by an impulse she doesn't quite understand, Ev tries to find her. She has to see the woman's face. She threads her way between bodies, doing her best not to jostle drinks. She arrives in the area where the woman had been but she's no longer there. Ev turns to a bored-looking man standing on his own.

"Did you see a blond woman?"

"Where?"

"Here. A few seconds ago."

"Nope."

"You sure?"

"I think you're the only blond here." He squints at her. "Maybe you saw yourself in one of the mirrors?"

Someone taps her shoulder.

She spins around to see Kelly's bearded husband. He's carrying an enormous platter of cheese. "Would you mind getting some more cups?" he shouts over the music. "They should be in the storage room behind the coat check."

She nods and threads her way to the storage room and gives the heavy door a yank. Inside is Sean.

He's facing away from her, on the phone, tracing the logo on a cardboard box with his finger. He doesn't turn around, just keeps murmuring to whoever's on the other end. She would get the cups and leave except there's something about his posture that's troubling.

She crosses the small space and puts her hand on his shoulder. He turns around and shakes his head slowly.

"Okay, then," he says. "Just have them call when they need me to come out." A few moments later he says goodbye and slides the phone into the breast pocket of his sports jacket.

"What's going on?" Ev asks, distressed by how shaken he is.

"Dad," he says.

"What's happening?"

"The bruising from his fall still hasn't gone away. Plus now he's experiencing weakness, thirst, and a bunch of other weird stuff. He finally agreed to see a specialist and it turns out he has multiple myeloma."

"That's cancer?"

"Blood cancer."

"It's not—?" She can't bring herself to say it.

Sean shrugs. "He's going for chemo right away. Then he'll need a bone marrow transplant. For that, they have to find someone compatible. Since he doesn't have siblings, they're going to test us kids."

Ev steps closer. She puts her arms around him and lays her head on his shoulder, not wanting to see the fear that's in his eyes. "So you're going out there?"

"Peter's going first since he's close by. Annette will go out next Tuesday and I'll take Zach while she's gone. When she comes back, I'll go out."

"Makes sense," says Ev. She can see that Sean feels better discussing strategy and plans. She keeps him on that track, talking logistics for a few more minutes. Ev spies a stack of cups and picks it up. They go back out, put the cups on the bar, find Kelly, offer congratulations, and say goodnight. They walk to the subway, their footsteps loud and rhythmic on the silent sidewalks.

"How did this even happen?" Ev asks.

"No idea. It can run in families," Sean says. "Though it doesn't seem like there's a history of it in ours. And the doctor says it's not related to my lymphoma at all."

"I guess the party's off, at least for now, huh?"

"Actually, no."

They arrive at the next street and have to wait for some cars to pass.

"Dad doesn't have to be hospitalized till the transplant. He's tired but wants to do the party for Mom's sake. Plus everybody already has their plane tickets. And knowing Dad, I think it'll be therapeutic. To look around the room and take in everything—everyone—he has to live for."

"Right," says Ev, impressed by Erik's bravery and stoicism.

"Maybe we can take Zach to a Mets game," Sean says as the light turns and they step off the curb.

"Hmm?" asks Ev.

"When Annette's in Chicago. With everything the poor kid has going on in his life, we should do some fun stuff with him."

Ev furrows her brow. She realizes he mentioned this earlier, but it doesn't make much sense. Won't Zach miss school if he stays in the city?

But there's surely no one else he'd rather be with at this moment than Sean. And with his dad starting a new life, his school troubles, and now his grandfather sick, he deserves some cheering up.

On the subway platform, Sean goes quiet again, and for the first time in a long time, she thinks about her mother's illness.

. . . . .

To this day, she doesn't know exactly when Greta got sick. Greta kept it from everyone, including—Ev suspects—her husband, for as long as she could. But if Ev had to, she would guess that Greta must have known on the April day that she insisted the three of them go to Stinson Beach. It was way too cold, but if you wanted to get Anton out of the lab, the outdoors was the way to go. So they put swimsuits on under their clothes and Anton loaded up the car with a hamper of sandwiches Greta had made, his camera, and a blowup raft.

The seagulls screeched above as they waded into the water. A strong undertow tugged at their ankles, nearly knocking them over, but Anton grabbed the arms of his wife and daughter and steadied them. Later, when Ev wandered down the beach to look for shells, she glanced back to see her parents holding hands, locked in what seemed like an intense conversation. A few minutes later, they collapsed on the blanket together, Anton clinging fiercely to Greta.

Everleigh, a knot in her stomach, waited until they pulled themselves apart before going back. Once she did, Greta acted as if everything was perfectly normal and suggested Everleigh and Anton build a sandcastle together while she put out the lunch. Everleigh and her father had scraped up handfuls of wet sand, packing it into various sizes of buckets and plastic cups to create turrets. But he told her she wasn't stacking hers carefully enough, that they were going to fall over. He said he was only trying to teach her about the fundamental principles of physics, but to eight-year-old Everleigh, it felt like criticism from Captain Killjoy. She threw down her shovel and stalked off.

When her empty stomach forced her back, her father was taking pictures and her mother was blowing up the raft. They munched on sandwiches silently for several minutes before Greta spoke.

"Daddy wants to take you out on the water, honey," she said.

Anton looked up in apparent surprise. After a pause, he nodded in assent, saying, "Might help us cool off."

They waded out, Anton placed the raft on the water, and she hauled herself aboard. She let him pull her around while she closed her eyes, concentrating on the sensation of bobbing up and down.

"I'm sorry about before," he said finally. "We shouldn't be fighting."

She was still smarting but knew her mother would expect her to act like a grown-up. She turned over. "Me too," she said. "Sorry for acting like a brat."

He winked in a strange, humorless way and began to tug the raft farther out. Once they were in deep water, he used his elbows to pull himself halfway aboard and they floated silently.

"Just you and me, kid," Anton said, swallowing.

Together, they looked back at the shore but Greta was almost too small to see.

The next day, Meryl calls out from her desk. "Gareth on the phone."

Ev picks up. "Hey." She used to say "hello," but with her impending status change she thinks she can be less formal.

"I seem to remember you play a little golf."

"I'd say I'm an enthusiastic dabbler," she says. She's taken a series of classes designed for women executives and even has a set of clubs. "Why?"

"Frank Marchant loves it and I thought, once I tell him about my desire that you replace me—which will be soon—it might pay to get you off to a good start with him and a few of his most relevant cronies."

Ev doesn't know what to say. She dimly imagined she'd meet

Marchant at some point once she assumed the presidency, but an intimate golf game just like the big boys do? This had never occurred to her.

"I had to prove myself to him and his minions show by show, budget by budget, share point by share point. It was excruciating. I finally realized it was a fool's errand and hit on this golf thing." Gareth takes a breath. "I'm not great at it and neither are they. But we humans are creatures of the heart more than the head. Even suits. They have to like you before anything else."

"Right," Ev says.

"I happen to know Frank loves a nice club. I have a friend who runs an exclusive place up in Hastings that Frank once said he wanted to try. I'm thinking we all go up there. We swat a few balls, retire to the clubhouse, and you turn on that charm of yours." She expects him to laugh when he says this but he doesn't. "Let them get to know you as a person. Their trust will follow and could save you years' worth of headaches."

Ev can't believe her luck. Not only is the way being paved for her, it's being laid with soft, fluffy carpeting. "Sounds wonderful, Gareth." She'll get Meryl to book her a brush-up session with a pro at Chelsea Piers in the next couple of weeks. "When are you thinking of?"

"ASAP," says Gareth. "We agreed to get in a last game before everyone heads to their country houses for the summer. I can do Saturday after next. Let's see if they can, too." He doesn't ask if this is good for her.

In fact, it isn't. It's the day of Sean's parents' party.

It's 10 p.m. and Ev is in the office, watching the broadcast of her show. Outside her door, the newsroom falls away in darkness.

Breaking is on each of her seven monitors. It's a decent potpourri tonight: an in-depth exploration of a congressman's bribery scandal, a feature on research indicating that babies already have a sense of morality, and a behind-the-scenes look at a young country star who's about to cross over into pop. The girl suffers from MS so this one's a heart-warmer.

The bribery story is killer. Aviva was coproducer. Just before the layoffs, she'd flown to Washington to interview the congressman's wife. The wife is mortified by her husband's behavior, and though she did nothing wrong herself, she's been taking a beating on social media. The interview is handled with nuance and sensitivity, hallmarks of Aviva's work.

Ev wonders where she is now, whether she's found another job.

Tab, too, who worked on the country singer story. What is she doing?

The show ends. The credits go by quickly so the eleven o'clock news can lure viewers in before they change the channel. The credits include the names of the producers and crew on the individual stories and a series of courtesies for footage and music they've used. And then, at the very end, there it is:

EXECUTIVE PRODUCER
EVERLEIGH PAGE

Her name, gracing approximately six million homes simultaneously. It's childish to care, but she can't help it. Probably because there was a moment, the day she packed up and left Lawton for the last time, when she was fairly certain she'd never work in journalism again.

This will be one of the last times her credit appears on *Breaking*, so she tries to savor it. But in a heartbeat, it's gone.

. . . . .

Ev has her leg balanced on a railing overlooking the Hudson River, stretching. Stretching and waiting. She left Sean at her place to drop off her dry cleaning while he called his parents. They were supposed to meet here fifteen minutes ago but he's nowhere to be seen. She uses the time to think about how she's going to tell Sean what she has to tell him. Things have been changing fast. Too fast.

Since Erik's diagnosis, the doctors have changed the plan for testing Sean and his siblings. They want to do it more quickly, testing all three of them on a single day—next Friday. Also known as the day before the anniversary party.

The problem is Zach. He was supposed to stay at Sean's place while Annette was away, but now Sean will be away as well.

And so, three nights ago Sean asked if she would host Zach. "We'd bring him to Chicago but all the adults will be at the hospital and we don't want him having to sit in the waiting room for hours and hours," he'd said, clasping her hands. "And I've talked to Annette. Made her understand that nothing like the museum incident will happen again. That you'll be careful about what you say to him and basically 'stay in your lane.'"

Ev had nodded her agreement, suffering this "ding" by Annette with good grace. And she found herself looking forward to spending some time with Zach, even trying to think of a Broadway show he might like. But the next day, Sean had upped the ante. Apparently, Zach forgot to tell everyone that on Friday, he has the State Assessment in Science standardized test. So Sean asked Ev if she'd accompany Zach up to Westchester on the train and bring him back afterward. Which meant missing a day of work, a day when Gareth wanted her to attend a meeting with a team of consultants about managing the ARC brand. When she told him she couldn't make it, Gareth was naturally confused. Nights, weekends, she's never *not* been available, and here she was taking a day off just as she's become privy to the inner workings of the highest levels of management. She'd mumbled something about a mammogram, but it hardly sounded adequate even to her own ears.

So Ev had politely inquired: If she dropped him off at Grand Central, and picked him up afterward, could Zach possibly take the train by himself? Holy Jesus, did she catch an earful. This just *isn't okay* when you're talking about a thirteen-year-old, no parent would allow such a thing. Never mind that crime statistics reveal New York's safer than it's ever been. And that when Ev was Zach's age, she took a forty-five-minute bus ride to an afterschool job at a fried chicken place.

"Look, I know this is rotten timing," Sean had admitted, "with your new job coming up and all. And I know kid stuff isn't really your thing. I'm sorry about that. But we're in a tight spot. So I'd like you to do this one thing," he'd said, exhaling. "For me."

She softened. "Of course," she'd told him quietly. "I'm sorry. Don't give it another thought."

Finally, Sean appears, walking briskly across the West Side Highway. He doesn't kiss her hello.

"Want to get started?" he asks.

"Sure," she replies, but he's already jogging. She catches up. Side to side, she can feel energy coming off him, an almost physical thing.

Usually they chat as they run, but Sean remains silent, going faster and faster, seemingly obsessed by the ground five feet in front of him. When they come up behind a group moving more slowly, he circles around them, not checking to see if Ev is keeping up. Finally, after some fifteen minutes, he slows abruptly and pulls her off the path.

"I was going to buy your tickets today," he says, puffing lightly while she wheezes and grips a pole. "For you and Zach."

"Tickets," she says, trying to understand what he means.

"Plane tickets. For you guys to fly to Chicago on Saturday morning." He raises an eyebrow.

Ev's heart sinks. Naturally, if Zach can't ride a train by himself, he can't very well take a plane alone. But she must have missed where this leg of the favor was first introduced, or she would have admitted to Sean that she's not coming to Chicago, that she's going to miss the party. What's puzzling is that Sean's tone is terse. He's not apologetic about how this favor keeps mushrooming; he's not entreating her to say yes. It's more like he's daring her to say no.

Of course, he has no idea how her thinking about all this has been evolving. Her heart aches for what he's going through with his dad but she's starting to get concerned that his family's current needs are only the beginning of something long, slippery, and painful. Erik is very sick. Even if he gets well, and she dearly hopes he does, there could be relapses. Either way, he's not getting any younger. Neither is Carmen. As the years go by, they're going to need increasing amounts of care.

Peter may be the closest geographically to his parents, but he's got his hands full with three young children and a job that demands lots of travel. And Annette's a single mother trying to get a business off the ground.

Anyway, Sean is the eldest and the one everyone depends on. When things get difficult, he'll need a girlfriend who can be a true partner, not one who's covering breaking news, obsessing over ratings, and running off to board meetings. He deserves that. So does his family.

"You with me?" asks Sean.

"I'm not sure about all this," says Ev, looking out at the river.

"Ah," replies Sean, sounding unsurprised.

"I'm not sure I'm up to it."

"Up to what exactly?"

She shrugs. "Now, it's Zach. Later, it's something else. It feels like things between us were one way for a long time and now, suddenly, they're changing." She takes a deep breath. "I'm just not sure I can be there for you the way you all want me to be. I wish I could, I do. But I think it's better if I'm honest about this."

"We *all*?"

"Your family," she says.

"Trust me, they want nothing from you."

Ev looks at him sharply. "What's that supposed to mean?"

"Let's just say they're not so happy about this match."

She remembers the Zoom session she overheard. "I know Anette's feelings about me. And Carmen's—"

"Oh, I have my own thoughts. I know you like me, probably even think you love me. But you don't really care about what's important to me. Especially if it in any way becomes inconvenient." Sean looks up at the sky. "I'm good for you, I think. But you're not good for me."

Ev pauses, trying to process. "It's my new job, right? Just be honest."

"Uh, *no*," Sean says. "I'm happy for you, in case you hadn't noticed. But I'm seeing a different side of you."

A cramp convulses her left calf and she winces. "A different side? Or a successful one?"

"Absolutely," Sean agrees. "If success means firing people you used to care about and killing important stories. You know one of the things I actually found most attractive about you when we met?

Your obsession with your work. You were so into it, always talking about the stories you wanted to tell and the issues you wanted to tackle. I thought it was sexy. Passion is sexy. *Caring* is sexy. Now it's all about climbing the ladder. But to quote a cliché, a job doesn't love you back."

She crosses her arms. "It does if you do it right."

Sean shakes his head with an ironic smile, as if he's just realized what an utter sweetheart he's spent the last two years with.

For a moment, Ev sees herself as he must: Stunted. Selfish. Ruthless.

She knows she isn't any of these things. But she hates that Sean has cause to think she is. She hates that to get where she deserves to be in this world, she has to make choices that are so unfair. And there's this: If Ev were a man who'd married into the family, would the Andersens expect her to drop everything like this? She sincerely doubts it.

A question pricks her consciousness: If she could change—if she could somehow not want the things she wants—would she?

She might, for Sean.

But she does want what she wants. And she's not wrong to.

She scrunches her eyes closed, trying to reorient herself. "Look, what's going on?" she asks. "Why are you so angry all of a sudden? Everything was fine when I left."

A group running three abreast goes by and Ev can feel the heat they carry.

"You're not coming to Chicago," Sean says.

She can't tell if this is a statement or a question. "You don't want me to come?"

"No, I mean you're not coming. You just haven't told me yet."

Her eyebrows shoot up. How does he know?

"You got a call while you were out. Your pal Gareth. Saying *tee time* on Saturday was moved up so you'll have time for a nice long dinner afterward. I thought maybe you two were having an affair."

Ev starts to interrupt—she can't have him thinking this—but he cuts her off.

"Relax," he says, putting a hand up. "An affair would at least be something hot-blooded. You two barely have a pulse between you."

Ev clears her throat. "I was planning to tell you," she says quietly. "I can't get out of it. I have to meet Frank Marchant and—" but she can see this is not helping. She thinks of telling Sean about her idea to come out first thing Sunday morning. But she can see now he won't care. The party is Saturday, and as far as he's concerned, it's a zero-sum weekend.

Anyway, he's walking away. He gets about fifteen feet before he turns back to her. "Oh," he says. "And don't worry about Zach. Not that you were."

"What do you mean?"

"He'll fly out with me and Annette on Thursday."

"What about his test?" asks Ev weakly.

"He's missing it. Too late to find anyone else to take him. Thanks for that, too."

Ev can't think of anything to say but it doesn't matter because Sean's disappeared. He's been absorbed by swarms of happy humans and she is left standing alone.

The contents of several shopping bags lay spread out on the bed. Who knew there were so many spins on plaid?

She needs to wear the right thing for golfing on Saturday. It's not so easy for a woman, this business of looking attractive but not sexy. Or maybe a little sexy. The idea is that the men you need to impress realize that you hold this power but also understand that you are not trying to—and don't need to—use it on them. They respect a woman with allure more than one without it, but that respect goes out the window if they think you're so lacking in talent or confidence that you actually rely on it.

She goes to the kitchen, pours a glass of wine, and heads back to the bedroom. One by one she tries on the options: the slim pedal-pushers, the flirty skirt. Which color polo sets off her eyes best?

She feels reasonably good about keeping up with the others. She played every evening this week, smacking balls down the fairway. Ten balls without a break. She was so focused she sometimes forgot to check to see whether someone was walking behind her.

"Watch it!" hissed Brady, her pro. "On the other hand, nice power."

She feels okay about the golf. But she'd caddy for these guys if it meant she could finally talk about her new job and the big plans she has for it. She's sat on this secret for weeks now and it's been excruciating.

Well, she did tell her father. She emailed him and received a response the following morning.

Everleigh dear,

Congratulations. What a proud and humbling moment. Think hard about the impact you intend to have and use your new influence well.

Dad

All these years in Europe seem to have left a mark; he sounds like an aristocrat from another century. Proper, polite. The formality isn't a surprise anymore, but the lack of warmth—the lack of anything like father-daughter intimacy—stings like it always has.

Ev shakes her head, not wanting to dwell on this. It isn't relevant to anything now.

She refocuses on the meeting with Marchant. Adrenaline pumps at the thought of finally sharing her ideas. She does a little model walk in front of the mirror, wine sloshing out of the glass as she spins.

The skirt is flattering but perhaps a tad short. Pants it is. The lemon polo makes her gray eyes pop. But what about the visor? She slips it on. It's a bit costumey, but if she wears sunglasses, she might appear standoffish.

Somewhere down the hall her phone goes off, indicating a text. Her first hope is that it's Sean even though she knows it isn't.

Thinking of Sean reminds her of Zach. The kid was supposed to be here tonight. What would he have been doing? Studying for his test, of course. She pictures him sprawled on the floor, the way he does when doing his homework. Maybe he would have turned to her for advice; maybe she could have given him the kind of help she could have used so desperately at his age.

The phone goes off again. She paces into the living room and finds it under a pillow on the sofa. The text is from Gareth.

Did you get previous msg?
Confirm pls.

Frowning, she scrolls up until she sees it.

Marchant canceled. Emergency
shareholder meeting. Have to reschedule.

She sinks down on the nearest chair, processing this news. The golf game is off, along with the dinner with the power brokers. There will be no expounding on her goals and strategy. No one appreciating the plans she's been working so hard on. Not until they can reschedule, anyway. But isn't everyone off to their country houses soon? This whole thing might have to wait till fall now.

Deflated, she goes to the kitchen to pour some more wine. The long, empty weekend stretches before her with nothing to do but ponder this disappointment.

For a moment, she thinks of going to Chicago after all, surprising Sean. She might be able to turn things around with a bold gesture.

But at this point, she's pretty sure Sean wouldn't buy it. He'd guess that something had gone wrong with her plans. He'd be quite certain that she hadn't suddenly turned down Gareth and chosen him and his family instead.

She picks up the phone and texts Gareth back. *Gotcha* she writes, trying to sound breezy. She pours the rest of the wine into her glass but there is no rest. The bottle is empty.

Slumping, chin in hand, she scrolls idly back and forth through weeks and months of previous texts. Dozens and dozens fly by, mostly from Sean. There are plenty from Gareth as well, of course. Some are from Meryl, letting her know that a meeting had been canceled or moved. Aviva pops up a lot, too. Aviva confirming the whistleblower was safely on tape, Aviva inviting her to a bar near the office after putting in a long day in the edit room on Armitage.

She scrolls faster now. Nouns and verbs, names and places zooming by with little relation to one another: her life in abstract. Meaningless. Like when you stand close to a pointillist painting and all you see is dots.

She blinks and, as she slows down her scrolling, one particular text reconstitutes its discrete elements into something that does make sense.

Dilly wants to see you.
She has something to say

Ev reads it three times before switching her phone off.

TWENTY-ONE

S he looks up from the paper. Land and sky open up all around her and the roar in her ears is invigorating.

Empire Service. Two and a half hours north from New York City to Albany, where the train hangs a left, rolling west toward Rochester and beyond to Niagara Falls. The last time Ev rode this line, twenty years ago, she was in coach. Back then, she didn't know there was any other class of service. Now she pushes away the tray with the remains of her Niçoise salad, releases the footrest, and stretches out her legs.

It's good to be going somewhere. She can practically feel the cobwebs clearing.

Schenectady, Amsterdam, Utica, Rome: stops she once knew like her ABCs. During college, she and Dilly spent weekends riding these rails back and forth to visit a friend of Dilly's mom in the city. Back then, they'd had this habit of draping themselves conspicuously on one another, she remembers. On the lawn or in the drawing room, Ev would throw her legs across Dilly's lap as they read. Or Dilly would lay her head on Ev's thigh as they smoked cigarettes and talked. It was a common thing among the girls at Lawton. She can't think why. Maybe they craved physical contact but didn't have boyfriends. Maybe it was a sisterhood thing. Maybe they enjoyed broadcasting their alliance.

Ev recalls a group of guys, local kids, walking down the train's aisle once and catching her and Dilly in one of these characteristic displays. "Hey, dyke," one had guffawed at Dilly.

"At least I can *get* a girl," Dilly had yawned back.

Ev smiles in spite of herself and goes back to the paper.

At Syracuse, she switches to the bus because the train doesn't stop at hole-in-the-wall Lawton. The bus, with its cracked vinyl seats and wad of gum stuck to the window, is quite the comedown. She should have rented a car. But all the years in Manhattan have atrophied her driving skills. When she produced, she drove a lot, all over the country. Overseas, too. Which wasn't always easy. A Japanese map could give you an aneurysm. But for years now, if she's in a car, it's been a taxi. Or Sean has been driving.

They pass a beautiful stretch of farmland. Grain silos, rolling hills, cattle grazing. Half an hour later, a sign announces that they're in the heart of the Finger Lakes region. There are eleven lakes in all, she remembers. Though narrow, they're among the deepest in the country, some more than six hundred feet.

The lakes bear names that evoke the area's Native American history: Otisco, Skaneateles, Owasco, Cayuga, Seneca, Keuka, Canandaigua, Honeoye. Ev repeats the names sotto voce, feeling their once familiar taste on her tongue like a childhood dish.

The bus pulls into the Seneca Falls station, the one just before Lawton, and a few people file out. She spies a plaque outside the ticket office:

WHERE YOU ONCE BELONGED

SENECA FALLS
PROUD HOME OF THE FIRST
WOMEN'S RIGHTS CONVENTION
JULY 19–20, 1848

Was the plaque always there? She doesn't remember it. Lawton College's proximity to such a historic location was well-known by the students—it was even featured in the school catalogue—but few ever visited. May and Belina had organized an outing at one point but half the house had gotten the flu and the trip was canceled.

The bus pulls out and some twenty minutes later, they snake through Lawton's formerly industrial area. Lawton, like so many upstate towns, was hit with factory closings in the '70s, and when she lived here some two decades later, this part of town still felt creepy with its long, low buildings blighted by broken windows like black eyes and scrawls of graffiti like scars. Now most of the hulks seem to have been cleaned up. Several have trucks unloading outside, and through an open door Ev sees what seems to be an art gallery inside.

Up ahead, the bus station reveals itself and Ev is hit by a wave of nausea. It builds as they chug the final blocks and pull up to the curb. Is she experiencing motion sickness now, in the last seconds of the journey? The bus stops, and with an expulsion of air, the doors jerk open. A family in the back heads out but she feels too queasy to move.

Then she realizes what she's feeling: butterflies.

She stands, pulls her bag off the overhead rack, and heads to the door.

"You have a great day now," says the driver, looking at her over his sunglasses.

221

She nods absently and negotiates the steps down to the sidewalk. She wobbles on the last one, which seems particularly steep.

The B&B has modernized since her day: gone are the brocade curtains and needlepoint cushions. The furnishings are now in soothing, neutral shades, the bathroom fixtures square and minimalist. She rests her bag on the bed and kicks off her shoes.

When she'd called May to tell her she'd be coming to Recommitment after all, right after slinging the golf clothes back into their shopping bags, May's reaction had not been what Ev had expected. May had sounded surprised and relieved but there also seemed to be a tinge of worry in her voice. Which, given how hard she'd pushed for Ev to come was, frankly, odd.

May assured her that there would be a room waiting for her at Foster House.

"Your old room, in fact," May had said. "The view out to the garden will be glorious, everything's in bloom and—"

"Everyone's staying together at the House?" Ev had asked, frowning. For some reason, she'd imagined the other three in scattered Airbnbs around town.

"The girls are gone for the year and the place is empty. Why pay for a hotel?"

Ev wasn't ready for that much togetherness. "I'll stay at McBride's," she'd said. McBride's was, and according to the internet still is, the only place to stay in tiny Lawton besides a fleabag on the other side of town.

"You sure?" asked May. "Everyone else will be at Foster."

Precisely, Ev wanted to say.

"And you may not feel like—" May stopped herself. "You may not feel like traveling afterward."

"*Traveling*? It's a twenty-minute walk. Five in a cab."

"You may not want to, is all I'm saying."

"I'll take my chances," Ev had insisted.

Ev gazes around the room. It looks like the same one her father stayed in during his one and only visit.

A short walk along Main Street and she enters what passes for Lawton's business district. Like a childhood bedroom, it looks smaller than she remembers but also a good bit more cheerful. Many of the empty storefronts and dusty hardware stores have been replaced by bustling little businesses. There's a vegan café, a custom skincare boutique, and a yoga studio.

Her phone chimes, signaling the arrival of a text. Again her first thought is to hope it's Sean, but it's not. Of course, he's having his blood testing done today. Maybe she should call and ask how it's going. Would he take the call? Does he consider them broken up? Or just taking time to think?

Which does she want it to be? She doesn't even know.

There's something new across the street. A sign says "The Iroquois League: Six Nations Museum."

Inside, over the admissions desk, an entire wall is given to a black-and-white rendering of Native Americans and European settlers. The Native Americans wear buckskins and furs. The men's heads are capped by an ebullient profusion of feathers like the leafy green part of a pineapple. The women have long braids and wear tunics with heavy beading around the collar. The settlers wear pilgrim hats. The men, anyway. There are no settler women in the picture.

She pays the entrance fee and goes in. The exhibit details the six tribes of the Confederacy: Mohawk, Seneca, Onondaga, Oneida,

Cayuga, and Tuscarora. Display cases feature weaponry, cooking pots, jewelry, and clothing. There are also interactive exhibits where you can take quizzes or design your own longhouse.

She heads into a series of side galleries. The last is titled "Women of the Six Nations" and a stencil high on the wall gets her attention. It says "In the nineteenth century, Iroquois women were the most powerful in the United States."

A series of illustrated panels adorns the walls. The first few describe the status of women in early America, from Black women who endured the hell of slave life to white women who were unable to own property, enter into contracts, get an education, or vote.

The next panel explains:

Women's second-class position in Western society had been in place for centuries. Even in the 1800s, most Americans were still guided by the biblical notion that God made Adam first and subsequently, Eve, created to function as his "helpmate." Genesis states that after Eve ate the forbidden fruit, for her disobedience, she, and all women after her, would be under the authority of men as punishment. "Thy desire shall be to thy husband," the scripture says, "and he shall rule over thee."

How convenient. It's nothing she doesn't know, but it's nevertheless eyeroll-inducing.

She moves along to the next panel and is immediately reminded of what Dr. Long told her so many years ago:

LIFE WAS DIFFERENT FOR WOMEN
OF THE IROQUOIS NATION

Unlike in other Native tribes and American society at large, Iroquois women were the ones who defined the political, social, and economic norms of their nation. While women were not themselves sachems (chief-leaders), it was women who chose each tribe's sachem and replaced him if they believed it necessary in a process called "knocking off the horns." Women were so powerful that when European American women were captured by the Iroquois and later given the opportunity to return to their own people, they often elected to stay.

The next panel shows scenes of Iroquois and white women together, talking, trading, and tending a garden. The text says:

Early American feminists wondered: Was woman's lesser status really God-ordained as a punishment for Eve's sin? If true, they reasoned, the oppression of women would be universal. But when they discovered the authority and respect women commanded right under their noses in Iroquois tribes, they realized that their subjugation was man-made—*men*-made—and they resolved to fight for their own equality.

The next few panels flesh out the story of how Native women inspired and assisted the suffragists, leading to the landmark convention in Seneca, the first gathering of its kind, making the first-ever official demand that women be granted the right to vote.

. . . In fact, the bond between the Iroquois women and the suffragists turned out to be so potent that one local reporter, Matilda Joslyn Gage, wrote that it appeared capable of creating "magic."

Ev almost turns to go but she spies a wall in the back with a single painting on it, a finely wrought portrait of a white woman in a gossamer gown. She has pale skin, raven hair piled high, and shrewd brown eyes.

Aurora Foster. There was a similar, much smaller, picture in Foster House's foyer.

There's a panel next to the frame.

A SPECIAL RELATIONSHIP

It is a local Seneca woman who must be credited with key funds that helped make this museum a reality.

River Cloud* (birthdate unknown) was the greatest of the Iroquois medicine women. So acclaimed were her talents that white families often called upon her and she became well-known throughout and beyond the Finger Lakes.

In 1838, she treated the five-year-old daughter of wealthy Lawton banker Augustus Foster and his wife, Emma. The girl, Aurora [left], had contracted scarlet fever. Traditional bloodletting had nearly killed her. River Cloud took Aurora to her own home, where she is said to have applied a poultice and held Aurora in her arms for three days and nights. At the end of this time, Aurora was cured. Her father declared that River Cloud's "magic" had saved his daughter, and she became an honorary member of the Foster family.

In later years, the liberal-minded Augustus Foster became a friend to local suffragists. As it became more and more dangerous for them to meet, Foster created a secret subterranean parlor in his home for their final gatherings before the Women's Rights Convention, where a fifteen-year-old Aurora served tea. She asked to accompany the women to the convention where she was transfixed by the speakers. Three years later, Aurora applied to the all-male Lawton College. She was, of course, denied entrance. In response, she took up an ad hoc medical apprenticeship with the Iroquois and began a campaign to force Lawton College to accept women. A charismatic figure, she easily recruited women for the fight.

Over the years, though, as these young female activists married, moved away, and started families, many drifted from the cause, and Aurora, who never took a husband, found herself pressing her case largely alone.

Her dearest friend and confidant remained River Cloud, who moved, along with her family, into Aurora's home after her parents passed away.

In 1885, Aurora's health declined and she despaired she would not live long enough to see her campaign through. River Cloud was able to slow, though not derail, Aurora's slide toward death. But she did offer something else. According to Aurora's diaries, River Cloud induced a trance allowing Aurora to "see through time," revealing that indeed the day would come when Lawton College would admit women.

With this knowledge, Aurora Foster passed away in peace. She bequeathed her family home to River Cloud, and her descendants, to hold in custody for the women who would eventually enter the college.

Here was the information that Dr. Long said had been lost over time. She wonders if the doctor has swung by the museum and seen all this. If she even lives in Lawton anymore.

Aurora feared they would face fierce opposition to their presence and desired that they have a quiet, safe place away from campus to live. The home, on Indian Street, still stands. It is called Foster House and is home to twelve Lawton College women each academic year.

Aurora left the rest of her estate to River Cloud herself, who turned much of it over to the Council of Matrons. This money was invested and the proceeds provided the funds to build this museum.

~~~

*There are no records of River Cloud after about 1886. It is believed she traveled north to Montreal around that time to treat victims of a smallpox epidemic.

Ev takes a long look at Aurora Foster. She was right about Lawton College. Women were admitted, but it didn't mean they were accepted.

TWENTY-TWO

The shouts are guttural, primal.

Ev shades her eyes against the light, gazing across the enormous electric-green field. About ten or fifteen boys run back and forth in the distance, their lacrosse sticks clicking faintly when they clash.

She's had a good night's sleep and feels ready for the day—and more important, the night—ahead. She walks along the north side of the field toward campus, where her meeting will be. Carla Santiago, director of the college's TV station, called several times over the last two months, inquiring as to whether Ev would be attending her reunion and, if so, if she'd agree to an interview. Like Foster House, Carla doesn't seem to care that Ev was expelled. Or maybe she just doesn't know.

She has some extra time and takes a seat on the bleachers to watch the kids. Many of Lawton's lacrosse players took summer school to lighten their course loads during the school year. This meant they remained on campus after the other students left, often meeting for informal pickup games. The practice evidently continues.

It's been two decades since she watched a game but her eyes

adjust quickly. She spots the standouts: The guy in the red shirt is good at scooping, the lanky guy cradles well. Most of them seem to enjoy checking—the act of forcefully dislodging a ball from another player's stick.

After a few minutes, she pushes herself up from the bench, noting the beta-blocker head-rush that follows.

The athletic complex is just as she remembers it, massive and imposing as a piece of Soviet architecture. She steps into the lobby, which is set up for some kind of reception with long tables draped in bunting. Beyond it lies something she doesn't remember: the "Hall of Winners." She approaches and finds a series of large flags hanging from the ceiling, bearing the likenesses of Lawton's sports greats. The first flags feature black-and-white portraits from the early 1900s. The later ones are in color. Ev walks underneath, staring into the eyes of men who in their day were doubtless the biggest fish in this little pond.

She's just wondering if Lawton's caught up with the Title IX times and whether any female athletes have gotten the hero treatment when she sees him.

The pitiless hazel eyes. The sharp cheekbones. The chipped front tooth as if an artist had been called in to soften his formidable visage with a hint of boyish innocence.

Dan Daggett.

His flag flutters faintly yet somehow ominously. She tries to conjure Dan's voice but can't. His presence loomed large on campus but, like a king, though he was seen constantly, he was rarely heard.

In all her time at Lawton, he'd said exactly four words to her.

Dan was the only son of Barclay Daggett, who'd played lacrosse for Lawton in the early '70s. Barclay had gone on to become a Wall Street titan and wrote check upon check to support his old team. Dan was five times the player his father was and could have easily played Division I, but he chose to play for Lawton to help realize his father's dream of the school winning an NCAA Division III championship. This sacrifice was treated by the administration, the faculty, and most of the student body as evidence of a sterling character.

For nearly a decade, Lawton had been eliminated in the semi-finals by schools like Hobart and Ithaca. With sophomore Dan, Lawton made it to the finals. On the shoulders of junior Dan, Lawton won the elusive title.

By senior year, the trustees probably would have renamed the school Daggett College if he'd wanted. He was untouchable and—

"Ah, Dan the Dodger." A burly janitor with hairy forearms comes out from a supply closet, nodding up at the flag. "A favorite of yours, is he?"

Ev had forgotten Dan's nickname, which came from the lacrosse term *dodge*, meaning to evade a defender while driving with the ball.

Something occurs to her. She can't believe she didn't think of this before. *Is Dan here, at Lawton?* It's his twentieth reunion, too. The thought triggers alarm, like in a movie where the girl wipes steam from the bathroom mirror and sees the monster behind her.

"You want me to take a picture of you and him?" the janitor asks, using his thumbs and forefingers to create an imaginary frame encompassing Ev and Dan's flag.

Ev cocks her head, weighing the appropriate way to respond to this.

"Oh fuck no," she says.

The quad is teeming. Hundreds of alumni, waiting in long lines to pick up welcome packets while calling out to one another and hugging. Ev takes a seat on one of the benches ringing the square.

231

Everyone looks so happy to be here, like they've been waiting two decades just for this. As if their college years were their best.

She leans back and crosses her legs. As her eyes rove over the exultant faces, she can't help but wish that she were rushing into an old friend's arms right now. Instead of counting the hours till score-settling time.

"Well, *hey*," a woman says, approaching her. She lifts her sunglasses above her eyes. "Leigh Page, right? I thought that was you." She sits down on the bench, turquoise jewelry jangling. "Kim Masters. Well, DiLeo back then. Kimi."

"Right—hi," Ev says, realizing she's going to spend this whole weekend being called Leigh unless she wants to correct people every time. She regards Kimi's square face with its features huddled in the middle, trying to place her.

"We had Twenty-First Century Society together, right? Freshman year?" Kimi says.

"Yes. Of course. Nice to see you." Leigh remembers Kimi as a real "school spirit" type. A member of one of the more rah-rah sororities. "What are you up to these days?"

Kimi explains that she lives in Austin where she teaches middle school. She asks Ev what she does and, just for a moment, Ev weighs whether she can drop her news about becoming ARC News president. No, she can't. She shouldn't tell anyone before it happens, although she's going to do just that tonight. She's giving herself permission to drop this bombshell once, so she can relish the looks on her sisters' faces when they realize what she's made of herself, despite them.

"Remember Addison?" asks Kimi suddenly. She's pointing up at the third floor of Bendix Hall, where Twenty-First Century Society had been held. "I wonder if he's still here. I think about him a lot," she says.

"He was a good egg," Ev says.

"I'm always trying to get my students to debate each other the way Addison did with us. Remember our discussions? What am I saying?" she asks, laughing. "You were smack in the middle of most of them. You and your friend. What was her name? Della? All your women's rights stuff. *Why don't we have a women's lacrosse team? Why hasn't Lawton ever had a woman dean of students?*" Then she sobers a bit, as if afraid Ev might take umbrage. "Not that you were wrong, it was just like, 'Not this again, you know?'" Before Ev can answer, Kimi launches into more memories of the class, seeming to remember it in extraordinary detail.

"I guess you're doing something at Foster House tonight?" Kimi asks.

Ev nods.

"I thought about pledging there. Well, not pledging. Whatever you guys called it."

"There wasn't really a word for it," Ev says. Foster House wasn't part of the Greek system and had no rush week. There were no parties, no socials where you were paraded in front of older girls in hopes of demonstrating you had whatever they were looking for. "You just sort of got picked."

Kimi takes off her sunglasses and wipes the lenses on her T-shirt. "Foster was gorgeous, I remember," she says. "A hike from campus, but it put our house to shame." Kimi puts her glasses back on and clears her throat. "Anything weird ever happen there?" she asks, a little too casually.

"Weird?"

"There were stories, back then."

"What kind of stories?" She's not going to help Kimi out on this, that's for sure.

Kimi clears her throat. "That it was, like, you know . . ."

"I don't."

Kimi shrugs. "Haunted or something."

"You mean that we were witches, right? Crazy lesbian witches?"

At least Kimi has the good grace to look embarrassed.

Ev glances at her watch. It's nearly time to meet Carla. "Afraid I have to run. Really great seeing you, though," she says, standing.

"Sorry if I offended you," Kimi offers faintly, but Ev doesn't answer.

She nearly trips over a raised brick and looks up to see a sleek, modern building. Large letters are affixed to the front: LCTV, Lawton's college TV station.

After checking in with the guard, Ev follows signs to the newsroom, containing a series of pods with three desks each. The computers and TV monitors on the wall are all dark.

Down a hallway on the far side, one office shows signs of life: A light is on and sounds of shuffling emanate from within.

"Hello?" Ev says, peeking around the doorframe.

A woman with gray hair in a chic bob looks up from a moving box and smiles. "Ah! Welcome," she says, coming out from behind her desk and extending a hand. "I'm Carla."

"Good to meet you," Ev says. She takes the seat that's offered and Carla plops down across from her, beaming.

"Let me first say, I know you probably have a lot of events to get to and I really appreciate your time," Carla says.

"My pleasure," Ev says, feeling no need to explain that she isn't attending any of the college reunion events. "This place is great. None of this was here in my day."

"Not bad, right? For a school of three thousand."

Lawton is obviously growing. It was a little over two thousand students when she was here. Carla tells her about the college's evolving broadcasting program and the station's various achievements. "I wish the kids were still on campus so you could meet some of them," says Carla. "I wanted one of our journalists to do this interview. But this will be great. It'll be part of our new podcast series. I've wanted to talk with you ever since the Channel Surf piece."

"You saw that?"

"Are you kidding? It was shared by everyone," Carla says. "We all appreciated what you said about the need for more full-throated investigative work. There's less and less of that being done these days, and if we don't have people at your level committed to it, I'm afraid of what might happen."

Ev feels a bit uncomfortable but shakes it off as Carla pulls out a list of questions and turns on the recording function on her phone. She begins by focusing on some of *Breaking*'s more famous stories of years past and moves into the various challenges of keeping up such a high level of work.

"I'm actually trying to form an investigative unit here at the student station next year," Carla says. "I think there are enough kids interested. And there's a bunch of stuff going on in the Lawton town council I'd like to turn them loose on. Some true sleaze going on in this gentrifying little burg of ours."

"Sounds like a great opportunity for some real-world experience."

"Unfortunately, without me around I'm not sure it'll come together. The new dean wants the kids to focus on the *business* of journalism, reporting as 'content to be monetized.' It's becoming a battle."

"The bottom line's becoming the bottom line everywhere," Ev says wryly. "But—you're leaving?"

"I'm moving to LA. Taking a position at Annenberg. It's a step up, of course. But I'll miss this place."

"Who's taking over at LCTV then?" Ev asks.

"An open question," says Carla. "The dean wants a marketing person. I'm trying to find a real journalist with a sexy enough résumé that he can't say no." Carla leans forward, looking at Ev over her glasses. "I don't suppose you'd be interested in returning to your old stomping grounds, if you're sick of the rat race? Salary's not awful. And shaping the journalists of tomorrow, well, it's quite special."

"That I know," Ev says. She tells Carla about her writing clinic while politely ignoring the woman's offer. When it comes out that Ev's becoming ARC News president, Carla will understand.

TWENTY-THREE

Ev grabs coffee at a hipster place just off campus. It isn't till she's paying that she realizes she's ordered her coffee as Sean takes it —dark with three sugars. She apologizes to the barista and they do it over.

She sips as she walks in the general direction of the B&B. After several blocks, she finds herself on Owasco Street. She looks both ways and realizes why it feels so familiar. It's frat row.

At the far end of the block lies Delta Sigma Phi. She approaches slowly, coming to a halt in front of the steps that lead up to the porch. She wonders if they're holding an event here tonight, like they are at Foster. She wonders if Dan will be going. Could he be here now?

The thought unsettles her but Ev finds herself entering the alley that runs down the left side of the house. She threads her way past some garbage cans and stops beside a small window. Inside is the staircase that leads down to the basement.

Even on this warm day, she can feel the way the chill seemed to rise up and envelop them.

. . . . .

Dilly's pale neck almost glowed in the dark, her gold hoops swaying gently as she moved down the stairs. The deafening music pulsed in Leigh's ears and the taste of vodka lingered on her tongue. She felt queasy. The punch must have been stronger than she'd realized. They reached the bottom step and found themselves in a small space with a concrete floor lit by a bare bulb hanging from the ceiling. Across the way was a door, halfway open.

"Cam's either left the party—or she's in here," Dilly said. "Let's go."

Inside, Leigh could make out a large TV and a pool table. Otherwise it appeared empty. There must have been speakers somewhere because the music was as loud as in the rest of the house. One of their favorite songs came on and Dilly started to dance, wrapping her arms around herself in a mock display of ecstasy. Leigh tried to copy her but mostly just staggered unartfully.

After a few moments, Dilly leaned in to Leigh's ear, close enough that what she said next tickled the tiny hairs deep inside. "We're not alone." She pointed past the pool table.

Ev craned her neck and made out a couple on a mattress on the floor. The guy, muscles straining against his T-shirt, was moving slowly back and forth, almost completely covering the girl, whose brown hair was fanned out around her.

"That's not Cam, is it?" Dilly asked.

Leigh shook her head. It wasn't, but she did look familiar.

The guy began to move down his partner's body, revealing that the girl was naked from the waist up.

"Jesus," said Dilly, turning toward the door. "We're out of here."

But Leigh didn't move. It looked like Shannon, a girl she'd met in the laundry room of their freshman dorm. They'd both been short on quarters and had shared a machine and a funny, rambling conversation as they waited for their clothes to be done.

Whoever this girl was, did she want to be there? Leigh crept toward them.

The boy pushed himself up on his elbows and began fumbling with the girl's belt.

He turned his head and a sliver of light from the doorway illuminated his face.

Dan Daggett.

The song ended and was replaced by the sound of faint arguing from upstairs about what to play next.

In the relative silence, Leigh wobbled, feeling the alcohol careen through her system. Dilly was already out the door and she was about to follow when something caught her attention.

Dan's arm. Was it resting next to the girl's neck or *on* it?

She cleared her throat. Nothing happened. She cleared it again, loudly.

Dan turned and his drunken eyes locked on hers.

"*Get the fuck out*," he hissed.

Leigh bolted for the door and stood just outside it, her heart thumping. She strained to listen in case the girl called for help. But from upstairs, the first notes of "Stairway to Heaven" filled the air, triggering whoops and hollers that drowned out everything else.

Ev turns her back to the window and leans against the side of the house, blinking, the confusion of two decades ago swirling around her once again. The guilt comes roaring back, too. Was the girl a willing participant or was she being assaulted? It was a full year before she'd written the article where Cam accused Dan, so she truly had no idea what she was seeing.

If she'd done something differently, she might have found out. But it wouldn't have changed her own fate, about that she's sure.

Thanks to her "sisters," there's a through line from that night in the basement to the moment she dragged her suitcases down the Foster House steps and heaved them into the taxi.

Isn't there?

Suddenly, she isn't so sure about what exactly she needs to say tonight. If she's going to let Dilly and the others have it, she realizes, she could be at a bit of a disadvantage. There are things she no longer remembers well and other things she has no way of knowing.

Which means there's someplace she has to go. She can't believe she didn't think of this before.

The *Lawton Leader* hasn't moved. It's still in the low, ugly building near the administrative complex.

A guard sits behind a desk reading a paperback. There was always security at the *Leader*, which she came to depend on during her last weeks on campus.

"I need to visit the newsroom," Ev says.

"Are you here for your reunion?"

"Ah—sure."

"Do you have your badge?"

"No," Ev says. "I haven't registered yet."

The guard tilts her head. "Would you mind doing that first? Then come on back."

Ev isn't signed up for the reunion and therefore can't register, but she's not about to get into that. So she looks at her watch. "I'm not sure I have time. I have to be at Foster House in—"

"You're Foster House?"

"Yes."

"That's off campus?"

"Yes."

"Oh."

The guard says nothing further and Ev performs an exaggerated shrug as if to say, "*And?*" People upstate have no sense of urgency.

"I guess it's okay. You have a driver's license or something?"

Ev produces her ARC ID and heads into the large newsroom with its battered desks, stacks of folders, and crammed corkboards.

It's surreal to be back. The place is nothing to look at, but it's where her career began, where she started to figure out who she was and what she could do. Her eyes sting and she presses her palms into them. No time for this, she's on a mission.

She calls out to the only person in the room, a girl at a desk about midway down, fingers hovering over her keyboard.

"Excuse me?" says Ev.

"Yeah?" the girl says, looking up.

"Can you tell me where the archived papers are? In some of these filing cabinets, maybe?"

"From this year or before?" the girl asks.

"Before."

"Library, fourth floor."

In the library building, she moves quickly up the marble stairs, past the reading rooms and offices. It's quiet and dark, the only light coming in through the windows at the opposite ends of the long hallway. A sign directs her to the *Leader* archives. Once inside, she flicks on the fluorescents to reveal a room about ten by fifteen feet, walls lined with floor-to-ceiling shelves full of bound volumes. Each contains two months' worth of papers, their dates printed on the spines.

The familiar scent of the *Leader*, pulp mixed with metal, envelops her as she scans the volumes looking for the ones that represent her years at Lawton. She locates them on the far side of the room and zeroes in on the spring semester of her senior year. Her final article came out the last week of March, she guesses, pulling out the appropriate binder.

After hauling it over to the table in the middle of the room, she takes a seat and starts flipping through the pages till she gets to the paper that came out right after her article about Dan.

ALLEGED VICTIM RECANTS ACCUSATION AGAINST DAGGETT

LACROSSE STAR CLEARED INITIAL REPORTING QUESTIONED

By Blair Bykova

Camilla Overton, the Lawton senior who maintains she was sexually assaulted at the Harvest Bonfire more than three years ago, is taking back a key element of her account as reported in this paper: the identity of her attacker. Overton says she doesn't know the name of the student who led her into the woods and raped her but confirms that it was not Leopard attackman Dan Daggett.

A surge of bitterness floods Ev's insides.

She'd suspected that Blair had held a grudge ever since freshman year when her piece about failing students supplanted Blair's own. Then she'd published the Lawton-lacrosse-as-cult story, which had brought her major recognition. And then she'd broken the campus rape story.

Blair herself wasn't particularly good at interviewing people but she did have enough talent to spin a few quotes into a good twelve inches. She had worked hard to become a favorite of Jeremy Rubin, Gil's deputy editor, who had seemed to want to groom her as his own female protégé, maybe as a challenge to Gil, and constantly advocated for Blair to do bigger stories with better placement.

The moment there was an opportunity, of course, Blair was only too happy to take Leigh down.

Overton says it was not her intention to falsely accuse Daggett or anyone else. She says she did so under pressure from a Leader reporter who, in saying she was trying to help Overton "recover" memories lost to time and trauma, fed her Daggett's name, claiming she needed a "big name" for a powerful story.

It's all Ev can do not to rip the page out and crumple it into a ball.

Dean Sykes said he was not surprised by the clearing of Daggett. "Dan Daggett is one of the finest students, athletes, and student-athletes we've ever had. Lawton is a better place because of his presence."

The reporter, Everleigh Page, declined to comment in time for this edition of the Leader.

What a joke. Blair hadn't even contacted her.

She pulls out the next paper and immediately spies the little box in the lower right-hand corner of the first page.

A NOTE FROM THE DEPUTY EDITOR

Here at the Lawton Leader, nothing is more important than earning your trust. A recent story that included an accusation of sexual misconduct against a student is currently under scrutiny. We want to assure you, our readers, that we are thoroughly investigating how this story was researched and reported. Results will appear in a future edition of the Leader.

The reporter who wrote the piece is on leave until this process is over.

—Jeremy Rubin, Deputy Editor in Chief

It's horrifying to read about yourself like this. The *Leader*, apologizing for *her*. Which only happened because Gil wasn't around. He was interviewing for jobs around the Northeast when all this went down. No cell phones back then, he was impossible to reach. Jeremy was in charge.

And it wasn't like she had a recording of Cam accusing Dan to prove the truth. They didn't record interviews at college papers back then. People weren't as distrustful as they are now, and anyway, taping interviews would have required lugging around bulky machinery. Even if they did, recording one of your best friends while she spilled her guts about the worst thing that had ever happened to her? No way.

She doesn't want to read anymore. But, almost as if hypnotized, she continues to flip the pages and soon she finds another of Blair's missives.

. . . If the matter of potentially faulty and libelous reporting should come before a student tribunal, it could present a conflict of interest for student council president, Adele Dechanet. Dechanet is a housemate of both Page and Overton—and Page's roommate—at Foster House, the feminist-minded off-campus house.

Dechanet maintains that personal relationships will play no part in any adjudication. But she did sound a note of sympathy for Overton. "Cam went through a terrible thing as a vulnerable freshman. No matter what the truth is about the article in which she named her attacker, it's a tragedy that her earlier ordeal should now be compounded, and in such a public way."

Another member of Foster House, Tina Lapinski, concurs that Overton is paying a steep price. "In all the talk about how Dan Daggett may have been wronged, people are forgetting Cam and what she's going through . . ."

Ev doesn't need to read another line. It's all just as she remembered: no one defending her. Dilly and Tina, circling the wagons around Cam and only Cam. Resentment floods through her.

She stands up, heart pounding. It was a terrible idea to come back here. Should she go home? Leave all this in the past once and for all?

No. No way.

Defenseless little Leigh may be long gone, but Ev is here.

She looks at her watch. Just enough time to get back to the B&B and change.

TWENTY-FOUR

F oster House looms against the sky in cool serenity, shimmering in the day's waning light. The brick path, lined by rosebushes, leads her to the front steps and the deep porch.

The door is slightly ajar and Ev pushes it open.

"Hello?" she calls.

There's no answer. Aurora Foster appraises her coolly from the picture frame across the vestibule. The dining room on her left, with the polished wooden table and high-backed chairs, appears unchanged. The drawing room on her right, with a sweating pitcher and glasses on the sideboard, waits expectantly.

"Hello?" she says again, heading into the kitchen. The proportions are as generous as she remembers: The cutting board, built into the counter, is as long as a bed and the porcelain sink is large enough to sit in. The window seat in the breakfast nook is as inviting as ever. She places her knee on it and brings her face close to the glass.

Beyond the stone patio lies a lush lawn that stretches twenty yards or so to a large vegetable patch. From the back corner of the property, back by the tall hedges, a thin trail of smoke reaches up toward the sky. Ev kicks off her shoes and stands on the seat so she can see better. There's a woman out there, tending a large cast iron pot hanging from a rod over a fire. She wears a white dress, and black hair hangs like a licorice braid down her back. Dr. Long! Or her daughter? She hopes it's the doctor; she could use some support tonight. She thinks of running outside to check but she wants to gather her thoughts before the others arrive.

She slips her shoes back on, retraces her steps, and heads up the staircase. The first-floor landing has a door on either side and a short hallway. The last door on the left belonged to her and Dilly. They slept here sophomore and junior years and even senior year when they were each entitled to their own room on the second floor. They told everyone they were too lazy to move their stuff but the truth was they just liked being together.

She knocks lightly even though she knows the girls are gone for the year and steps inside.

She half-smiles in recognition. The two twin beds are in exactly the same position as twenty years ago. She and Dilly tried a dozen times to come up with a new layout but it never worked as well as this way: the two lying end-to-end along the far wall, under the windows that looked onto the backyard.

The beds are bare and she sits on the thin striped mattress of the one that used to be hers, taking in the two desks, two bureaus, and two closets. She lies flat and closes her eyes. Within a few minutes her lower back throbs and she slides a bare pillow under it. She can't believe this was ever comfortable.

Ev stares up at the ceiling, listening to kids playing outside somewhere.

Her mind goes back to one particular November night.

She held the letter from her father out to Dilly, who skimmed it with a knitted brow.

"He won't let you come home with me for Christmas?" she asked incredulously. "Why?"

"Keep reading," Leigh said, and Dilly's eyes moved back to the paper.

"He says you have to go back to California and box up your old house. Why the fuck . . . ?" She kicked off her shoes and sat cross-legged across from Leigh on the bed.

Leigh hesitated, not wanting to say it out loud. "He doesn't say but it's obvious, isn't it? He's going to sell the house. My mom's house. Where I grew up."

"Oh shit," Dilly said. She pulled out the cigarettes from the nightstand and lit one for each of them. They held them out the window as they smoked, the steady inhaling and exhaling calming Leigh's nerves.

"I'll go with you," Dilly said.

"Where?"

"To California."

"No way. Your family would have a conniption. Your mom lives for the holidays. So do you." She almost added, *so do I*. The previous Christmas at the Dechanets, with scads of siblings and cousins and drinking games in the basement, had been the best week she'd had in a long time.

"She'll manage. They'll all manage." Dilly shrugged and took a deep drag. "I've always wanted to go to California. We'll put up a huge tree and have a big feast on your dining room table. Which we will then chop up into tiny pieces and send to your dad COD. How's that sound?"

"Good," Leigh had said. "Really good."

. . . . .

"Hello?" comes a voice from downstairs. "Someone here?"

Ev swivels her legs over the side of the bed and stands, a light sweat breaking out on her upper lip.

"I saw a handbag," May says. "I was hoping it was you."

Ev grips the banister as she makes her way down the stairs to where May stands. May maintains her elegant, head-of-house bearing, and her sea-green eyes, though more hooded than they used to be, retain their beauty. She wears her still-shiny dark hair up and a linen apron over a calf-length sheath in peacock blue. As Ev reaches the bottom step, May wipes her hands on the apron. She opens her arms just as Ev extends a hand. There's an awkward moment but in the end, they hug.

"It's so good that you came," May says, pulling back and searching Ev's eyes. "I was just outside picking some roses. Cam's upstairs, I think. Did you see her?"

"No."

"Let me get you a drink." May hurries over to the sideboard, picks up tongs, and roots around in an ice bucket. This is a bit odd because May always frowned on alcohol at the house, except for welcome dinners, even for seniors, many of whom had reached the drinking age. "I've mixed up some vodka and lemon. I thought it would be refreshing, it's so warm," May says, tucking a sprig of mint into the glass. She hands it to Ev.

Ev takes a sip and almost spits it out. "Strong," she croaks, but May doesn't seem to notice.

"Why don't I go find Cam," May says. She turns on her heel and heads for the stairs.

Ev takes a quick look at herself in the smoked-glass mirror over the mantle. In a bout of deference to May's directive that they once again don 1920s-era duds, she's chosen a cream slip dress that's flapper-esque in silhouette. Her hair, in a low chignon, is still the white-blond it was in college, except for a spot at the nape where it's growing in a bit darker. No one but Sean ever sees that, though.

Footsteps approach and Cam appears. A rush of emotion is interrupted by an observation: Cam looks different. She's sort of puffy, at least compared to her birdlike college self. Her hair is still a soft brown but it's a little longer now, which has released a pretty wave it didn't used to have. Her eyes, with their familiar downward tilt at the outer corners, have a watchful look.

"Leigh," she says.

"Hey," she says noncommittally. Ev won't plunge right into her grievances; she'll hold them in reserve to uncork at just the right time, whenever that might be. That'll be a judgment call. For now she'll remain detached and calm.

"A drink?" asks May, coming in behind Cam. She's already heading toward the pitcher.

"No thanks," says Cam.

"Sure?" May asks, frowning.

"I'm fine."

Silence follows. The bell rings and May sets off for the door.

"Strange to be back here again," observes Cam, looking around the room.

"It is," agrees Ev.

"How was your trip?" Cam asks.

"Fine. Took the train up from New York. You?"

"Flew from Pittsburgh to Albany via Toronto. Out of the way but way cheaper."

Ev's wondering if money is an issue for Cam when the sound of low voices wafts back from the foyer. Ev can't tell who's arrived. Who would she prefer to deal with next? Whether it's Dilly or Tina, it's going to be unpleasant, though in slightly different ways. Like a game of Russian roulette, it just depends which color bullet you want.

A moment later, Tina comes in, dumping a large canvas duffel on the floor. Ev notices that her nose ring is gone. Her black hair's in a fishtail braid and she's chosen a batwing, cocoon-style dress. Her face appears a bit drawn but her mood seems upbeat.

Tina pulls Cam into a tight hug. Then she glances at Ev and raises an eyebrow, as if to say, *And what do you have to say for yourself?*

Why on Earth should Ev have to say anything? It's Tina who owes Ev an explanation. Since Dilly is surely going to apologize for her betrayal tonight, she'd assumed everyone else would as well. Now she's just confused.

May smiles with relief when Tina expresses interest in a drink. Its pouring, stirring, and garnishing use up another couple of uncomfortable minutes. The other women stand, awkwardly shifting their weight.

The last arrival is not signaled by the bell. One moment the archway that frames the foyer is empty, the next, it contains Dilly.

There is a force associated with the sight of her, a breath-removing thing.

Dilly's hair is even shorter now, showing off her long neck and giving her an elfin look. The color is still henna-red and rich, like a long-simmered sauce. She wears a drop-waist mustard-colored dress that hangs beautifully on her lithe frame.

"There she is," exclaims May. She moves quickly to Dilly and clasps her by the shoulders. They laugh and kiss each other warmly on both cheeks, which produces in Ev a surprising, annoying stab of jealousy.

Dilly and Tina embrace easily. It's plain they're still close or at least in touch. Then Dilly looks at Cam, pressing her lips together with a pained but hopeful expression. They hug and Dilly whispers something in Cam's ear. Cam nods.

Finally, Dilly turns to Ev. The apology should start here, shouldn't it? In the expression.

But all Ev sees in the amber eyes she remembers so well is anger. Anger of such intensity that it couldn't possibly stem from anything that happened twenty years ago.

"Why don't we all sit down?" May says. "Can I top off anyone's drink?"

Even Ev will need a few more minutes to finish the one she has, and Tina shakes her head as well. They sit, Dilly and Tina on the couch, Cam and May in club chairs, while Ev perches on an ottoman.

"It's incredible to have you all here," May says, looking at each of them. "Maybe I'm prejudiced because you represent the first year I had any say on new members. But I was sure that you four would constitute a true gift to Foster House. And you each fulfilled your promise, becoming vital members of the Lawton community. Dilly at the student council. Leigh at the paper. Tina, the activist. I don't think Lawton would ever have tried composting if it weren't for you. And Cam, the academic star who, despite some difficulties, remained the essence of compassion."

Ev almost spits out her drink at this last one.

"It's precisely your strengths when you were young women that are going to make tonight so rewarding," May says. Her voice takes on a wistful tone. "I can still picture you, so strong, so fierce. I used to wonder about what you four might achieve together in this world."

Ev and the others squirm a little.

"I realize things have changed. That there's some tension here tonight," May continues. She crosses her legs. "But it's important to put that to the side as much as we can."

This claim is greeted with silence.

"This is an important gathering. I'm confident that it will be wonderful, but that doesn't mean it will be easy. The more you can free yourself of any hostility and be in the moment, the more you'll get out of it."

Briefly, the crosscurrents of bitterness seem to abate as everyone tries to figure out what May is talking about.

"I hope everyone read their packet?" May asks.

The other three nod and Ev follows suit.

"Good. That information, I feel, is critical for context. That's why I sent it. Neither Iris nor Maggie prepared us for our Recommitment last year and I dearly wish they had. I hope whoever among you takes charge of next year's will forward the same material to the women in the class behind you. Or perhaps you'll dig up some research of your own."

Ev experiences a pinprick of concern. What could be so important? She threw out the packet when she thought she wasn't coming, so she has no idea.

"I'd like to offer a reminder of why we're here tonight," May continues. "Upon your initiation here at Foster, you went through Commitment. Many sororities at Lawton had elaborate rites, as you all know, in which members endeavored to prove their loyalty to the sorority house itself. At Foster, while loyalty has always been considered important, loyalty to yourself—your *essential* self—is considered far more critical."

Dilly and Tina widen their eyes at each other in a gentle *Here we go* kind of way, and Ev wishes she had someone to make faces with.

"So. How did 'Commitment' and 'Recommitment' come about? You may well be wondering." She doesn't wait for them to answer. "You might remember that Aurora Foster worked tirelessly to get women into Lawton College. She believed intently in the importance of higher education for women. Building her case, she traveled to women's colleges like Holyoke, Barnard, and Wellesley, speaking to students. She observed that girls who had been through four years of peer companionship in an academic setting had a unique confidence and a heightened sense of altruism."

With the lecture, it feels like they're back in college. Ev feels her drink kick in and tries to follow what May is saying.

"Meanwhile, from her exposure to the Iroquois people, Aurora knew that women could flourish in leadership roles. Her dream was that a select group of young women could enjoy the best of both worlds: studying at Lawton while immersing themselves in Iroquois culture. Of course, since Aurora's time, Native influence in this part of the country has fallen off dramatically. But it was her hope that generations of young women would come into their own here, in this house that bears her name, committing themselves to a life of doing good works."

May takes a sip of her drink. After she puts it down, her eyes linger on her glass for a few moments.

"But Aurora also knew from her own experience that even hard-won wisdom and deeply felt fervor can be fragile things. She'd worked with too many women whose passion for the cause had dimmed when the challenges of life piled up. She'd seen too many fires go out. 'Recommitment' was her answer to this problem."

Ev wonders if May picked this all up at the Iroquois museum. Maybe there was an Aurora Foster book in the gift shop. But who cares? What does it have to do with anything now? She wriggles in her seat, wanting to move along to the confrontation portion of the evening.

Finally, May continues. She seems to have forgotten what she was talking about because she moves on without quite buttoning up her thought. "I don't mean to sound so ponderous," May says, with a vague smile. "As I said, this is going to be a marvelous night. And I want to assure you that there's nothing to worry about."

If you don't want people to worry, how about not telling them there's nothing to worry about? Ev downs the rest of her drink in one gulp.

"I believe we have a few minutes before everything's ready," May says, looking at her watch. "Since not everyone's in touch, why don't we go around the room and everybody say where they're living and what they're doing these days? Camilla, will you begin?"

Cam looks startled by the sudden spotlight. She sits up a little straighter and takes a deep breath. "I'm living outside of Pittsburgh. Married, no kids." She twists her wedding ring as if considering saying more about this but doesn't. "For the last six years or so I've been working part-time for a friend who has a small mail-order business. And once a week, I teach a painting class. Which I love."

Painting? Ev doesn't remember Cam doing any art at Lawton.

"Lovely, Camilla," says May. She nods at Tina.

Tina clasps her hands on her lap. "As *most* of you know, I'm back in Iowa."

Ev takes it that everybody knows this but her.

"I got a master's in agriculture and did some government work. But my family's farm was struggling, so a couple of years ago I went back. I'm trying to modernize it and do the whole organic thing." She pulls out her phone and scrolls through some pictures. "The change was tough on my husband, who prefers city life. I'm not sure how that's going to go. But my kids love it." She holds the phone up for everyone to see. A boy and a girl, who appear to be middle school age, sit one behind the other on a tractor.

"Sounds like an adventure," May says, smiling warmly. "But we better move this along. Adele? What's going on with you?"

Dilly, looking suddenly sober, speaks quietly. "I'm in quality control."

It's the last thing Ev expects. "Quality control?" she asks.

"Yes. For various . . . corporate interests."

It's not like Dilly to be evasive like this. "Like . . . ?" Ev asks.

Dilly gives her the side eye. "I'm between jobs right now. And I've decided not to look for another position right away. It's been a stressful time for us and we could use a break. So Darius and I are going to take the boys down to Louisiana to spend the summer with their cousins."

"Still smoking?" Tina asks with a grin. "Last summer you said you were determined to quit."

"I did quit," Dilly says, smiling. "Though occasionally, when I have some thinking to do, I still indulge."

Despite herself, Ev nods in recognition.

"Good for you," May says, clapping, clearly hoping to lighten the mood. She glances at her watch. "All right, then. Last but not least, Everleigh. Tell everyone what you're up to."

Finally. Ev is fairly bursting to talk. She stands and slowly walks to the sideboard, the better to draw out the moment. "Another drink for anyone?" They all shake their heads, and she takes her time using the tongs to stack large ice cubes into her highball, which she fills with the vodka lemonade from the pitcher. Feeling all eyes on her back, she throws in several sprigs of mint, one by one, and retakes her seat.

"We can't stand the suspense," May says. "You told me on the phone you aren't married. But were you ever? Do you have kids?"

This throws Ev. She was all set to talk about ARC.

"Mmm," she says, figuring out how to spin this. "Never married, no kids," she says. "No time!" She expects the others to chuckle out of politeness at least, but only Cam looks understanding. She pivots to firmer ground. "I do have a boyfriend," she says quietly. Her voice catches. Does she? "His name is Sean." She stops and swallows. "And he—" To her surprise the others, except for Dilly, nod, taking her emotion for joy, not seeing it for the uncertainty it is.

"Anyway," she continues. "For the last five years, I've been the EP—that's executive producer—of *Breaking*, a primetime news-magazine on ARC." She looks around the room, trying to gauge whether they know the show; their expressions remain neutral. "It's fascinating, challenging work that I like to think is important . . ." She goes on for a bit, trying to make the others understand her job and what a quality show *Breaking* is. When she's done, she pauses for effect. "But I have some exciting news, and you're going to be the first to hear it."

Discreetly, May looks at her watch again and Ev feels a burr of irritation. She doesn't want to be hustled out of here for whatever else they're doing tonight. As far as she's concerned, this is the main event.

"I'm about to be promoted to president of ARC News," she says. There's no immediate reaction. "This means I'll be in charge of all the news programming, directing strategy and policy for our flagship operation as well as our bureaus around the world."

May and Cam nod politely, Tina looks indifferent, and Dilly appears nothing less than flabbergasted.

This is strange but Ev barely notices because she's saved the best for last. This part will impress the feminists of Foster House. "The thing that's so thrilling about this is that I'll be the first woman to ever hold the position at my network." She presses her palms together, trying to sum up how she feels. "It's an honor to be considered worthy of the responsibility. Both as a manager—but even more importantly of course—as a journalist."

"Congratulations," says May with warmth in her voice.

"Nice," says Cam.

But Dilly is shaking her head, muttering something under her breath.

"Excuse me?" says Ev sharply.

"I said, 'unbelievable,'" Dilly replies.

"Why?" asks Ev. "Because the last you saw me, I was being kicked out of Lawton for being just that—a journalist?"

"What are you talking about?" asks Dilly.

May looks concerned. "I think we—"

"I've had a fun afternoon going through the *Leader* archives," Ev says, turning on Dilly. "You should do it too, if you have some free time. I was doing some good stories back then—stories that might have helped the girls at this school. Or at least they could have if my reputation hadn't been trashed thanks to you. All of you."

"Okay, let's—" May tries.

"Thanks to us?" Dilly leans forward. "May I ask how far you got in reading those papers?"

"How far?"

"Yes. Which issues did you read? As a 'journalist,' surely you did your research." Her tone is scathing.

"I—I don't remember the *exact* dates," Ev says impatiently. "But I did read where Cam lied about me pressuring her to give up Dan Daggett's name. And where you both"—she wags her fingers at Dilly and Tina—"said you felt sorry for Cam, painting me as some kind of callous liar who used her for my own ends. You got me *kicked out of school*. So—yes. Thanks to you."

"*What?*" asks Dilly. "You—"

"Stop!" May is standing now. Her eyes are wild and pleading, her composure gone. "You've got to stop and I mean now."

"No way," Ev says, determined to finish her point. "You don't understand—"

"No, *you* don't understand," May says, chest heaving. "You cannot do this. Not now." She checks her watch again.

What is this incessant obsession with the time? Ev wonders.

"Gather your things and let's go."

"I—" Ev starts.

"*Now*," May says.

"Go?" Cam says. "Where are we going?"

"Isn't it obvious?" asks May. "Downstairs."

They gather in the hallway, Ev standing slightly apart from the others, fuming. The bookcase that usually blocks the stairs to the basement has already been pushed slightly aside. May opens it all the way, flicks on a light switch overhead, and steps out of the way. They file down: Dilly first, then Tina, Cam, and Ev. May brings up the rear, maybe to make sure no one turns around and hightails it. They reach the bottom and May brushes past them to the low door, which she pushes open. Inside, a fire is glaring in the simple hearth and 1920s jazz plays on a gramophone. A woman beckons them in.

It's Belina. Her chestnut hair, which used to be shoulder-length, now surrounds her pale face like a river around a stone, cascading over a deep garnet dress. She does a bit of the Charleston. "Isn't this a hoot? Back inside the suffragists' secret lair." She approaches each of them and kisses their cheeks. "Welcome back to the Lucretia Mott room," she says.

Ev looks around at the art nouveau rug and the brocade sofa, where Clan Mothers helped suffragists plan the Women's Rights Convention of 1848. After all their struggles and suffering, if they could have only seen how the country celebrated the hundredth anniversary of women winning the right to vote. Most, probably, with very little idea of exactly who'd secured it and how much they'd risked to do so.

She takes the same seat she took on Commitment night when Dr. Long took their blood. Ev spies herself and Dilly in a rectangular gilt mirror hanging horizontally by a thick ribbon. They look like two magnets that repel, their bodies turned firmly away from one another.

"Let's get started," says May. "Belina, would you like to read the invocation please?"

"Yes, love," Belina says, dipping her chin and looking up at May in a flirty manner. She seems impish, giddy. Maybe because she's seeing May again and what's rekindled between them is thrillingly new. She takes a piece of paper from a polished wooden side table and winks at them before starting. "Try to loosen up, okay?" she says. "It'll be much more fun if you do. Now, from the top: *We gather tonight in this special place to summon the forces of . . .*"

Ev couldn't follow even if she wanted to. Her blood is still boiling over the encounter upstairs and she's planning what she's going to say to the other three the minute this thing is over.

"*. . . Sisters who acted so bravely to ensure women would control their own destiny. We recognize their sacrifice . . .*"

The jazz, with a trumpet's lively, nasal sound, picks up its pace. The notes slide dizzily up and down, and Ev watches the firelight dance across Dilly's face. Despite everything, she feels a twinge of tenderness as it illuminates the fine lines that now radiate from the corners of her eyes.

"Thank you," May says, which must mean Belina is done. "And now, would you please?" May looks toward the velvet curtain. Someone's standing there. The figure steps into the light.

It's Dr. Long. Ev immediately feels her heartbeat slow. She's still angry about everything, but for just this moment, there's a reprieve.

The doctor is older now, of course. Her mahogany skin has a few more lines, and her hair has a little gray in the front, but her left eye, with its two tiny planets, still reassures somehow.

Dr. Long approaches them, carrying a tray of teacups. Her gate is steady; the cups do not rattle as the vials did on Commitment night. She sets the tray down on the same side table as last time, but this time Dr. Long doesn't need to check what she's brought to see whether she's remembered everything. She's had two decades of experience under her belt, and you can see it in her lifted chin and serene expression.

She nods at the others, then crosses swiftly to Ev and hugs her. It's unexpected, and such a relief to feel something other than loathing coming her way that Ev almost cries.

"Good to see you," the doctor whispers into her ear.

"You too," Ev breathes.

The doctor presses a small piece of paper into her hand. "I've been thinking about our conversation that day with the knives. That question you asked . . ." She pauses. "If you want to talk again one day, we can."

Ev looks at her quizzically and accepts the cup the doctor hands her.

Ev unfolds the paper. It contains a phone number. She can feel the curious eyes of the others on her as she sniffs the contents of the cup. More booze? Sometimes, at suffragist-themed events, they'd pour their hooch into teacups. But she doesn't smell alcohol.

"Something to settle your stomach," says May simply.

Ev takes a sip. The liquid has no flavor but coats her insides.

The trumpet hits a string of high staccato notes. The fire flares and shadows ripple along the sepia walls.

"Okay, everyone," May says. "Please turn off your phones and leave them here."

. . . . .

They're ushered into the same corner from which Dr. Long emerged, where the velvet curtain hangs. "In a few moments, I'm going to open this," says May, pulling the curtain aside and revealing a small unpainted door. "You'll file into the hallway behind it. It's tight quarters, just to warn you. Off the hallway, you'll find four doors. Tina, you stand in front—wait, Dr. Long, do I have this right?" She shares a scrap of paper with the doctor, who nods. "Tina, you stand in front of the first one, Adele the second, Everleigh the third, and Camilla the fourth. When I tell you, you'll each open your door, step through, and shut it behind you. It'll be dark inside but don't worry. We'll bring up the lights from here. If at any point you decide you need to leave, knock on the door. We'll come get you."

Christ, thinks Ev, seeing her chance to confront the others slipping further and further away. She taps her foot impatiently, not caring who hears it. "How long is this going to take?" she asks.

May clears her throat. "Not long," she says flatly, apparently not liking Ev's question or tone. "Seems to last five or six minutes."

Seems to last?

"Anybody want to visit the bathroom first?" asks Belina, as if they're six years old and about to be packed into the family station wagon. They all shake their heads.

May opens the door. They have to duck a little to pass through the doorway into the narrow hall beyond. A single low-wattage bulb in the ceiling barely reveals the space. They actually have to feel along the left wall to find the first door where Tina takes up her post. Dilly stops at the next one and it's awkward when Ev has to squeeze by her, their hips skimming against one another. Ev makes her way to the third door and feels Cam push by to the fourth.

"Can everybody hear me?" calls May.

"Yes," they call back.

"When I tell you," May continues, "go inside and close the door behind you. It's possible you may hear one another . . . if that happens, try to ignore it and focus on your own experience."

Ev clenches and unclenches her fists.

"All right," May says. "Go on in. And remember, there's nothing to be afraid of."

Ev turns the knob. It resists at first, then yields once she tries counterclockwise. There's a click and the door opens. As advertised, it's pitch black on the other side. She feels her way in. When she hears Dilly's and Cam's doors close on either side, she pushes her own shut.

The temperature feels a few degrees lower, which isn't surprising since they're in a corner of the basement and this room is nowhere near the fireplace. The wall on the right feels like wood paneling and she moves along it till she comes to an indentation or groove of some kind. A wave of claustrophobia passes over her and she steps back, fumbling for the doorknob. She almost twists it but pride stops her. She's not going to be a baby. Her hand falls to her side.

She stands still. Nothing happens and she rubs her upper arms with vigor. Her mind starts whirring again about Dilly. Why was she asking about which issues of the *Leader* Ev had read? What was the point?

The lights start to come up, pulsing on and off as if on a malfunctioning dimmer. Ev can see she's in a small room, about five by seven feet, with a low ceiling. She can just make out a shape, a piece of furniture, on the other side. She presses into the floor with her toe and can tell she's on a rug. There's a sudden feeling of vertigo and she squeezes her eyes shut.

After several seconds, there's a noise and her lids fly open.

She's not alone.

Ev brings a hand to her mouth and presses her back against the door. Her breath comes fast and shallow.

Through the dim, she can see a woman sitting on a chair against the far wall. She's looking down at her lap, long blond hair obscuring her face.

Slowly, she straightens. The hair falls away and Ev looks into her own eyes.

The woman—the girl—on the chair.

It's Leigh.

TWENTY-FIVE

"*Mom?*" The figure's voice is hoarse, more air than sound. Ev's confusion is absolute and she spends several moments trying to unwind the tangle that's replaced her mind.

The figure in front of her doesn't look quite real. It's faint and limpid as if diluted with water from an Alpine lake. But as seconds go by she fills in a bit, her edges sharpening. Soon, she is almost lifelike. Most of the details are eerily perfect, including the slightly knocked knees, the pale eyelashes, and the nails with chipped purple polish. But she is too beautiful: the skin too luminous, the teeth too white. She stretches and wriggles as if testing her form.

She wears a black tasseled flapper dress paired with high-tops.

With a jolt, Ev wonders if this is who she saw—or dreamed she saw—on the subway and at the art gallery. A figment. Ever since the invitation to Recommitment came, triggering so many memories, her young self has been there all the time, hovering on the periphery.

But those "sightings" were just Ev's brain playing tricks on her. This girl doesn't seem to be a trick. She seems real. But of course she isn't.

Ev holds her breath and advances three steps. She's close enough now to see individual strands of hair and the chest moving gently up and down.

Ev reaches her hand out and the figure shrinks back. Ev nods and smiles to show she's friendly—whatever that means in this context—and tries again. Her hand hovers over the left arm. If she touches it, it will surely evaporate like fog.

Her fingers alight near the left wrist. But it isn't skin she's feeling. It's too smooth, too springy, a foreign substance.

She lightly rubs a small patch, shivering as she realizes it is indeed the feel of skin—young skin. Her own, now, is slightly looser, drier.

She pulls her hand back, her mind spinning. This is impossible.

She thinks of May, wondering about the material she sent.

What the hell was in that packet?

"Mom?"

Why does she keep saying that? *Unless . . .*

Ev looks very much like Leigh herself, just older. But does Ev look like Greta? She hasn't looked at a picture of her mother in years. There's one tucked in a notebook inside her nightstand and she used to take it out from time to time. But it hurt too much so she stopped.

This hurts, too. To see herself this young, this vulnerable.

The young one squints as if finally understanding. With her index finger, she points to Ev then to herself.

Ev nods.

"When?"

It takes Ev a moment to figure out what she means. "Forty-two," she says.

The girl blinks as if this is an age she can't imagine being.

There's another chair near the door. Ev pulls it forward and sits.

"You—"

"I—"

"We—"

"Do—?"

They both speak at once, stop, and start again.

"Where did you come from?" Leigh asks.

Ev points toward the door.

"What's out there?"

Ev shrugs. "The world."

The girl nods again. Then she raises her eyebrows as if possibilities are dawning on her. "Can—"

"What—"

"Do—?"

They're wasting precious time, so Ev decides to just shut up.

"—at the *Times Union*?" asks Leigh.

"What?"

"Do you—do I—work at the *Times Union* now?"

Ev almost laughs. The first thing she wants to ask about is work? But it's this detail, even more than the physical ones, that rings the most true. She was so wrapped up in her burgeoning life as a journalist, especially after, as Gil had speculated might happen, her pieces at the *Leader* caught the attention of the *Lawton Patriot*. Someone had even called to discuss her becoming a stringer.

"No," Ev says.

Leigh looks crestfallen. It's weirdly painful to see.

"Forget it," Ev assures her. "Much bigger things are coming your way." She tells the girl about ARC.

"Television?" Leigh's nose wrinkles.

Ev starts to speak, then stops. She doesn't have a ready explanation. TV carries a different kind of power than print. And not enough people are reading papers anymore. But that doesn't sound good. So she tells Leigh about how ARC is the place she's going to make history.

"President of news," Leigh says, frowning. "What does that mean?"

Ev is startled. Why is there a need for her to elaborate? "Well—"

"I hope I'm doing something real," Leigh says, interrupting. "Like, what's the biggest story I've done?" Leigh leans forward, eyes wide.

Ev bites her lower lip. It can easily be argued that it's Armitage. It might not be the bringing down of a corrupt president or exposing a secret war, but its importance can't be denied; the issue of drug and vaccine safety touches virtually every American family. She's done her best to put this out of her mind since Gareth told her Armitage will never run. But the truth is, it's still eating away at her. She keeps playing the story in her mind, hearing the whistleblower's damning account and thinking of how devastating it will be if anyone should be hurt by an Armitage product because ARC has abdicated its responsibility. She'd like nothing more than to tell Leigh about her part in this important scoop. But Armitage is not running and, as Ev looks into the shining eyes on the unlined face with its tiny spray of acne across the chin, she knows she can't lie to her. Not in this or any parallel universe.

"There's not quite as much time to do actual reporting once you get into management. But managing journalists is just as important as being one. You'll understand that later."

Leigh's shoulders sag. She brings her ring finger to the tips of her eyelashes and absently moves it lightly back and forth.

Ev wants to offer something else, something comforting before this thing ends, which could be any second. But the reality is that the news business is not going in a direction Leigh will understand.

"Gil said the same sort of thing after he became editor in chief," Leigh says, sighing. She sits up straight, her face brightening. "Wait, does he work at ARC too?"

"No," Ev says. She pauses. "I don't know where he is."

Leigh's cheek dimples as though she's chewing on the inside of it. "Did—" She exhales, then almost squeaks: "Did Dad come back?"

"To us, you mean? Like, does he live in America now?"

Leigh nods and Ev hesitates. The painful truth, that she was being abandoned, crept up on her slowly, a series of disappointments over months and years. But for Leigh to have to absorb it in a single blow? That seems too cruel. And yet, if she, Ev, had heard the truth straight out, how many of those later disappointments would have been avoided? "No. I'm sorry. He didn't," she says. She'll leave it at this though; no point mentioning that Anton and Ronja go on to have a baby of their own, one who will reap the benefits of Anton finally understanding, as he himself once said, "what it is to be a father."

Leigh leans back in her seat. "Am I married?" she asks.

"Oh—no."

Leigh blows out her cheeks.

Ev thinks of telling her about Sean. What a good person he is, how lucky she is to have him. Things she has not always admitted, even to herself. But then she'd also have to confess that she doesn't know if they'll ever see each other again.

Leigh has sunk into some kind of funk. "I miss Gil," she says.

"I know."

"With him on the road, I finally get it."

"He's a great editor," Ev says.

"Yes. But he's a friend, too. And—I don't know. It sounds weird, but he's kind of like a dad sometimes," Leigh mutters, pulling at a thread hanging from her dress.

Ev nods. She remembers thinking this, though she never told anyone. It was something she appreciated more than she could have fully expressed, anyway.

Leigh seems to refocus. "What about Dilly?"

"What about her?"

"We're still best friends."

"Well—"

"This I know: We drive across country after graduation. It's all planned. Captain promised Dilly a car if she gets a 3.75 GPA, which is in the bag. I've been planning the route. We're taking the longest possible way, across the North, around the Great Lakes, and . . ."

Ev wants to shake the girl, warn that her friends—especially Dilly—are frauds. But as she gets caught up in Leigh's enthusiasm, she can't help but wonder if Leigh's faith in Dilly could possibly be justified. Leigh's a smart girl. More intuitive, more focused, than Ev remembered.

And yet at some moments, when her eyes go wide and she repeats a detail as if to make sure Ev truly *gets it*, the girl's exhilaration seems forced. Like she's papering over a secret fear.

Leigh stops talking. She crosses her arms and fixes Ev with a stare. "What?" she asks.

"Nothing." Ev shrugs.

"You've got this look on your face like I'm way off. So, whatever it is, just tell me."

"There's nothing to tell."

"Are Dilly and I friends when we're old?"

It takes Ev a moment to absorb that "old" from the young one isn't an insult. It's just how she sees things.

It's a terrible moment. "To be honest—"

"You're telling me my life is going to suck," Leigh says, making a slicing motion with her hands. "No. You're telling me that *you* ruin *my* life."

Ev falls back in her chair so hard it hurts her spine. She's wondering what to say when a low rattle fills the room. The hanging light bulb sways. The walls shake. It sounds like the house is about to collapse.

"What's happening?" Leigh cries, putting her hands over her head.

Ev jumps up and covers Leigh's body with her own, trying to figure out what the hell is going on now. She holds Leigh tight until she realizes that the moving walls are actually pocket doors on both sides of the little room, rumbling as they slowly slide apart.

On her far left, they reveal Tina. And young Tina.

On her near left, Dilly and young Dilly.

On her right, Cam and young Cam. Who appear to be crying.

TWENTY-SIX

Everyone freezes.

The young ones look apprehensive but as soon as they spot one another, they relax. Leigh throws Ev off and rises to her feet. She and the others move toward each other and plop to the floor in a small circle, knees touching, their youthful bodies untroubled by the hard surface. Briefly, they lean in, touching foreheads, their arms around each other. A beat or two goes by, as they appear to synchronize their breathing.

Young Cam rubs her sleeve across her eyes and the others comfort her: Young Tina strokes her hair while young Dilly murmurs encouragement. Leigh pulls Dilly toward her fiercely and looks into her eyes with urgency. They whisper, something passes between them, and Leigh nods, exhaling.

Ev approaches them, wanting to hear. The other grown-ups inch forward as well. But they stop in their tracks when the girls' outlines start to soften. One moment, they are as real as they are, the next, their edges bleed into the objects around them. Their forms undulate and shimmer like sun on the ocean. Their low voices grow faint.

"*No*," grown-up Cam whispers as the girls fade from view.

Ev raises her arm, trying to catch Leigh's eye before she disappears.

And she succeeds, sort of. Leigh flicks her storm-gray eyes at Ev, giving her an even look. There's a message in it, though for the life of her, Ev cannot decipher it. Before she can respond, Leigh returns her focus to her friends, and moments later, they slip back to whatever strange dimension they came from, leaving only a barely perceptible disturbance in the air, like heat rising off asphalt.

Ev places her palm on the nearest wall to steady herself, concentrating on her heartbeat.

"Holy shit," Tina says.

"Is anyone else on medication?" Cam asks.

Dilly and Tina snort softly.

"I'm serious," says Cam. "One of the side effects of lithium is confusion."

We're certainly letting our hair down, Ev thinks. She's read a lot about prescription drugs while working on Armitage. Lithium is used to treat mental illnesses.

"I take something for diabetes," says Tina. "Some nausea when I started but that's about it."

"I take a statin," says Dilly. "A few muscle aches, nothing more."

Everyone looks at Ev. "Beta-blockers," she admits.

The women smile wanly at one another. They pull chairs into a rough circle, Ev slightly apart from the other three, and Tina helps Cam, who seems weak-kneed, into a seat.

"Did that just happen?" Cam asks.

"That tea," Tina says. "Was it made from the stuff we smoked at the picnic?"

"Don't think so," Dilly replies. "This was something else altogether. We weren't just seeing things. Those girls were *here.* Weren't they?"

They sit silently for several moments. "We were something," Cam says. "Wish I'd realized it then."

"I guess that was Aurora Foster's point." Tina puts her elbows on her knees and leans forward, massaging her temples. "I can't believe how much energy I had. Kind of depressing."

"What was in May's packet?" Ev asks.

"Stuff about vision quests and ghost dances," Tina replies. "Nothing to prepare anyone for . . . whatever that was."

Ev realizes she never told the other three about the night in the drawing room, with the circle of chairs and the fire's thundering rebirth. She wonders why she withheld it. She could bring it up, but it doesn't feel like the time.

"This is what I don't get," Dilly says, her voice steady and clear, as if she's recovering more quickly than the others. She and her young self probably had a fine old time together. She turns toward Ev. "Why did you leave?"

"Leave where?" Ev asks.

"School. Us." Dilly waves in the direction of the departed girls. "*That.* We were best friends. And you left without a word. It was the most shocking thing I've ever experienced." She shakes her head. "Before tonight."

"You don't know?" Ev asks.

"Not a goddamn clue," says Tina flatly.

"Don't," says Cam, raising a finger in the air. "There are things she wasn't aware of."

"Things she would have been aware of if she'd stuck around for five fucking minutes," says Dilly.

"Or opened a letter," says Tina.

"What wasn't I aware of?" Ev asks, exasperated.

Everyone starts to talk at once but Cam shushes them. "Me first," she says. Cam pushes her hair behind her ears and sighs. "I get why you're mad. So let me start by saying this: You did nothing wrong when you interviewed me, okay? I want to make that clear. You did ask me to name the guy who attacked me. When that Blair girl questioned me about it later, I had no idea what she was after. I told her that you had said 'a name is important because that will make it real.' But I never claimed you said, 'a *big* name is important'—like she put in the article. Okay?"

"You said that I fed you Dan's name."

"She mischaracterized that."

"Did you tell her I pressured you?" Ev asks.

"Yes. But only because you did."

"Did not."

"You *did*." Cam waves away Ev's protest. "At least I felt like you did. But I also told her you weren't wrong to. It was important that someone be brave enough to name a guy. The right guy."

"So was it or wasn't it Dan who attacked you?" Ev keeps her voice low though she wants to shout.

Cam exhales and her eyes flutter. "It was," Cam says, the answer clearly paining her. "Of course it was."

"Then why did you say it wasn't?" Ev grips the edges of her chair.

"I was scared." Cam swallows. "The whole school was apoplectic. And I doubted myself. My memory. I'd started forgetting things."

"Forgetting things?" asks Ev.

"It can happen when you're bipolar."

"You never told me you were bipolar," Ev replies, irritated.

"I didn't *know*. It was undiagnosed. I only started to put all this together in retrospect. Years later. But talking to her tonight—" Cam's eyes go to where the girls just disappeared from. "—it's so obvious. Back then, though, it wasn't talked about like it is today. I tried to comfort her, tell her things will work out. And—"

"But why did you talk to Blair at all?" Ev asks, unable to stop herself from interrupting.

"I didn't know she had an agenda. She said she was just doing a follow-up piece." Cam looks uncomfortable. "Plus—they told me to."

"Who?"

"Dean Sykes. He had me pulled out of class. When I got to his office, the athletic director was there, too—Maddox. They told me that alumni were furious, that the school could get in trouble. That it could be forced to close."

"You believed that?" Ev says, shaking her head.

"I was a kid, okay?" says Cam hotly. "And there was other stuff going on, too."

"Like what?"

"Like those creepy notes," Cam says. "Remember?"

Ev squints. She does remember—ravings about ugly feminists who deserved rape and worse—printed out in all caps and shoved under the front door of Foster.

"And something else, too. I was being followed."

"What?" Dilly says. "You never told us that."

"A couple of times, when I was walking alone on campus at night, I heard someone behind me. I'd turn and see shapes moving just out of sight. Once, someone I couldn't see said my name. Scared the hell out of me."

Ev jerks in recognition. This is spookily similar to her recurring dream, the one that rears its head when she's under stress. Could this be what it stems from? She has a hazy recollection of being followed, too.

"You weren't imagining it," Ev says.

They all look at her, apparently waiting for her to elaborate. But she doesn't want to get off topic.

"Still," she continues. "I tried to talk to you after Blair's first piece came out. I went to the common room where we hung out before class on Tuesdays but you didn't show up. Were you avoiding me?"

"I was in the infirmary again."

"Why?"

"They were afraid I was going to hurt myself. My mood swings were out of control. I wound up going home."

"To Phoenix?"

"Yes. I needed my parents. I think Sykes was only too happy to oblige, too, since it meant getting me off campus. He told me that because of my history on the dean's list, he'd let me take my finals by mail."

Ev doesn't know what to say. Several moments go by and then she turns to Dilly. "So why did *you* trash me to Blair?"

"That's hardly fair," Dilly says, not missing a beat. "Like Cam, I didn't know what kind of story she was writing. But frankly, I was glad to have an opportunity to defend myself. I had to reassure everyone that, if anything happened, the student council could be fair. Sykes was demanding I recuse myself from any proceedings that might involve you or Dan. Frankly, he had a point. But I wanted at least *one* person in that room to be on your side."

"But you defended Cam to Blair. Why couldn't you defend me?" she asks.

"Why do you think you know every damn thing?" Dilly practically explodes. "I *told* Blair that you were a great reporter, that there was no way you did anything wrong. She didn't put that in. I called Jeremy, too." Dilly exhales. "But to be honest, I did have some questions of my own. About the Dan thing."

"Do tell," says Ev, glaring.

"I knew you were furious at yourself for not stopping him at the party, when we saw him with that girl in the basement. You beat yourself up for months, sure that Dan was taking advantage of her and that you could have stopped it. Don't you remember? I thought it was possible, even just subconsciously, that you might have pushed Cam into naming him, if only to make it up to that girl."

Ev crosses her legs but doesn't say anything.

Dilly continues, "I wouldn't necessarily have blamed you, either. You were right about him. I'm sorry I didn't talk to you. But you were never around. Days and days went by when all I saw was your byline."

"I was sleeping at the *Leader*," Ev says. "They had security."

"*I* defended you to Blair too, though you might not believe it," Tina says. "But I hope you understand how cornered Dilly and I felt. You on one side, Cam on the other. We loved and believed you both. It was awful feeling like no matter what we did, we'd be letting one of you down. The whole house was coming apart at the seams, the younger girls freaked out by what was going on with us seniors. You just weren't there to see it."

Ev's face is hot. "I didn't think about that," she admits. But it's true, the atmosphere all across campus was charged. Boys against girls. Administration against students. Professors against one another.

"We could have talked about all this back then," Dilly says. "So I repeat: Why did you leave?"

"Um, I was thrown out of school?" Ev says.

"You *were*?" Dilly says.

"Sykes called me in, did you not know that? Told me he was convening a disciplinary hearing. A mere formality before being expelled."

No one had been scarier than Dean Sykes the day he summoned her to his office. His hair slicked back with so much gel it looked wet and his eyes the deepest black, he'd gazed at her with the menace of a cobra. He'd informed her that at the hearing she'd face Dan, "the injured party," his father, his coach, and members of the athletic department. In turn, she'd be allowed to bring one member of the faculty from a preapproved list, or a parent. He said she was in legal jeopardy.

That night, long after everyone at the *Leader* had gone home, she'd dialed her father. As ring after ring echoed in her ear she'd paced, almost pulling the phone off the desk. He might be angry but her hope was that he'd stand up for her like other parents did whenever their kids got in trouble. She imagined him swooping into Sykes's office, using scientific method to dissect Blair's story and destroy the dean's argument.

"My dear," Anton had said when he answered, sounding wide-awake though it was just after dawn in Geneva. "How extraordinary to hear from you at this moment!"

"What's going on?" she'd asked, confused about why he sounded so happy.

"It's Ronja." He made a strange whooping sound. "We just found out. I'm going to be a father!" There was a pause before he added, "Again."

Leigh had slid down the wall to the floor. For a girl with decent brains, she somehow hadn't seen this coming.

She couldn't bring herself to tell him about the disciplinary hearing at such a moment. The contrast between her personal unraveling and the perfect child on the way would be too humiliating.

Anyway, he never did ask Ev why she was calling.

She'd tossed and turned on the *Leader*'s sagging couch all night, planning to call Dilly first thing in the morning. At 5:30 a.m., a rumbling engine and a loud *thunk* outside announced the arrival of the paper. She'd lugged the stack in, cut the twine, and pulled the top copy to her, immediately spying Blair's second story. She'd read it through exactly once.

Later that morning, when she was sure everyone at Foster would be out of the house, she'd gone home, packed some clothes and a few books, and called a cab. By lunchtime, she was on the train to New York.

"We knew about the hearing," Cam says now. "But why didn't you want to fight? I was going to go with you and tell them about Blair making things up."

Tina scoots forward in her seat. "We were all going to be there. Dilly and I were even going to go to Talbot. He wasn't a very strong president but he actually cared more about student integrity than sports. Gil was going to come, too."

"How did he even know what was going on?"

"Dilly called around to all the papers where he was interviewing," Tina says. "She finally found him somewhere in Massachusetts, right?"

Dilly nods.

"She told him what was going on."

"You did?" Ev asks.

"Yes. He canceled the rest of his trip and came back to be a character witness. And he wrote an editor's note defending you as a journalist."

"It was the deputy editor who wrote the note and it was *against* me."

"Again, how far did you read?" asks Dilly. "As soon as Gil got back to campus, he wrote another one. He got quotes from other girls you'd interviewed who backed you up. He said you were the paper's best reporter and that he was behind you all the way."

Ev screws her eyes shut. "I was so sure . . ." she says, trailing off.

"For a reporter, you sure make a lot of assumptions," says Dilly.

Ev can't do much more than nod. "Did other girls come forward?" she asks. "Did Dan ever get in trouble?"

"No," says Cam. "He was MVP and graduated the hero everyone thought he was." Cam rubs the armrest of her chair. "But some things *did* change."

"What?

"The year after we graduated, they finally started to take security seriously," Tina says. "More lighting on campus, a shuttle bus for students walking home at night, and a crackdown on drinking at the frats." She shifts in her seat. "I guess they weren't ready to punish rapists, but they were willing, at least, to try to prevent assaults from happening in the first place. I mean, you told some powerful stories in the paper. You basically shamed them into taking action."

Ev nods. "And Dan?" she asks. "Does anyone know what happened to him?" She imagines he became a professional athlete. Or a captain of industry.

"He was killed in Iraq," Tina says. "It was the cover story in the alumni magazine."

Ev rubs her forehead.

"I tried writing you," Cam says. "We all did. We got your dad's address in Geneva from an envelope in your room. Didn't he give you the letters?"

"He tried to, I think," Ev says, remembering. "But I wasn't easy to find. I took the money he sent for a plane ticket to Switzerland and used it to go to Greece. I was at hostels all summer."

"Gil said he wrote you, too," Tina says.

Ev nods. At this point, anything's possible.

"Why did you shut us all out?" asks Tina.

Ev looks down at her lap and shakes her head, thinking of the girl she just saw, the girl she once was. The brave front, the pouncing on any perceived transgression. Attempts to cover something Ev can only now begin to identify.

She hadn't been able to hold on to her mother. Then she'd lost her father, not to death but, maybe even worse, to someone he liked better. When she perceived even a glimmer that her friends had "betrayed" her, it felt less like a shock than part of a pattern.

In her mind, she was only leaving them before they could leave her.

Ev sags against the back of her chair. "I shouldn't have," she says.

There's an excruciating silence that seems endless. Finally, Cam stands and holds out her hand. Ev stares at it for a moment before clasping it with her own. Cam pulls Ev to her feet and hugs her. Ev stiffens at first, then exhales. She feels a set of arms come around them both. Tina.

She waits for Dilly to join them but she doesn't.

Back in the Lucretia Mott room, the gramophone needle has slid to the center of the record and now bounces lightly, making a soft scratching sound. The fire is out and the room is chilly.

May, Belina, and Dr. Long are gone, probably having been surprised at how long this particular Recommitment was taking.

Ev looks at her watch. Almost two hours have gone by. Without thinking, she fishes the phone out of her bag and hits the power button. Tina pours four glasses of water and hands them around. Ev downs hers in two long gulps and then looks at her phone.

There are four messages from Gareth. Why would he be calling on a Saturday night? Her heart starts pumping and she hits the button to call him back. The others are heading out the door. Cam and Tina are already gone and Dilly is just a few paces behind them.

Ev hesitates. "Wait," she says, ending the call just before it goes through. She crosses to Dilly and reaches for her wrist. Dilly turns, her amber eyes with the yellow near the iris watching Ev intently. Just like they did that night in California.

It had been a long week, cleaning out her childhood house. Dilly had taken on the entire kitchen and garage, while Leigh had sorted through the personal items. She had tossed most of her dad's things but found herself saving every last button and bookmark belonging to her mother. On the last day, she and Dilly had tackled one final chore: a cavernous upstairs closet at the end of the hall. Leigh had found the old inflatable raft, nearly flat. She was about to yank out the clear plastic plug to empty it when Dilly put a hand on her arm.

"When was the last time you used that?" Dilly asked.

"I don't know."

"Think."

"As a kid. Years ago."

"With your mom? Didn't you tell me she took you to the beach not long before she died?"

"Yes," Leigh had said, remembering. "We spent the day at Stinson. I think that was the day she told my dad she was sick."

"Did she blow this up for you?" Dilly asked.

"Yes." And just like that, Leigh had understood.

They sat on the floor, cross-legged, knees touching. Dilly had tugged on the plug and put her finger over the hole. She placed it under Leigh's chin. Leigh nodded and Dilly took her finger away.

Leigh closed her eyes, feeling the last of her mother's breath move over her lips, across her cheeks, and through her eyelashes.

$\cdots\cdots$

Dilly tries to pull away and Ev grabs her wrist tighter. She swallows and looks at her old friend. "I'm sorry," she says.

Dilly regards her for several long moments. "Me too." She turns and walks out.

TWENTY-SEVEN

Ev's never been to Gareth's house. But he claims that everything's happening so fast that they have to meet Sunday afternoon.

A cab from Penn Station to the Upper East Side, having to circumvent various street fairs, was a bad idea. She rolls her shoulders. Her head hurts and her insides churn.

The taxi deposits her in front of a large baroque building. A doorman ushers her to an elevator that contains an attendant and a low upholstered bench. Even though she's going only a few floors, Ev sits.

Gareth's is one of only two apartments on the floor. She rings the buzzer.

He appears in a blue sweater and chinos and beckons her into the foyer, which has protective paper taped to the floor. The sound of loud banging echoes from another room.

"Sorry about this," he says, gesturing vaguely around. "They're removing some installations I'm taking to Napa and I don't think they know Hirst from LeWitt." He glances at her carry-on bag. "You can leave that here in the foyer."

They head into a palatial kitchen. A middle-aged woman in a

black uniform with a white apron sets two china cups on an enormous marble island. She pours coffee from a silver decanter into each.

"We can handle the rest. Thank you, Gabrielle," Gareth says.

She nods and departs.

Ev hikes herself up onto the stool Gareth indicates. He pushes sugar and cream toward her but she waves them away impatiently.

Gareth throws several lumps of sugar into his own coffee and stirs briskly, his spoon clanging against the insides of his cup. He doesn't sit.

"On Friday evening, I informed Frank about my leaving and you replacing me. He wanted to talk about it but in general was on board," Gareth begins. "He called back the next day though, directly after the emergency shareholder meeting. Apparently there's been fresh drama with a daughter company—riots at a factory in Malaysia or something—who can keep up? Anyway, it threw the board for a loop and made them nervous about any big changes to their portfolio. And while ARC News represents barely 2 percent of their holdings, everything to do with the news these days is high-profile and they're suddenly concerned about someone new coming in."

Ev puts her cup down. "Is it that they don't want you to go? Or is the problem specifically with me?"

"A bit of both," he says. "They know me, they like me. I've done well by them. You're new. And, though they would never say it, you come in a different package than they're used to. They're insisting I stay on."

Ev looks up at the ceiling. The coffee turns to acid in her stomach.

"But I have an idea," Gareth says.

"Yes?"

"It will require careful orchestration and we have to act fast."

Ev sits up straight.

Gareth pulls his stool closer to hers and sits. For the first time, he looks at her as something other than his employee. As a fellow soldier, maybe. Or a friend.

"The lady of the hour," says Frank Marchant, taking her hand.

It's like meeting God, if God had an office in midtown. Frank Marchant, CEO of the parent company, fabled figure among the city's elite, practically hums with vitality and authority. He's younger than she expected, early fifties, with a head of lustrous blond hair. He reminds her of Apollo as seen in children's books of Greek myths.

She has to give him credit. He's so solicitous you'd never know he was against her ascension to ARC News president just days ago. But since then she and Gareth have delivered a one-two punch: Gareth created a vineyard "situation"—something to do with a root fungus on the vines—that required him to leave for California immediately, and Ev followed up with a presentation of her vision, including ideas such as streamlining news-gathering procedures, deepening the connection between editorial and technological staff, and detailed plans to bolster the public's faith in news by including some of their journalistic process in the final product. It was nothing short of a triumph.

The look on Marchant's face told her an offer would be in her hands within hours, and it was.

Now she's here on the seventy-second floor, in a conference room off Frank's office, to meet the board and talk about the up-coming transition.

"Please have a seat," Frank says, indicating the chair next to him. The table is ringed by seven men and one woman, all of whom have gotten to their feet. They introduce themselves, each reaching across the table to shake her hand.

"I want to say that everyone here is delighted to welcome you to the team," Frank says. "I trust the lawyers sent over the relevant material?"

"Yes," Ev replies. The "relevant material" turned out to be a contract as long as a novella, complete with stock options, a golden parachute provision, and free financial counseling. Even her attorney whistled when he saw it.

"So we're here today to talk about your rollout," Frank continues.

Ev nods.

"We're thrilled that you've accepted our offer and that you will be taking over as president of ARC News. You were far and away the best candidate."

Ev wasn't aware that they considered anyone else.

"But we're also cognizant of the fact that your appointment represents a milestone. One we may want to capitalize on."

Ev can guess what Frank's getting at but cocks her head respectfully.

"As you know, our company, thanks to a couple of rogue subsidiaries, has taken a black eye in the press recently. There's a factory scuffle now that's presenting a bit of a headache."

Board members hold absolutely still as if not wanting to admit, even tacitly, that all is not well in their world in front of an underling like her.

"So we thought this would be a smart time to make a little news—a little *good* news—here at ARC."

Ev raises an eyebrow in friendly interest.

"With this in mind, we want to celebrate that a woman is finally taking the helm of our News Division. We have reason to think it can be a 'feel good' moment for everyone. Plus we believe it's evidence of the, ah, *modern* approach that our company is now ready to take when it comes to problem-solving. So we're planning an extra special introduction of you to the media."

So being a woman is suddenly a plus? Ev smiles and opens the bottle of water in front of her.

A bushy-eyebrowed board member watches intently as the bottle touches her lips. Ev puts the water down and angles her body away from his.

Frank continues, "Of course we'll lead with your many accomplishments and your comprehensive cost-cutting ideas for the future. But we don't want to ignore the innovation that your new title represents. In fact, we want to underscore it."

"For the record, I want to reiterate that we have to be careful how we go about this," pipes up a bald, pockmarked man on the opposite side of the table. "Can't have folks thinking this is an affirmative-action hire."

The lone woman on the board frowns. "I thought we were going with Ms. Page because she is a world-class journalist," she says, giving Ev what looks like a nod of appreciation. "I say we promote her that way."

"Agreed, Cecilia," says Frank. He slides a stack of folders her way. "Please take one and pass it on." Then he says to Ev, "Inside is a general outline of our plan. Eventually, we'll be flying you out to meet with all the O&Os and setting up Zooms with the foreign bureaus. But first we want to bring the top media reporters to a lunch next week and have you meet them face-to-face. Most of us will be there, too, to signal our unequivocal support."

For media-averse Frank to grace an event like the one he's describing is surprising. But if he wants attention, this is the way to do it. Any industry reporters not inclined to get off their duffs to meet the first woman to helm ARC News sure as heck will turn up to see Frank Marchant in the flesh.

"I hope I can justify your faith in me," Ev says demurely, opening her folder.

It's the first night since Recommitment that she doesn't have a pile of work to bring home. It's been a sleep-deprived ten days, plotting with Gareth, writing a speech to deliver to the entire News Division, and preparing an excited but flustered Malcolm to take over as EP of *Breaking*.

She unpacks the bag of takeout on the kitchen table and takes chopsticks to a tray of *shumai* while paging through her Lawton yearbook from senior year.

She stops at a two-page spread of the *Leader* newsroom and staff. There's a photo of Blair interviewing some students at a table in the library.

In Ev's mind, Blair has lurked like a monster. But here, with her pixie cut and earnest expression, she looks like a baby. Was she really as terrible as Ev remembers her? Ambitious, yes, but so was she. Blair had Jeremy in her corner but she herself had Gil. And Cam *did* recant her story. Someone had to cover it. Instinct still tells her that Blair hastened, and took joy in, her downfall, but Ev feels a fresh stab of shame at how wrong she's been about so many things. How ungenerous.

She turns another page and lands on a large picture of Gil putting together a layout, hair flopping over one eye.

He looks so earnest and vital. She wonders where he is, if he's still a journalist. She hopes so. Maybe she'll try to find him.

She runs a finger along the curve of his face. His blue eyes have the kindness, and conviction, of Sean's.

Sean. *Sean.* She repeats his name out loud, a name that was always a comfort to her, like a smooth little stone you could slide into your pocket and hold whenever things got rough.

She wonders where Sean is tonight and how Erik is doing.

Across the courtyard, her neighbors arrive home from work, reuniting with partners and children and pets, each apartment a tiny quotidian universe. She's always thought of Sean's clan as self-absorbed. Worse: as baggage, a time suck. But maybe they simply present the starkest possible contrast to the abandonment at the center of her own story.

She fishes out the phone in her bag and dials Sean's number. His mailbox is full.

It's a little after nine. Sometimes he works this late. She calls his office and gets the voicemail of his secretary.

"Hi, Tracy, Ev here. Could you let Sean know I'm trying to reach him?"

She pulls some sake from the fridge, pours it into a tiny ceramic cup, and heats it in the microwave. Back at the table, she sips thoughtfully.

What she knows is how little she knows. About herself. About anything.

She's successful, soon to be powerful. But inside, she's . . . blank.

Gently, she swirls the sake. Is there anything good about being blank? Maybe.

A blank, at least, is space. Space you can fill.

The big media reporters have indeed turned out. They sit, along with a couple dozen handpicked ARC staffers, at tables of five in the largest of the ARC conference rooms, which has been transformed for the day with white curtains and gigantic orange peonies.

Ev sits on a small dais along with several members of the board, listening to Frank at the podium. It's such a rare appearance that people are actually taking pictures of him with their phones. Frank talks about what a fantastic organization ARC is and describes in detail its proud history. He talks about why his company coveted ARC for years before purchasing a majority stake and how gratified they are to have this particular jewel in their crown.

Finally, Frank says her name. He's talking about her career and, boy, does he lay it on thick. She is "the journalist of a generation" who has "integrity in spades" and "unerring news judgment."

"If Everleigh Page says something is news, you better believe it's news. And you better watch," Frank says.

She had imagined she'd love no moment more than this one. Hearing this kind of praise in a room full of witnesses, surely it would be the best feeling in the world.

But it's actually kind of embarrassing.

"And so, in short, we are proud to make this woman"—he puts just the tiniest emphasis on *woman*—"the standard bearer for ARC News. Now, and for many, many years to come." Frank beckons Ev to join him. She rises and moves to his side. "Our company has its share of critics. But we believe this choice of ours will, for so many reasons, go down as one of our great achievements." Frank turns over the last page of his speech, sweeps his gaze around the room, and, seemingly carried away by the moment, utters an unscripted thought: "This woman is our future and we are behind her one thousand percent. In short, mark this one down, folks, you'll find no daylight between this board and Everleigh Page. Not now, not ever."

A light bulb goes off in Ev's head. In front of the world, Frank has tied their fates together. He and the board now need her as much—or more—as she needs them. Giving her a kind of power that even Gareth didn't have.

And she's just figured out how to use it.

"Thank you," she says, lifting her voice over the polite applause. She meets his eye. "You have no idea just how grateful I am."

Ev bustles around her new office on the fortieth floor. She'd assumed she was getting Gareth's old office on fifteen, but Frank wanted to make a bigger splash for her. She isn't crazy about being so far away from her staff, but she plans to spend as much time as she can in the newsrooms and edit suites anyway. It's not fully furnished yet, so most of her things are in boxes, but the light is spectacular. She can hear Meryl just outside, loading files into her desk drawers. Every half hour or so, she comes in with another delivery of flowers.

News is on most of her monitors, of course. But Mac 'n' Cheese is there, too.

She has some time before her next meeting and uses it to hang the photo of Dilly, Tina, Cam, and herself from the suffragist picnic. She sliced it from her yearbook with a box cutter and had it framed. Now it gets a place above her desk.

Next, she pulls another small framed photo from her tote. She sets it on the desk, facing her chair. It's the picture of her mother that she kept in her nightstand, taken by her father that day at the beach. Greta, a windbreaker over her bathing suit, a brave smile on her lips and ocean spray, or tears, on her cheeks.

Ev sits down and flips through a few articles about her ascension. Most of them carry the same AP photo of Frank behind her, beaming as she began her speech. "A Woman Slides into Driver's Seat at ARC News," the *New York Times'* Business section proclaims.

When she's done reading, Ev laces her fingertips and stretches her hands overhead. Time to take this thing for a spin.

She picks up the phone and dials.

"Hello?"

"Tabitha?"

"Yes?"

"This is Ev. Ev Page."

There is silence on the other end.

"Hello?"

"Oh," Tab says. She sounds guarded.

"I—" Ev begins, realizing she should have thought this through. "How are you?"

"Okay."

"How's your health? I hope no more scares?"

"Nope," Tab says flatly.

"So, what are you up to these days?" Ev asks.

"Why?"

"We miss your face around here," Ev says, cutting out an article dubbing her "the most powerful woman in news."

"That's a bizarre thing to say."

Ev puts down the scissors. "Let me rephrase. What I want to say is we—I—regret letting you go." There's no response and she swallows. "So, you know, if you haven't found anything else, we'd like to have you back."

"You fired me."

"I know. That was—"

"Actually, no. You had Malcolm fire me."

"I'm sorry about that," Ev says. "I was meeting with—" she starts to explain about the lunch with Gareth and then realizes how dumb that will sound. "Never mind. There's no excuse. That was wrong."

"I'm glad to hear you say that." Tab sighs. "But I could never trust you again."

The words are like a slap. But they are not unjustified.

"I understand," Ev says, exhaling. "But if you change your mind, you'll always have a place at ARC."

Tab says nothing.

"Okay?"

In answer, she hears three high-pitched beeps. She's not sure whether they signal a dropped call or whether Tab has simply hung up.

Well, that sucked.

She tries again. The phone rings six times, and then Aviva's husband picks up.

"Hi, James, it's Ev Page." She tries to keep her voice light, friendly. "How are you? Michaela?"

"Um, hi. We're . . . fine." James speaks slowly as if figuring out how to handle this.

"I won't keep you," Ev says. "I was just wondering if Aviva's there? She's not answering her cell."

"She's out," James says. "And probably not answering on purpose."

"Has she found another job? Because—"

"I'm sure she wouldn't want me to share that with you. But I will say that it's not exactly easy out there. Not a lot of staff jobs. You know, with benefits? And after all she did for—no. I'm not saying any more. Except I'm fairly sure Aviva wouldn't work with you again if you were the last person on Earth."

After they hang up, Ev stares out the window. Meryl comes in with another delivery of flowers and Ev tells her to keep them for herself.

. . . . .

In the afternoon, she ventures back down to her old office, now full of sports posters and small glass boxes containing signed baseballs.

"How's it going?" she asks Malcolm, taking a seat across from his desk.

"Spectacular," he says, though his cheer seems a bit forced. "Everyone's pumped for a strong summer."

Summer is not traditionally a great time for network TV. But the last couple of years, *Breaking* has been capitalizing on the fact that everyone else is in reruns and has been airing some of its bigger stories in June and July, now that people can take their favorite shows with them on vacation. It was Ev who came up with this strategy and it's often delivered in the ratings. Malcolm knows it's up to him to keep up this streak.

"Glad to hear it," says Ev.

"What's it like upstairs?" Malcolm asks. "I need to hear all about Frank Marchant. Can't believe you've seen him in the flesh." Malcolm wears a tie that does not go with his shirt. She doesn't need to look to know that under the desk, his feet are in bright sneakers. She makes a mental note to take him shopping; she can't invite him to meetings with the brass looking like this. And she very much wants him to meet the brass. She wants the other ARC News executives to get face time with them, too. Gareth being the only person the parent company felt comfortable with didn't serve anyone very well. As he himself reasoned, the board needed to get to know you before they'd start to trust you.

Ev shares a few tidbits about Frank and the board, as well as her plans for her "first hundred days" as head of ARC News.

"'The first hundred days'—just like the president," he says, laughing, but also with a bit of awe in his voice. Though he's a smart producer with good managerial skills, he isn't yet an ace at office politics. He doesn't always agree with her directives—he was deeply resistant to firing a string of colleagues while she was off with Gareth—but she can tell he admires her toughness.

"I want to talk to you about Thursday," she says.

"Thursday's show?"

"Yes. How's it looking?"

"Well, we're waiting for that police brutality trial to end in Boston. If we get a verdict even as late as tomorrow afternoon, we'll lead with that. But the prosecutor says it's highly unlikely. If we don't get a verdict, I've got two other story options." Malcolm picks up a stress ball and starts squeezing it. "But we're in a bit of a jam because we don't have enough editors to polish three stories at once. *Smell the Coffee!* took two of them for that 'Sexy Summer You' series. Plus—"

Ev smiles and cuts him off gently. "I've got a little present for you."

"A present?"

"Going to solve all your problems. For this week, anyway."

Malcolm stops squeezing. "I'm all ears."

"I have a story for you."

"A new story?" He looks flummoxed. "How would we turn it around in two days?"

"It's already done. An hour-long investigation, good to go. Even the music and photos are cleared. All you need to do is get a statement from the accused and drop it in."

Malcolm blinks. "What story is this?"

"It's the last one Aviva did before she left."

"The one that was all hush-hush?"

"Yep."

Malcolm puts the ball down. "What is it?"

Ev hesitates. She was tempted, before she got here, to simply provide the highlights, without letting Malcolm in on the backstory, the reason Armitage is never supposed to see the light of day. But that wouldn't be fair. He's EP of *Breaking* now; this is his show.

"I'm going to tell you everything," she says. "But I need to warn you, there's probably going to be some backlash."

"From whom?"

"The board. From what I've heard, they may care more about profits than principles. But they put themselves in the journalism business. It's time they find out what that means. And once this story is out there, I'm confident the wider world will agree with *us*."

Malcolm appears stunned but also riveted.

Ev leans forward. "After I fill you in, if you don't want to air it, I'll understand. But if you do, I want you to know that I, and I alone, will face any blowback."

"Jesus," he says. "Tell me."

She fumbles with the keys security gave her and opens the door. Aviva's office looks like something out of the Rapture: papers everywhere, file drawers open, and books stacked on the floor as if she was plucked from a busy workday with no notice. Which she was. That's how they do it here; when you're fired, you're escorted from the building almost immediately to protect the network's proprietary information.

Ev sits in Aviva's chair and looks around. It appears Aviva was at least given time to take down family photos and her daughter's artwork because the walls are full of ugly black marks and sad little holes.

Malcolm was beyond excited about Armitage, as she was fairly sure he would be, but Ev realized he was going to need Aviva's research and notes for a final fact check. She doesn't have to look hard to find what she's here for. Armitage material is spread out all over the desk.

She makes a pile of all the documents she can find. Then she flips through the Armitage files in the open drawer on her right. They're in alphabetical order and toward the back she finds one labeled "Whitney." Whitney the Whistleblower. She never did learn her identity.

She opens the file. Inside is a Xerox of a driver's license belonging to an Adele Dechanet with an Ohio address.

Dilly stares out at her from the small photo.

Ev drops the file and stands up. Then sits down again. This can't be right. Dilly was the one who called Aviva all those months ago, offering herself up as a source?

Was it a coincidence? Or did Dilly know Ev worked at *Breaking*? Maybe Dilly had Googled her and seen the Channel Surf interview, where she said she wanted to do more investigative work. Clearly this was a story Dilly wanted to tell, but maybe it was Ev that made her determined to work with ARC. But why would she want to help Ev at all?

Is it possible Dilly was feeling bad about everything that happened twenty years ago, even though she did nothing wrong, and wanted to do Ev a good turn? Her mind reels.

The rest of it, at least, makes sense. Dilly was a chemistry major. Easily could have gone to work in the drug industry. And she said she's between jobs now, which could be because her whistleblowing was discovered and she was fired.

And it explains why Dilly was irate from the moment Ev walked in the door at Foster House and extra furious when Ev announced she was being made ARC News president. Thanks to Ev, she'd lost her job for nothing. But then why didn't Dilly bring it up while they were all laying their cards on the table?

She can think of only one reason: That night was so humiliating to Ev—she was forced to admit so many mistakes—that Dilly had taken pity on her and not gone in for the kill.

She looks at her friend's picture again but it's too much to bear and she slides it back into the file.

Ev's head swims as she picks up the stack of papers. She pauses in the doorway, sweeping her eyes around the office where a good person once did great work.

God, what a mess.

"Tracy called," Meryl says when Ev arrives back at her office. "Said to tell you she's in the office now."

"Thanks," Ev says. She starts dialing before she even sits down.

"Flowform. Tracy."

"Tracy, it's Ev Page."

"Oh, hi. I'm sorry I just got your message. I've been at an offsite for a couple of days." Tracy sounds breathless. "Have you heard back from Sean?"

"No," says Ev. "What's going on?"

"I—I thought . . . shoot."

"What?" Ev asks.

"Sean's father. He had a blood clot a few days ago. I think it was a side effect of the chemo? Anyway, it traveled to his lungs and he had to go into the hospital. Sean went back to Chicago."

"Is his dad all right?"

"It wasn't looking good, but I haven't heard anything. You can call the house. Sean's staying there."

"I don't have their number," Ev says.

If Tracy's surprised, she doesn't show it. "I'll give it to you."

. . . . .

The gate is packed with the kind of people who actually commute between New York and Chicago for work: little or no luggage, on their phones with colleagues back at the office, yammering about clients and meetings.

Ev fits right in. In the end, she didn't use the number Tracy provided. She hopped in a cab for LaGuardia with only her purse. And she, too, is on her phone, trying to squeeze in a couple of calls before departure. She scrolls through her contact list and dials just as they announce boarding.

"Carla Santiago."

"Carla, it's Everleigh Page."

"Hel*lo*," says Carla with obvious delight. She congratulates Ev on the new job. "It's thrilling," she says. "And so inspiring for our girls here at Lawton. Speaking of which, how was your reunion?"

"Oh," says Ev, caught off guard, though this is a perfectly natural question. She clears her throat. "You know how those things are."

"Awkward and boring?"

"Exactly," says Ev.

Over the loudspeaker, the gate agent calls her row.

"Look, I was wondering if you've found anyone to replace you for the director position at the station."

"There's a guy the dean likes but I can't stand," Carla says. She pauses. "Why?"

"I've got someone for you."

"Who?"

"She's the best I've ever worked with and Lawton would be lucky to have her. Watch *Breaking* Thursday night and you'll see her work."

"Intriguing."

Ev stands and hoists her bag onto her shoulder. "But I need to caution you."

"About what?

"If you talk to her, don't mention that I was the one who gave you her name."

"Why on Earth not?"

"If you do, she probably won't take the job."

"Well, okay then," says Carla. "What's her name?"

"Aviva. Aviva Abramowitz."

After they hang up, a flight attendant comes over the loud-speaker. "In a few moments, we'll be asking you to turn off any electronic devices."

Ev slides into the window seat and takes a deep breath. She touches the edge of her phone briefly to her forehead. Before powering it down, before she loses her nerve, she creates a group text to Dilly, Tina, and Cam.

Anybody up for meeting to help plan next year's Recommitment?
Maybe give them some info that's actually helpful?
Happy to host.

Immediately, Cam responds:

I'm there.

Ev bites the inside of her cheek as she waits. A minute later, Tina replies:

Okay.

Her knee bounces as she awaits Dilly's reply. Dots appear and pulse at the bottom of the screen, but the seconds drag on with no words appearing. Finally, the dots disappear.

Ev exhales. She types a text to Dilly alone:

I know everything now.
I have no right to ask this but please watch
Breaking Thursday night.
And then, if you'll let me, I'd like to talk

The pulsing dots reappear . . . disappear . . . reappear.

I'll watch.

It's all Ev can hope for. She can't control Dilly's actions, only her own. From now on she'll try to do better.

She gets through to Meryl just as the flight attendant sweeps through, telling them they really must turn off their phones.

"Where are you?" asks Meryl.

"On a plane," Ev says. "I want to tell you I'm going to be out of town for a few days. Maybe a little longer."

"Everything okay?"

"Yes," Ev says. "But Frank Marchant may be looking for me after Thursday's broadcast. Maybe even during." Ev has realized that at that point, she might be somewhere she can't have her phone on. Like the hospital. "If he can't reach me, he may call you."

"Okay."

Ev waits for her to freak out but she doesn't. "Aren't you going to ask what's going on?"

"No. You need me to cover and I will. It's not a problem. Anyway, I can hear them telling everybody to shut their phones off."

Ev smiles. Meryl misses nothing. "Do I ever tell you how much I appreciate you?"

"No." Meryl says this so dryly that Ev laughs. "What should I tell Marchant if he calls?" Meryl asks.

"Tell him . . ." Ev fastens her seat belt, pulling it tight against her abdomen. "Tell him I had a family emergency."

TWENTY-EIGHT

With afternoon traffic, the drive takes more than an hour. The neighborhood, when she reaches it, is lovely with generous homes, wide lawns, and porches with bicycles propped against them. Puddles dot the pavement, gleaming in the sunlight. It occurs to her that she might have come all this way for nothing. Everyone could be out. At church, praying or, God forbid, a funeral.

She parallel parks, bumping lightly into the cars in front and back. When she gets out, she's relieved to see they're undamaged. She pulls a bouquet from the back seat, and, since it's so warm, shrugs off her blazer.

A breeze tosses her hair around her face as she approaches the large Georgian Colonial. It's white with dark green shutters, an open veranda on one side of the front door, a screened-in one on the other. A vine with huge creamy blossoms weaves in and out of the railing.

She makes her way up the path and presses the doorbell. She can't hear whether it's rung. Several moments go by. She's wondering whether to knock or maybe just leave the flowers and run when the door swings open.

It's Annette. She's in sweats and a T-shirt, blowing on a steaming mug.

"Got it," Annette calls over her shoulder, as she appraises Ev without smiling.

"I just heard about Erik," says Ev.

In response, Annette takes exactly one step to the side so she can come in. Ev slowly wipes her feet on the mat, delaying the moment of impact, and enters the house. It smells like laundry and garlic. Ev holds out the flowers, but before either of them speaks, Peter comes shuffling down a polished wooden staircase.

"Look who's here," he says. He puts his hand over his heart and pats it with exaggeration a couple of times. Maybe it's a sweet gesture meaning he's happy to see her but more likely it means *be still my heart, the princess has deigned to show up*. At least he has the good grace to take the flowers out of her hand. "I'll see if we have a vase left," he says, and heads down a hall toward the back of the house.

Ev and Annette stand silently for a few moments. "Erik?" Ev finally prompts.

"Sleeping," says Annette.

"Is he—"

"And Sean's not here."

Just then Carmen comes in from the direction Peter left. She is barefoot, her sleeves rolled up. She wears an apron that says, "I'm Not Arguing, I'm Just Explaining Why I'm Correct."

"So it *is* you," she says. Again, the tone isn't clear. There's barking from somewhere outside and Carmen turns to her daughter. "Let Roger in, will you?"

"You know he makes me sneeze."

"You'll manage," says Carmen.

Annette flicks her eyes at Ev again and leaves. Carmen pushes an escaping dreadlock under her stretchy black headband. She wipes the back of her forearm across her eyes. "This is a surprise."

"I heard about Erik from Sean's office just today," says Ev. She shifts her weight from side to side. "But I can leave if you prefer."

Carmen tilts her head back and exhales. She looks at her watch and starts back down the hall. After a few steps she turns and beckons impatiently for Ev to follow.

The kitchen is enormous, with two islands, a professional stove, and an overhead rack from which a dozen pots dangle. There are bowls and open cookbooks covering the counters along with a stand mixer, jars of spices, olives, and bags of flour and sugar.

"Give these a rough chop," says Carmen, pushing a bag of pecans toward Ev.

Ev stares at them dumbly, needing a moment to catch up. She puts her purse and phone down on the counter and looks for a knife. Carmen goes back to the stove to stir something and Annette comes in from the yard, followed by an ivory speckled spaniel with long silky ears. He nuzzles the back of Carmen's knee and accepts a piece of smoked salmon from Peter, who's deftly slicing a side of it that's at least three feet long.

No one seems inclined to give Ev a knife, so she starts opening drawers until she finds one. She grabs a cutting board and gets to work. The dog ambles over. She crouches and caresses the side of his face. He, in turn, plants himself next to her and leans into the side of her leg.

No one speaks, let alone tells her where Sean is or if he's coming back, so she keeps her head bent to her task. Long minutes go by. She finishes the nuts and looks around. Annette is posted on the other side of the island, studding an enormous ham with cloves. Ev walks over, picks up a few, and raises her eyebrows at Annette. Annette shrugs and Ev begins pushing them into the cold meat.

"We had to cancel the party last weekend," says Carmen finally.

"But Erik came home yesterday and the doctor says he's well enough for a small gathering tonight. If we keep things quiet."

Ev starts to say how glad she is to hear it, but Peter is already talking.

"Please tell me Cousin Denise isn't bringing that investment weasel boyfriend of hers," he says, rolling plastic wrap across the salmon.

"Oh, but she is," says Carmen, ladling some stock from a small pot into a larger one. "No smart remarks, though." She turns to face her children. "Tonight, there's only love, babies."

"Can we just admit he's a sleaze?" Peter asks under his breath.

Carmen flicks a dish towel at him and they resume their tasks. Annette and Ev finish with the cloves. Ev looks around. No one pays any attention to her. Should she say something? Offer to leave again? Finally Carmen points at the bag of flour and a sifter.

"Three cups," she says.

As Ev scoops out a cupful, Annette clears her throat.

"You have some nerve," she says, picking up a pastry brush and starting to paint the ham with glaze.

Neither Carmen nor Peter look up, but they pause their work. Roger, who's rolling on his back, freezes, legs in air.

Annette continues, "He told everyone you were coming: the aunties, the uncles, the cousins. Probably the mailman. He was more excited about you being here than the damn anniversary. And even though the party was canceled, they all swung by, one after another, hoping to meet you. And here he is—alone."

Ev had expected Annette to be annoyed at her presence because of her possessiveness over Sean. But in this moment, Ev has to admit, Annette really does seem upset on her brother's behalf.

Peter pipes up from the other side of the room, where he's now polishing silverware. "Annette, please chill."

"It's okay," says Ev. She pours the cup of flour into the sifter and squeezes the metal handle. It's stiff at first and takes all her strength to move, but finally it loosens. "I screwed up," she admits.

She watches the fine white dust float down into the big glass bowl. The repetitive flexing of her hand muscles helps ease her tension.

Carmen circles the kitchen with a spoonful of some kind of pilaf. She blows on it and holds it in front of Peter, who takes a taste. Then Annette. Carmen starts to head back to the stove but then changes direction. She offers the spoon to Ev. Ev isn't wild about putting her lips where Annette's just were, but she takes a bite, noting the sweet pop from some currants.

She starts to offer a compliment when she hears the front door open and voices approach. Sean and Zach appear. Sean is wearing a wrinkled dress shirt over a tee and carrying a case of wine. He looks tired.

"The guy says there's almost nothing that goes with artichoke." Sean edges toward the table and puts the case down with a plunk. "So we—" He spots Ev beside his mother and stops talking. There's a raw quality to his expression that's immediately replaced by suspicion. "What are you doing here?"

It's overwhelming to see Sean again and she wants nothing more than to throw her arms around his neck. But as she moves in his direction, she finds her gaze pulled toward Zach, too. After everything that happened at Recommitment, his messy vulnerability, previously irritating, strikes her as deeply moving.

He was all but defenseless when she carelessly dropped the bomb on him that day at the museum. She felt mostly impatience with his helicopter family and annoyance at Annette for blowing her transgression out of proportion. But Annette wasn't wrong to want to protect Zach. It would be so easy for him to draw the wrong lesson from his dad's decision to leave, to think there's something wrong with him.

"I'm so sorry," she says.

"They let me take the test here," Zach says, shrugging.

"What?" she asks.

"The State Assessment in Science?" His tone says *duh*.

"Right," she says. "Right, of course." She dabs at the skin under her eye with a knuckle to stop a tear. "That's good, very good."

Sean seems momentarily mystified by her emotion but then regains his composure. "What are you doing here?" he repeats.

Ev presses her lips together. She turns and walks back to the counter where she picks up the sifter again and starts squeezing.

"She's helping," says Carmen, picking up a sweet potato to peel.

"Mom—" Sean starts, but Carmen cuts him off.

"We've got fifteen people coming tonight and your dad's eaten nothing but hospital food for two weeks. You want to sit there complaining about artichokes and unexpected guests or do you want to pitch in?"

Sean folds his arms, unmoved. "I've got work to do," he says. "I've been out of the office for eight days."

"So has everybody else," says Peter.

Sean looks at the ceiling. "What do you need me to do?"

"Put that softened butter in the mixer and add six eggs. Then a cup of whole milk and a teaspoon of vanilla," says Carmen. "Zach, can you please get all your stuff out of the living room?"

Zach nods, and after a puzzled glance at Ev, departs.

Sean takes a carton of eggs from the refrigerator and sets up in front of the mixer on the far island. He puts everything in the attached metal bowl and starts it up. Ev's grateful that the noise inhibits talking. Several minutes go by, everyone working, Roger pacing the room and whining softly.

Sean flicks off the machine. "Done," he says.

Carmen turns toward Ev. "Now you take the flour you sifted and pour it in." She wipes her hands on her apron. "Sean, put the mixer on low. Ev, pour as slowly as you possibly can."

Ev carries over the bowl with its perfect cone of pure white. Sean looks at her with no expression, then grudgingly edges back, allowing her access to the bowl. She tips in a few tablespoons of flour and Sean puts the machine on its lowest setting, labeled "slow mixing." The large, anchor-shaped blade sputters to life and begins its work.

The bowl of flour shakes in Ev's hands and she rests it on the counter.

"I've missed you," she says, just loudly enough for Sean to hear but not the others, who've gone into the pantry.

"More," murmurs Sean.

It takes Ev a moment to understand that he means the flour. She picks up the bowl and shakes some out.

"You asked what I'm doing here," Ev says. She takes a deep breath. "I want to try again. I was wrong about—well, pretty much everything." She's afraid to look Sean in the eye and keeps her gaze focused on the batter.

Sean shakes his head. "Sounds like you've had some kind of epiphany," he says with muted sarcasm. Like he can't even get worked up enough to be angry.

"You could say that. I think—" she says, trying to put her finger on what she wants to say. "I think I can do better."

"Putting aside my skepticism that you really believe you did anything wrong, what would be the point?"

"What do you mean?"

"You are who you are. Wrapped up in your job. A job that just got a whole lot bigger. Forgive me but I can't really see how you'd even have the time to try again. Let alone do better. And that's okay. You should do you." Sean scrapes eggshells off the counter into his hand and throws them away before wiping his hand on a dish towel.

"I've been thinking about that," she says. "I'm thinking I'm not going to do the job the way Gareth did. He lived to work, micromanaged. Didn't trust anyone. In the end, he had to move across the country to get some space from ARC. I'm going to show everyone that there's another way to do this. I'm going to let my EPs do more on their own. I'm going to give them room. And give myself room, too. For a life." She edges a little more flour into the bowl.

Sean uses a spatula to push down the batter on the sides of the bowl.

"That's good," he says reasonably. "Probably healthy. But it doesn't change what's going on with me. And everyone else under this roof. It is what it is. Life is curveballs. Things change. I'm not saying it'll always be as crazy as it is now, but it's not going to get easier any time soon."

"I realize that," Ev says. "I wouldn't have come here if I didn't. But you need to understand something, too." She turns in his direction. "You and I are different. We grew up differently." She shrugs. "Maybe I haven't been very good at understanding your . . . connections. I see that now. I also haven't been great at explaining where I'm coming from. I didn't really understand it myself till now. The bottom line is that all this"—she gestures around them—"doesn't come naturally to me. And that's not a crime. I need to ease into it. I'll still need time to work. I'll still want time alone. We'll have to talk about it as we go."

Sean blinks. "Hang on. You, *you*, want to talk about something?"

"Well—"

Her phone, on the counter, vibrates and a text fills the screen. It's from Carla.

> Just reached Aviva.
> She's fantastic.
> Going to meet next week!

"Gareth?" Sean asks, folding his arms.

"No." Ev turns off the phone and pushes it into her bag. "It's about Aviva. I'm trying to get her a new job."

Sean raises an eyebrow.

"Look, you asked me to be here and I am," Ev says. "I'm a week or two late. But all I want is to stay for dinner. With your mom and dad, Peter, Jasmin, Annette, Zach, your cousin Denise, and her 'investment weasel' boyfriend."

Sean's eyes widen. For a second, she thinks he's going to laugh but he doesn't. He points at the flour again and she starts to tip more in. But her hand slips and the entire bowlful lands in the mixer. The blade twists through it, but the nascent batter is overwhelmed and enormous dry lumps form.

Ev winces. She's ruined it. She should never have tried this, any of it. She closes her eyes, seeing herself on the plane home next to some stranger, hailing a cab, and arriving at her silent apartment where nothing is waiting for her but a stack of takeout menus.

From inside the pantry, there's a crash that sounds like tin cans falling to the floor. There's a rush of swearing and then laughter.

"Everleigh," says Sean. "Look."

Ev opens her eyes. The lumps have begun to fold themselves into the mix. She edges in for a better view and her shoulder touches Sean's. Through his shirt, she can feel a hint of warmth from his skin.

The thrumming of the machine echoes inside her. The blade is turning and working, cutting its way through, like time. Ev reaches for Sean's fine-boned hand, the one that's spent so many hours drawing her in the kind of detail no photograph could match. He doesn't pull away and their palms press together, sweating lightly, like teenagers'.

They stand there, watching the batter and flour entwined in their circular dance. Each takes turns holding back, refusing to succumb. But with every revolution, every pass of the blade, they disappear, bit by bit, one into the other.

THE END

ACKNOWLEDGMENTS

When it comes to writing a book, no one does it alone but not everyone falls ass-backward into such an incredible network of supporters and inspirations.

First, my heartfelt thanks to Susan Golomb, the delightful paradox: somehow the fiercest agent and sweetest friend (and my birthday sister).

I'm deeply indebted to She Writes Press, in particular to publisher Brooke Warner, who's created the closest thing to a publishing "family" that I've been part of, as well as the terrific Shannon Green and Lauren Wise.

I don't know how I got so lucky as to have Elena Stokes and Tanya Farrell to help me get the word out about this book, but I'll forever be grateful and look forward to our next Zoom.

As always, my greatest appreciation goes to the incomparable Jessie Sholl, whose editing skills are exceeded only by her generosity.

Gratitude to my earliest readers and smartest critiquers: Paulina Porizkova, Laurie McCall, Doug McLeod, Beryl Holness, Renee Silverman, Shizuka Otake, Lisa Wixon, Kate Brown, David Simonetti, and Cate La Farge Summers.

Thanks to Pat Mulcahy, whose shrewd appraisals helped me shape this story, my beloved Aunt Joan, who gave me my first unconditionally positive review, and my dearest friend Colleen Hadigan, who cheers me on in whatever I'm doing.

For helping me understand the extraordinary story of how Native American women of the Iroquois Confederacy inspired some of America's most important suffragists, a shout-out to both the Women's Rights National Historical Park in Seneca Falls, New York, and the Six Nations Iroquois Cultural Center in Onchiota, New York.

And lastly, I can never repay the talented news people who've taught me, over the years, all I know about journalism, from my colleagues at WPIX, to the inaugural team at NY1, to my merry band of fellow writers at *Good Morning America*.

But most of all, I must thank the members of my *Dateline NBC* family, the kindest and most gifted team I can imagine anyone assembling. Each has taught me something about the elegant dance of storytelling on the solid floor of truth. Special thanks to David Corvo, Liz Cole, Paul Ryan, and Allan Maraynes, who in some cases sat for interviews and all of whom demonstrate daily not only excellent journalism, but the exceptional management of journalists. (Most of us will admit the latter is far trickier.)

WHERE YOU ONCE BELONGED

Reading Group Discussion Guide

1. *In Where You Once Belonged*, Ev believes that even in these modern times, as a woman, she still has to "play ball" to succeed in her career in a way that men usually don't. Do you think that's true for her? For women in general?

2. Ev cares passionately about good journalism but is undeniably ambitious. This sometimes leads to poor decisions, both in her professional and personal lives. Did you relate to that aspect of her personality? Have you ever had to make difficult choices in your field because of this kind of push-pull? Would you judge her the same way if she were a man?

3. Ev, who lost her mother as a child and whose father moved abroad, struggles with the notion of family. She finds it uncomfortable, even painful, to be around Sean's close clan, and as a result, his parents start to believe that Ev is not a good match for their son. Do you understand where Ev is coming from? How did your childhood shape your feelings about family and how it fits into your life now?

4. The book builds up to the evening of Recommitment, when the women of Foster House return, twenty years after graduation from college. This brings up complicated feelings for Ev and her housemates Dilly, Tina, and Cam. What is your experience with reunions? How do they affect you, your friendships, and your sense of who you once were and what you've become?

5. If you met your younger self, what would you want to say to her/him? What do you imagine she or he would say to you? How might this be a helpful exercise for people who sense they're at a crossroads in life?

6. During Recommitment, Ev realizes she's been basing her beliefs about what happened with her Foster housemates on some wrong assumptions. Has that ever happened to you? To what degree do you think strained relationships that so many of us have with family and friends may stem from a long-ago misunderstanding or misremembering of a conversation or incident?

7. Following Recommitment, Ev makes very different choices. Have you ever experienced an event that made you re-evaluate your life and make significant changes?

8. *Where You Once Belonged* explores the history of how the women of certain Native American tribes inspired white suffragists in the 19th century in their fight for equality between the sexes. What do you think about this history? Did it surprise you? How does it fit into the larger story of American women's history?

9. Americans' trust in media has eroded. What did you learn about the inner workings of journalism from this book? Does this knowledge make you think differently about the news you consume?

ABOUT THE AUTHOR

LORNA GRAHAM is the author of *The Ghost of Greenwich Village* (Random House/Ballantine) and a writer at *Dateline NBC*. She has written numerous documentaries, including *Auschwitz*, produced by Steven Spielberg, narrated by Meryl Streep, and which competed at the 2016 Tribeca Film Festival. Across numerous films, PSAs, and speeches, she's written for Presidents Bill Clinton and George H. W. Bush, Tom Hanks, Harrison Ford, and Morgan Freeman. She graduated from Barnard College and lives in Greenwich Village.

Looking for your next great read?

We can help!

Visit www.shewritespress.com/next-read
or scan the QR code below for a list
of our recommended titles.

She Writes Press is an award-winning
independent publishing company founded to
serve women writers everywhere.